The Wife Upstairs

a novel by

FREIDA McFADDEN

The Wife Upstairs

© 2020 by Freida McFadden. All rights reserved.

Cover art by Melanie W.

To my girls, of course

NOVELS BY FREIDA McFADDEN

The Wife Upstairs

The Perfect Son

The Ex

The Surrogate Mother

Brain Damage

Baby City

Suicide Med

The Devil Wears Scrubs

The Devil You Know

CHAPTER 1

October, 2019

If I had hesitated even a minute, everything would have been different.

Her face would have slowly turned blue. She would have collapsed to the ground as her lungs screamed for oxygen. Then there would be an ambulance—too late. A trip to the hospital. Or maybe straight to the morgue. Somber calls to relatives—a husband, a daughter, a son.

I've never done anything heroic in my entire life. The leading candidate would be this cat I used to feed in an alley next to my building. But I'm not sure if feeding a stray cat counts as heroic. Also, I heard the cat eventually bit somebody, so maybe I was just aiding and abetting a bad-tempered cat.

But today, while I'm sitting in a booth in a small diner, now quiet after the early morning rush, I see the elderly woman at the table across from mine gasping for air. At first, she's coughing. Then the coughs stop and she grows silent. She clutches at her throat, the same way the woman does in the poster you always see about what to do when someone is choking.

I look around wildly, hoping to spot somebody who knows what to do. My stomach sinks—I'm almost alone in the diner. There's just one man in a business suit and he's all the way in the back, looking down at his phone. The waitress is nowhere in sight.

If I don't help this woman now, it will be too late. She will die.

I learned the Heimlich maneuver back in summer camp when I was thirteen. Kevin Malone practiced it on me, and I was so excited that Kevin was touching me, it was hard to focus on what I was learning. But it's not exactly rocket science. You wrap your arms around the choking victim, make a fist below the breastbone, then thrust. Hard.

I push my cup of coffee away and leap to my feet. The woman is tiny and probably weighs eighty pounds dripping wet. I easily haul her out of her seat and wrap my arms around her frail chest. Then I thrust upwards. Once. Twice. Three times.

It's not nearly as fun as when I was practicing with Kevin Malone.

Just when I'm scared it's not working, a hunk of sausage flies out of the woman's mouth. It lands on the table with a plunk, right next to her plate of eggs.

I saved her life. For the first time in my life, I'm a

hero.

"What in God's name is *wrong* with you? Are you crazy?"

I had thought the old woman would be tearfully thanking me right now. *Thank you so much for saving my life. How can I ever repay you?* But instead, she is somewhat less than grateful. Actually, that's an understatement. She's glaring at me with venom in her watery blue eyes, her jowls trembling with fury.

"You tried to attack me!" the woman yells as she steadies herself against the table. And then she picks up her half-full cup of coffee and throws the contents in my direction. Fortunately, the coffee has been sitting there for a while and is no longer hot. Less fortunately, the coffee is still *wet*. I'm drenched.

"You were choking," I sputter.

The woman snorts like she's never heard something so ridiculous in her entire life. "I was *fine*. Just a little water down the wrong pipe! You *attacked* me. I was minding my own business and you grabbed me!"

The middle-aged waitress finally emerges from the kitchen. She comes right over to us, making no effort to disguise the exhaustion in her bloodshot brown eyes. The waitress appears to be at the tail end of a busy shift and looks like she'd rather be just about anywhere than here, dealing with this. She wipes her hands on her blue jeans. "Is there a problem?" she asks in a raspy voice.

"Yes!" The old woman picks up her overstuffed pink

purse and clutches it to her chest. "This young woman just attacked me and tried to steal my purse."

Steal her purse? She can't be serious! "I didn't—"

"I think she broke my rib." The woman moans as she clutches her side. "I need you to call the police."

The police? Oh God, this can't be happening...

"She was choking..." I say weakly.

The old woman glares at me. "Tell the police I want to press charges," she hisses. "I'm going to make sure you go to jail for a long time."

Now I feel like *I'm* choking. She's not really going to press charges after I just saved her life, is she? And I can't afford to pay for a lawyer. My bank account is mostly cobwebs at this point.

Someone clears their throat behind me. I jerk my head around, and it's the man in the business suit who had been sitting at the other end of the diner. He's gotten up from his seat and is standing behind me.

"Excuse me," he says. "I saw the whole thing."

The old woman's eyes light up. "I have a witness then! You saw this horrible girl attack me!"

"You were choking!" I cry, for what feels like the hundredth time.

She clutches her chest and groans. "I think I have a punctured lung! We should probably call an ambulance."

I let out an involuntary gasp. "An ambulance?"

"*You're* my witness," the old woman says to the man. "You saw how she attacked me, didn't you?"

He glances at me with a raised eyebrow, and I just shake my head. "No, I saw how she saved your life," he says. "You were *choking*. You would have died."

Her eyes widen. "You're making that up!"

"No. I'm not." His voice is flat, leaving no room for argument. "She saved your life. You'd be dead if not for her. You should *thank* her."

The old woman looks between the two of us, the wrinkles in her face darkening. "Oh, I get it. The two of you are in cahoots!"

The man turns to the waitress. "There was no attack. You don't need to call the police."

It suddenly occurs to me the man is quite nice looking—and not just because he's standing up for me. He has a thick head of chestnut hair, vivid green eyes, and also, he fills out that suit pretty nicely. I don't usually notice things like that, but it's hard *not* to notice.

"I was attacked!" the old woman says, although there's less conviction in her words this time.

The waitress looks like she's barely stifling a yawn. She clearly wants this ordeal to be over with so she can get off her feet. "Do you want me to call an ambulance or…?"

"Don't bother!" the old woman snaps.

In spite of her alleged punctured lung, she stomps out of the diner with her giant pink purse, nearly getting floored by a taxi cab as she rushes across the street. As far as I can see, she hasn't bothered to pay her check. The waitress sighs and picks up her half-empty plate from the table, as well as the piece of sausage that nearly killed her.

"Hey," the man says to the waitress. "What did that woman owe you?"

The waitress glances down at the plate in her hand. "About seven dollars with tax."

The man hands her a twenty. "Keep the change."

The waitress smiles for the first time since I walked in here twenty minutes earlier. She pockets the money, then glances up at me. Her eyes drop to my shirt. "Bathroom is in the back, honey."

Bathroom?

As the waitress disappears into the kitchen, I look down at my clothing. This morning I had put on a clean, freshly ironed pink button-down top and gray pencil skirt because I've got my first job interview since I was laid off two weeks ago. It's nothing great, just bartending, but I need it—bad.

But when that woman threw her coffee at me, she got me square in the chest. There's a dark brown stain soaking into the fabric of my shirt. I can't go to an interview like this. I look like a slob. My only real option is to go home and change. Except my interview is in…

Fifteen minutes. Damn.

I'm new at this saving people's lives business. Does it always end up so crappily? Then again, I shouldn't be surprised. Everything going wrong unexpectedly seems to be a pattern in my life.

The man is looking at me with his eyebrows bunched

together. "Are you okay?"

"Fine." I look down at my ruined interview outfit. "Totally fine. Absolutely, completely fine."

He just looks at me. I don't know what it is about this guy, but something about the way he's looking at me makes me want to pour my heart out to him.

Or rip my clothes off. A little of that too. He *is* pretty hot. And it's been a while for me. A *long* while. I think there was a different president in office at the time. Kevin Spacey was still a respected actor. Brad and Angelina were a happy couple. You get the idea.

"I have a job interview," I admit. I tug at my coffee-soaked shirt. "*Had* a job interview. I don't think it's going to go well. In fact, I think I should just call it off."

He raises his eyebrows. "You're looking for a job?"

I shrug. "Yeah. Sort of."

Desperately, actually. My landlord informed me yesterday that if I don't have the rent by Friday, there's going to be an eviction notice on my door by Saturday. And then I'll have to live in a cardboard box on the street, because that's my last option.

"What kind of job was it?"

"Well, this one was bartending." At a seedy bar that would have paid minimum-wage. "But... I mean, that's what's available. At this point..."

I stop talking before I let on how desperate I am. This man is a stranger, after all. He doesn't want to hear my depressing life story.

He flashes an infectious grin that reveals a row of straight, white teeth. My parents couldn't afford braces, so I've got two crooked incisors that I'm self-conscious about. My dream, if I ever have enough money, is to get them fixed. But that's not going to happen, short of winning the lottery. And I can't even afford a ticket.

"Do you believe in fate?" he asks.

I cock my head to the side. Do I believe in *fate*? What kind of question is that? It seems like the kind of question that somebody who's had a very good life might ask. Because the cards I've been dealt so far have all been losing ones. Starting with my parents. And then Freddy. If fate exists, then all I can say is it doesn't like me very much.

"I'm here in the city for an interview myself," the man goes on, without waiting to hear my answer. "I was actually going to interview somebody for a job. Right here at this diner. Except she didn't show up. So…"

I stare at him. Is he saying what I think he's saying? "What kind of job?"

"Well, it's…" He hesitates, then nods his head at his table in the back. "Listen, why don't you go get yourself cleaned up and then we'll talk about it? I'll buy you a fresh cup of coffee—you look like you could use it." He grins at me. "I'm Adam, by the way. Adam Barnett."

"Sylvia Robinson."

"Nice to meet you, Sylvia."

He holds his hand out to me, and I shake it. He has a nice handshake. Warm and firm, but not like he's trying to crush the bones of my hand. Why do some men shake your hand like that? What are they trying to prove?

Of course, then I notice my own hand is sticky with coffee and cream. This just isn't my day. But Adam doesn't wipe his hand on his pants when we're done shaking—he doesn't seem at all concerned about my sticky palm.

"So what do you say?" he asks.

"I, uh…"

I don't know why I'm hesitating. A job is a job. And this man seems nice enough. He defended me when that old woman wanted to call the police. And he paid off her tab so the waitress didn't get stiffed. I need a job badly, and this is my only shot right now. Plus, I could use a nice hot cup of coffee after the morning I'm having.

But for some reason, I can't shake this awful feeling in the pit of my stomach.

I once read that when people have near-fatal heart attacks, they get a sense of doom. They describe a sinking sensation before the chest pain even begins, like the world is about to end. It's a commonly described phenomenon that nobody can explain. But when something terrible is about to happen, people *know*.

And when I look at Adam Barnett, for a moment, I get that sensation. Doom.

Like something terrible will happen if I follow him to his table.

But that's ridiculous. I've had a run of bad luck over my life, so of course, I'm going to be suspicious of everything. I don't believe in fate and I don't believe in premonitions. What I do believe is that I will be homeless in a few days if I don't get my hands on some money. And turning tricks in Times Square is not my cup of tea.

"Okay," I say. "Let me get cleaned up and then I'll join you."

CHAPTER 2

It's even worse than I thought.

I look at myself in the bathroom mirror and feel sick. I knew I had coffee on my shirt, but I didn't realize quite how much. Most of it is right on the front, like she shot me with a bullet of coffee, but coffee splatter marks are dotting the sleeves, on the collar, and even on my skirt. It's a disaster.

On further inspection, there are even a few flecks of brown on my neck and chin, and during the effort of performing the Heimlich maneuver, my dirty blonde hair has become partially unraveled from the elaborate French twist I learned how to execute from a YouTube video. I remove the clips and shake it loose, knowing I'll never be able to re-create it without step-by-step instructions from Yolanda the Hair Guru.

I turn on the faucet for the sink. The water is ice cold, of course. I wait a few seconds for it to heat up, but I'm not that lucky today. Instead, I have to splash cold water all over my face. Unfortunately, that makes my cheap mascara leak like I'm the Bride of Frankenstein, so I have to wipe it all off. I wore a lot more black eye makeup when I was younger, but I still wear a fair amount, and without it, my face looks pale and plain. But I don't have any in my purse, so there's not much I can do about it.

I start splashing water on my dirty pink shirt. I bought it last week on an online discount clothing store, which advertised it as a "salmon dress shirt." Except it's not so much "salmon" as "neon pink." The pink color is so bright, it hurts my eyes. I look like someone out of an eighties music video—all I need are a pair of legwarmers, a scrunchie, and some shoulder pads.

I manage to get most of the brown stain out, but now I've got dark wet splotches all over me. Also, it's becoming increasingly obvious that the wet fabric is see-through.

But what can I do? I don't have an extra shirt tucked away in my purse. Maybe it'll dry on the way out to the table. And perhaps a partially see-through shirt isn't the worst thing in the world in this situation.

Before I go out, I reach into my purse and pull out a tube of red lipstick. I apply a fresh layer, which brightens up my pale face.

There. That'll do.

The diner is cramped, and Adam snagged a booth that seats only two people. He's already ordered us coffee, and there's a cup waiting for me in front of the empty side of the booth. His eyes light up when he sees me, and he gestures for me to sit down.

"I got you a cup of coffee. Hope it's okay. There's cream and sugar on the table."

I slide into my seat. "I take it black."

Bitter and black. That's the only way I ever drink coffee.

"Same here." Adam lifts his cup of coffee and takes a long sip. He shudders. "What a day, huh?"

I nod. I know *I've* had a shit day. But I don't know what sort of day he's had so far. Is it just that the person he was supposed to interview didn't show? Something in his expression makes me think it's more than that, but it seems like it might be off-limits to ask. I don't want to be rude, especially since I'm now counting on this guy to keep a roof over my head.

"Do you want anything to eat?" he asks. "My treat."

I'm starving. I'm currently on the poverty diet. All I ate for breakfast this morning was a banana. I have eaten spaghetti every night in the last week for dinner, which means I only had to buy that one box of spaghetti and one can of tomato sauce, totaling $5.39. But the last thing I want to do is stuff my face in front of a potential employer, who also happens to be a cute guy. The coffee will have to be enough. "No thanks."

He stirs his coffee with a spoon, even though he hasn't added any cream or sugar. He tugs on his tie with his other hand. I don't know why he looks so nervous. *He's* the one offering a job. In this economy, it seems like anyone offering a job is in pretty good shape. I'm the one who's about to be homeless.

Of course, I don't know what the job is. Maybe it's something really awful. I try to imagine a job I wouldn't be willing to do for a reasonable salary. I would clean toilets. I would shovel snow for him on the coldest day of winter. I would take out his trash.

I wouldn't *eat* his trash. If that's the job, I wouldn't take it. I suppose that's where I draw the line. No eating of garbage.

"So I'm sure you want to hear about the job," he finally says. "Cut to the chase, right?"

"Well…"

He smiles crookedly. "You'd be working for me—at my house. Well, technically you'd be working for my wife."

"Oh!" I say. But what I'm really thinking is: oh.

Of course he has a wife. He's a nice, thirty-something guy who looks great in a suit. *Of course* he has a wife. Those guys are never single. I hadn't noticed a ring, but to be fair, I was distracted.

This is a good thing though. Because if he legitimately has a job for me, the last thing I need to do is muck it up with a pointless flirtation. I'm terrible at flirting anyway. If he's happily married, that will be off the table. And I can focus on a new job and getting my life back on track.

I take a second to check out his left hand, and sure enough, the simple white gold wedding band is there. How did I miss that?

I take a sip of coffee and shudder much the way he did. Wow, this stuff is high octane. "Your wife?"

"Yes." He plays with his wedding band, turning it in circles around his fourth finger. "Victoria has… she's been ill."

My heart sinks. "I don't have any nursing training…"

"Oh, you wouldn't need that." He takes another swig of coffee. "She's got a nurse to help her in the morning. And she's got me at night. But when I'm working, I want somebody around to keep her company."

She has a nurse who comes in every day? It sounds like this woman is pretty sick. I'm dying to ask what happened to her, but I feel like that might be rude. And he's not volunteering any information. If he wanted me to know, he would tell me. If I take the job, presumably I'll find out.

"She's alone all day," he explains. "I work from home, but I can't be with her twenty-four hours a day. I just want somebody to spend time with her. Maybe read to her. Sit with her during meals. Just be a friend to her."

"You're hiring me to be your wife's friend?" I blurt out before I can stop myself.

Adam's ears turn slightly pink. "Well, when you put it that way…"

"Sorry," I say quickly. "I shouldn't have said that. What you're doing for your wife is… nice. You don't want her to be lonely."

And I mean it. I don't know what's wrong with his

wife, but it's obvious he cares about her. He's willing to pay somebody to be with her while he's working. If something happened to me, I'd probably end up in some nursing home or something.

"You said you work from home," I say. "What sort of work do you do?"

I expected him to say he worked in computers, since that's what most people who work from home seem to do. But then he surprises me by saying, "I'm a writer."

"You're kidding!" I take a sip of my coffee. "Anything I would have heard of?"

He shrugs. "Maybe."

I'm not much of a reader, so he could be a bestselling author and I wouldn't know it. Presumably, he does okay if he's able to pay me to be his wife's friend. Or else, he's got a big inheritance. Or maybe Victoria has the money.

"Anyway..." He rakes a hand through his dark hair. "There's one other thing about the job..."

I raise my eyebrows. Uh oh, here comes the catch. Let me guess: I have to perform my duties while completely naked. "Yes?"

"It's not local."

"Not... local?"

"Victoria and I live out on Long Island."

I frown. "Where in Long Island?"

"All the way out."

"Like the Hamptons?"

"Montauk."

I stifle a groan. Montauk is at the tip of Long Island. Like, as far as you can go without being in the Atlantic Ocean. It would take me over two hours to drive there from my studio apartment in Brooklyn. And that's if I had a car, which I don't. I suppose I could take the Long Island Railroad. I can't even imagine how long a ride that would be.

"That's a bit of a trip," I admit. "And I don't have a car."

"Right." He stirs his coffee cup again. "That's why... I mean, if you took the job, you could live in our house. Rent-free, of course. And you can use Victoria's car for whatever you need."

My mouth falls open. I hadn't expected him to offer that. Of course, it makes sense. If you live out in Montauk, you can't expect to find somebody in the city to come work for you unless you offer accommodations.

"That's very generous," I say.

He offers that crooked smile again. "Work is keeping me very busy lately, and I hate the thought of Victoria being lonely all day. And I need to find someone before the winter sets in. The snow will make it more difficult for me to arrange interviews."

This job would solve all my problems. I'd have money coming in. I'd have a place to live. I'd be able to start crawling out of the hole my medical expenses left me in. I could start fresh. It would be amazing.

But for some reason, every fiber of my being is crying

out for me to tell him no. It's that same sense of impending doom I had outside. That if I take this job—if I go out to that house in Montauk—something terrible will happen to me.

Not just terrible. Worse than terrible.

I can't take this job.

"We should probably discuss salary," he says.

I clear my throat. There's no point in continuing this discussion. I have to tell him no. "Listen, Adam…"

"Would fifteen hundred dollars a week be okay?"

My mouth drops open. Is he *serious*? He can't possibly be. He's going to give me a free room *and* board *and* fifteen hundred dollars a week to hang out with his wife? How does he even have the money to pay me that much? It sounds too good to be true.

But if it's true, that money will change my life.

"And I can arrange health insurance too," he says quickly. "Also, you'll have Sundays off. And… two weeks of vacation? Is that enough?" When he sees my expression, he adds, "Three weeks. Three weeks of vacation."

I think I'm going to choke on my own happiness.

There's no reason not to take this job. Yes, my gut is telling me to turn him down. But so what? Freddy used to say to me that I always thought something bad was going to happen to me. *Doom and Gloom Sylvia.* But to be fair, I was right a lot. Bad things *did* happen to me. I've gotten burned so many times, it makes sense I'd be wary of an opportunity that seems too good to be true.

This job is a chance to turn things around.

"When do you need me to start?" I ask.

CHAPTER 3

The train ride out to Montauk is endless.

Adam offered to pick me up and drive me there, but I couldn't in good conscience make him drive six hours round-trip, and then another six hours to drive me home. If he drove twelve hours for me, I would feel obligated to take this job. Like when you go on a date with a guy and he buys you a lobster dinner, and then you feel like you owe him something.

Not that I date anymore. I'm done with that for at least the rest of this decade.

So I'm on the Long Island Railroad, and Adam has promised to reimburse me for my round trip ticket. I've snagged a window seat by myself, which wasn't that difficult considering I'm going against traffic, and I'm pretty sure nobody is commuting all the way out here on a daily basis anyway. I've got my earbuds in, but I've tuned out the music as I watch the scenery fly by. At first, there are lots of houses and buildings. Then fewer houses and fewer buildings. Then just houses. Now it's mostly green.

And I've still got another hour to go.

I get out my phone to try to find something to entertain me the rest of the journey. There's a text message from Freddy on the lock screen. I changed my number, but somehow he keeps getting it. One of our mutual friends must be giving it to him. He hasn't changed his number though, so I recognize the digits even without his name on the screen:

Please give me another chance. Please Sylvie.

I snort at the phone. By now, Freddy should know better than to think I'll ever give him another chance. It's because of him that I'm trekking out to Montauk to keep from living out on the street. This is his fault. My whole life is his fault. I start to block his number but before I can, another message pops up:

Please. I love you. I'll do anything you say.

And then he is officially blocked. But knowing Freddy, he'll figure out a way around it.

Adam told me he'd be waiting at the train station to pick me up. By the time the train pulls into its final stop, my neck feels stiff as a board. I take a moment to stretch myself out and gather my courage. That awful sensation has gotten worse and worse during the long train ride out to the tip of the island, but I do my best to push it away. I'm just feeling antsy because I've lived in the city for so long—that's all it is.

I brought a light jacket, but it's colder than I would've

expected out here. And windy. The moment I dismount the train, a gust of wind goes through my jacket like it's made of paper. I have no padding on my body anymore, so I'm cold most of the time even in warmer weather. I should've worn another sweater.

"Sylvia!"

I hear the familiar voice calling my name. I swivel my head to look down the platform—Adam is waving frantically at me. He's dressed more appropriately than I am in a warm looking blue jacket with a scarf and a black hat on his head. Clearly, he's very familiar with the weather out here.

He jogs over to me, a crooked grin on his face. In the last week, I had somehow forgotten how good-looking he is. Even in that bulky black wool hat, he's more than a little cute.

But he's also more than just a pretty face. When I went home and googled Adam Barnett after first meeting him, I discovered he had been overly modest when he called himself a writer. This guy has had three books that hit number one on the *New York Times* bestseller list. There are articles online that say he's one of the best modern writers of our time. The next Stephen King. This guy is a big shot. And apparently, a bit of a recluse.

Then I googled Victoria Barnett. I found nothing. And believe me, I looked.

"You get in okay?" he asks anxiously. "How was the ride?"

"Long." I hug my chest and shiver. "You know, it's like ten degrees colder out here than it was in the city."

He laughs. "Yeah. Today is cold. Do you want my scarf?"

Before I can say yes, he unwinds his dark green scarf from around his neck. I accept it graciously because I really am cold. It's such a gallant gesture. Also, it smells nice. Like expensive aftershave.

Okay, I should probably quit smelling his scarf.

Adam leads me out to the parking lot. I got a little spark of excitement when he hits his key fob and the BMW lights up. The guy drives a BMW. I've never known anyone who drove a BMW before. I haven't ever even *owned* a vehicle. Freddy drove a piece of junk car—a used Ford Fiesta with scratches all over it because he couldn't afford to get it repainted. Half the time, he had to ask me to come downstairs and give him a push to get it started. To his credit, Adam looks mildly embarrassed when he sees the way I'm looking at his car.

"Don't say it," he says. "I know."

"Know what?"

"I've got a rich asshole car." He slides into the leather driver's seat and I climb into the car next to him. Wow, leather. I run my hand over the material. "But it handles really well in the snow. And Victoria loved it."

I can't help but notice he referred to his wife in the past tense. We've talked on the phone a couple of times since our initial meeting and he's been very vague about his wife's illness. I'm not sure why he doesn't want to tell me.

I mean, I'm the one who's going to be taking care of her. I need to know what's wrong with her. Does she have arthritis? Lupus? Really bad food allergies? I can't even imagine.

Adam must sense what I'm thinking, because as he pulls onto the main road, he blurts out, "She had a head injury."

"Oh…"

"She fell down the stairs about nine months ago." He winces. "In our house. We have this crazy winding staircase and… I was in the city all day with my publisher, so I didn't find her till later. If I had been there…"

His voice breaks on those last words. I get an ache in my chest for him. It's bad enough to have to deal with your wife being ill, but worse to blame yourself. I wonder if Victoria blames him too.

After about twenty minutes of driving mostly in silence, we come across an iron gate extending the length of a city block. When Adam hits the button in his car and the gates open, I realize this must be where he lives. He lives in a gigantic house surrounded by a freaking gate. At least there isn't a moat and a dragon, but it wouldn't surprise me.

Adam must notice the way my mouth is hanging open. "Real estate is cheap out here," he explains. "You can get a huge house for next to nothing. That's why we wanted to move out here. Even though it's obviously not the most convenient."

"Yeah," I mutter, although I'm secretly thinking to myself that if I live to be a hundred, I'll never be able to afford a house that looks like this.

Given how magnificent the house is, it's surprising to see the grounds are so unkempt. The lawn is badly overgrown. There are leaves all over the place and branches hanging in the path to the garage. It gives the entire property a bit of an abandoned look to it. If somebody told me nobody lives here, I would believe it. Especially since there are no lights on inside the two-story house, even though Adam's wife is supposedly inside.

"We used to have a gardener," he explains. "But she... she's no longer with us..."

He gets a sad expression on his face. Despite how attractive and wildly successful he is, Adam looks like a man who has had a hard life. At least, he's had a rough go of things lately. It makes me like him even better.

The inside of the house is even more magnificent than the outside. I feel like I'm walking into an opera house or something. The living room is so large, I feel like it could swallow me up. I could fit five of my studio apartments in this room alone. There's an enormous sectional sofa abutting a real working fireplace and a widescreen television. Everything in this house is shiny new and painfully expensive-looking.

Adam is watching me, so I feel like I need to say

something. But all I can manage is, "Wow. This place is..."

"Big, right?" His face lights up at my expression—it's clear he loves this house. "That's why we wanted it. We used to live in this apartment in the city and it was so tiny. When Victoria first walked in here, she spun around in circles with her hands out."

I can relate to Victoria because I kind of want to do the same thing. This house is made for spinning around in circles with your hands stretched out.

My eyes rest on a photograph on the mantle above the fireplace. It's a picture of Adam with his arm around a young woman with blond hair. "Is... is that her?" I ask.

He nods. "Yes..."

I take a step closer to get a better look, hoping he won't think me rude. Victoria is... well, she's beautiful. She has long golden hair worn loose around her face and she's wearing a stunning black dress that she fills out perfectly.

But the thing I can't stop looking at is Victoria's face. She's pretty, but it's more than that. Her face is so open and honest and fresh and her smile is so friendly. I've always worn too much makeup, but Victoria is wearing hardly any, and it suits her. She looks like the sort of person that you meet and instantly like. She looks so happy in the photo.

She has no idea what's about to happen to her.

"She's beautiful," I finally say.

"Yes." His eyes drop. "She is."

He looks so sad, I wish I hadn't said anything.

He clears his throat. "She's upstairs. Do you want to meet her?"

I look at the flight of steps to get to the second floor. He wasn't kidding when he said it was a long and twisted staircase. The steps are almost painfully steep, with barely enough room for a foot on each landing. If somebody took a spill down that entire flight, they wouldn't walk away so easily. I look at the foot of the stairs, imagining the blond woman from the photograph lying there with her limbs twisted around her.

I shiver again. Is there a draft in this house?

I follow Adam up the flight of stairs, clinging to the banister for dear life. If I fall down the stairs and have a brain injury, I don't have a husband to hire people to take care of me twenty-four hours a day, so I better be damn careful on these steps.

"I don't leave her alone," Adam explains to me as we mount the steps. "Her nurse, Eva, is with her right now. That's where I'm hoping you'll come in. So Eva can have a break. And... me too."

He's embarrassed to admit he needs a break from his wife. But I get it. "No problem."

I follow Adam down a long hallway. This house is so big, there must be at least five or six bedrooms up here. He takes me to a room at the very end of the hallway on the right. "This is Victoria's room."

"You don't share a bedroom?" I blurt out.

Adam's green eyes widen. Why did I say that? Why

do I keep saying such stupid things? Who am I to judge his sleeping arrangements?

"No," he finally answers. "She needs a lot of equipment and… We just… No, we don't anymore. No."

"Of course," I say quickly. "I get it."

Adam raps his fist once against the closed door. Then we wait as I hold my breath.

"Come in!" an accented voice calls out.

I release the breath as Adam opens the door to the room. The first thing I see is an extremely large woman. She has close-cropped black hair and a light brown skin color. Her arms are easily the width of my upper thighs, and she looks like she could toss me onto her shoulder and jog around the house with me on her back. I try to guess her age, but she could be anywhere between thirty and sixty.

"Mr. Adam," she says in an unidentifiable accent. "You are back."

"Yes." He flashes a very forced-looking smile. "Eva, I'd like you to meet Sylvia. She's going to be helping out with Victoria. Hopefully." He winks at me. "Sylvia, this is Eva."

She narrows her eyes at me. "Hello."

I get the sense that Eva and I are not going to end up being the best of friends. I clear my throat. "It's very nice to meet you. I'm very much looking forward to meeting Victoria."

Eva swivels her head and I follow her gaze to the

window. And that's when I see the wheelchair set up to face the rear window. The chair has a headrest, but I can see golden locks flowing around the black material.

"Is that her?" I ask, even though it's ridiculously obvious that it is. Who else would it be?

"Yes." Adam smiles crookedly. "Come over and say hello."

I walk around the hospital bed, careful not to trip on what appears to be a mechanical lift for getting in and out of the bed. Adam steps aside to let me get close to the wheelchair. The chair is tilted just enough that I can see Victoria's face.

And before I can help myself, I let out a strangled gasp.

CHAPTER 4

This woman is not the same woman from the photograph downstairs.

Well, she is, but she isn't. If you know what I mean. She used to be that woman, but it's clear that she isn't anymore. She's a shell of that same woman.

She still has the same golden hair, but it's dull and limp instead of shiny like in the photograph. There is a scar snaking out from under her hairline on the left. Her blue eyes have lost all their expression, and they stare off in two completely different directions. Her left cheekbone looks almost dented and there is a jagged ugly scar running down the entire side of her face. For a moment, I wonder why, with all their money, they didn't give her plastic surgery, but the answer is obvious. She couldn't care less what she looks like anymore.

"Hey, Vicky." Adam's voice softens and takes on a tender tone I hadn't heard before. "This is Sylvia. She's really nice. She's going to be spending some time with you."

Victoria lifts her eyes to look at me. The right one looks straight in my face, but the other still points in the direction of the window. It's hard to tell if she's seeing me at all. She doesn't say a word.

"She doesn't talk much," he explains in a low voice. It's like he's hoping she won't hear, although she's about two feet away from us. "The injury to her head affected the part of her brain that controls speech. She can understand things, but it's hard to know how much. She can't get many words out. Sometimes she can say 'hi' or 'okay' but most of the time, she can't even tell you her own name."

His voice breaks slightly on the last thing he says. It must be hard for him to explain all this to another person. I can't imagine what it must be like for the person you married to not even know who you are or be able to say their own name.

"Hi, Victoria," I say. I realize that I'm speaking too loudly and too slowly, like I'm talking to a hearing-impaired child. If she's really in there and can understand what I'm saying, she must find it very patronizing. "I'm Sylvia. It's nice to meet you."

And then, for reasons I cannot fathom, I stick out my right hand.

It's an automatic gesture. At some point in everyone's life, they are taught to shake hands to be polite. But Victoria's right arm is resting in a trough attached to the armrest of her wheelchair. She is fidgeting with her left hand in her lap, but her right hand is motionless. She looks down at my own right hand like I have presented her with a foreign object. Eva is looking at me like I have done something epically stupid.

"She can't move her right side at all," Adam says.

"Right." My face burns, and I remind myself that if I do take this job, it won't always be this awkward. After a week, I'll know what to do and won't humiliate myself anymore. "Sorry."

"She does best with routine—same thing every day," Adam says. "Eva will help her to get up in the morning and one of us will take care of bedtime. You would just help out during the day. Meals, getting things she needs, and just keeping her company." He looks down at his wife's face, his brow furrowed. "I worry about her getting lonely. She just… She mostly likes to look out the window and maybe watch some television."

I follow Victoria's gaze out the window. She's got a view of the front of the house—of the overgrown lawn and the trees and a small shed. The gate is visible in the distance.

"What about taking walks outside?" I suggest. After I put on Adam's scarf, I realized the weather wasn't so bad once I was dressed for it properly. We have at least another good month before the bitter cold sets in.

He nods. "You would have to bundle her up really well, but if you want to do it, I can carry her down the stairs."

I realize what he's getting at. Victoria obviously can't make it down a flight of stairs on her own. But that makes me wonder why they keep her upstairs on the second floor. "Maybe she'd be better off sleeping downstairs?"

He shakes his head. "We only have a half bathroom down there and it's not big enough to fit her chair. And there's a much nicer view from the windows on the second floor. She likes it up here."

He looks down at her again with a tender expression on his face. It's not clear to me how she expresses that she likes or dislikes anything. Her face is completely blank. I would think she was dead except that her eyes occasionally blink and she's playing with a loose thread on her shirt with her left hand.

I chew on my lower lip. If I'm going to take this job, I have to find a way to connect with Victoria on some level. After all, it's clear we're not going to be having any heart-to-heart conversations anytime soon. I look down at her baggy T-shirt and sweatpants, recalling how stylish her outfit was in the photograph on the mantle. I can't imagine this is a woman who would have liked to dress in sweats every day.

Then I catch a glimpse of a gold chain around her neck—hanging from the chain is a tiny diamond snowflake. It looks beautiful and expensive.

That chain is like a glimpse of the old Victoria.

"That's a lovely necklace you have, Victoria," I say. I

figure every woman likes a compliment, whether she understands me or not.

Victoria lifts her blue eyes again. She stares up at me. "Thank you."

I almost jump out of my skin at the sound of her hoarse voice. I didn't expect her to talk. Her voice was slightly slurred, but it was very clear what she said. I glance over at Adam, who is beaming.

"She talked to you!" He's grinning ear to ear. "She almost never talks! That's amazing. She must really like you." He rests one hand on her shoulder. "Sylvia is nice, right?"

Victoria doesn't answer. She's staring out the window again. Oh well.

"You can't expect her to talk much," he says to me. "Believe me, it's huge that she said two words to you. Usually, we're lucky if we get one word." He shakes his head. "Anyway, let me show you the room you'd be staying in."

As I follow Adam out of Victoria's room, I take one last look back at Victoria. She doesn't look away from the window. She barely even seems aware that we were ever in the room. But Eva's eyes follow us like an arrow. She has a strange expression on her face that makes me very uneasy.

"It was nice meeting you, Eva," I say to her.

And much like Victoria, she doesn't respond. She just keeps staring at me. It's very unsettling. I hope I don't have to deal with this woman much. Adam said she's only around in the morning.

The bedroom Adam gives me is gorgeous. It's bigger than my entire studio apartment back in the city. It's already furnished with a bed and a dresser and a small bookcase. He's even got sheets and a blanket on the bed. The only thing missing is a mint on the pillow.

"I hope it's okay." He squeezes his hands together. "I can get a truck to help move your furniture out here if you want to bring any of it, but you're welcome to this stuff."

"I don't need my furniture." The furniture back at my apartment is hanging together by the grace of God. Every time I go to sleep, I'm scared my bed will collapse during the night. "This will be fine."

"Or if the room is too small for you, there are other rooms..." He glances at the doorway. "The one all the way at the end is mine, but you could have any other room. There's also the attic, but I work up there."

"No, I promise, this is wonderful." I take a seat on the bed and almost moan with pleasure. The covers feel so soft under my fingers. I can't imagine what they must have cost. I wonder if Victoria is the one who picked them out. "You sure have a lot of rooms."

Adam gets that sad look on his face again. "We had this idea about filling them up with kids."

Oh God. Everything about this man's life is so *depressing*. This poor guy gets married to the woman of his dreams, who he obviously loves very much, and then she's in a horrible accident and can barely speak and hardly seems to know who he is. And instead of stuffing her away in some nursing home, he's brought her home with him and is spending a fortune to try to make her life as good as possible.

Victoria may not be a lucky woman. But she hit the jackpot on husbands.

"So what do you think?" Adam's eyebrows bunch together. "I don't mean to pressure you, but... You could see how hard it is for me to get into the city to interview people. I just want to have this squared away before winter."

"I..."

I need to tell him yes. I need this job so badly. My landlord has told me I've got till the end of the week to come up with the rent, but I have nothing in my bank account. So that's not going to happen. This man is willing to pay me an incredible salary as well as room and board. And even health insurance, for God's sake. I would be crazy not to take this job.

So why am I hesitating? Just because everything else in my life has gone to hell, it doesn't mean this will too.

"Is it the money?" He bites his lip. "Do you need more money?"

"It's not that." Damn, why did I say that? This was my chance to ask for more money. "I just feel very isolated out here."

He nods thoughtfully. "I know what you mean. I felt that way at first too. But it's really not that bad. I mean, there's a McDonald's five minutes away. And you can use Victoria's car to go anywhere you like. I don't want you to feel like you're stuck here... You're welcome to go out in the evenings when I'm around to stay with Victoria."

"Right..."

"I think you'll love it here." He leans forward slightly, so that I can smell the aftershave that was on his scarf. Unwittingly, he's giving me another reason to stay—my boss is hot. "It's very quiet and the mall is right around the corner. Victoria absolutely loved it here. That is, until..."

I can't say to him what I'm really thinking, which is that this house gives me the creeps. Maybe Victoria loved it here, but I don't. And for that matter, his wife gives me the creeps too. There's something about her and that blank expression that terrifies me. It's an awful thing to say about a woman who has been through something horrible, but I can't help it.

But what can I do? I don't want to live on the street.

"Okay," I say. "I'll take the job."

CHAPTER 5

While I'm lying on my lumpy mattress back at home, I fantasize about the bed in the house out in Montauk. Those silky sheets and nice warm blanket. I bet in that house, I won't get woken up during the night by sirens at least three times. And one night last week by gunshots. I'm certain if I stayed here long enough, I'd get hit by a stray bullet.

I can't wait to get out of here. But at the same time, the thought of going to live in that enormous house scares me beyond all words.

I don't know what frightens me more—the house or Victoria herself. When I close my eyes, I can still see that blank expression on her face. When she moved into that house, she was healthy and happy. Now look at her.

I wish I didn't have to take this job. I wish I had any other choice.

My phone buzzes loudly on my tiny nightstand. I pick it up and stare at the words on the screen.

Come to the window.

It's an unfamiliar number, but that doesn't mean it's somebody I don't know. More likely, it means that somebody I do know got a burner phone so they could text me, even though I blocked them.

Meaning, it's Freddy.

I text back: *Go away.*

Not until you come to the window.

My studio is so tiny that it's less than a foot from my bed to the window. I cross the two steps to my second-floor window, and sure enough, there is Freddy. It's raining a little and his dark brown hair is plastered to his skull. He's blinking away raindrops as he looks up at my window.

I let out a sigh and wrench open the window. "Go away, Freddy. I mean it."

"Sylvie…" He digs around in the pocket of his baggy jeans while looking up at me. "You've got to give me another chance. I love you."

"Forget it."

He pulls his cell phone out of his pocket and holds it up in the air. A second later, Peter Gabriel's "In Your Eyes" is blasting loud enough to wake my neighbors. "Please forgive me, Sylvie."

I roll my eyes. Freddy is re-creating the classic scene from the movie *Say Anything* when John Cusack holds up a boom box blasting Peter Gabriel to get back Ione Skye. And it works in the movie. Because that's a *movie*. And also because John Cusack and Ione Skye were just a couple of kids who didn't go through what I went through with Freddy Ruggiero.

Anyway, Freddy knows *Say Anything* is one of my favorite movies. He always used to tease me that I would tear up during the scene with the boom box. So it makes sense he would want to give this a try. But he doesn't have a chance. Maybe if he brought a real boom box and not just a stupid phone. But even then, probably not.

"Good night, Freddy," I say, and I slam the window shut.

I can still hear him yelling my name, but I just ignore it. I'm never taking Freddy back. If he wanted to be with me, he never should have left when I needed him the most. One good thing about getting the hell out of Brooklyn is I'm going to make sure he can't find me.

CHAPTER 6

"That's really all you're taking with you?"

Adam insisted on coming in to the city to help me move out to Long Island. He offered to rent a truck, but I told him it wouldn't be necessary. And as promised, all I've got is two large suitcases and one backpack. He threw the suitcases into the trunk of his BMW, and now he's looking around like he can't believe I don't have more stuff.

I shove my hands into the pockets of my fall coat, which I've had since I was seventeen. The sleeves are frayed and the zipper gets stuck about twenty percent of the time. After I get my first paycheck, I'm going to buy a new coat. I've been fantasizing about it. "That's it."

"But…" Adam scratches his chin as he looks at the luggage one last time. "It's just not very much. I mean, Victoria wouldn't have even been able to fit her shoes into those two bags."

"Yeah, well." I don't want to give him the real answer, about how you can't accumulate that much clothing if you have no money to buy clothing with. "Let's go."

Riding in Adam's BMW is so much better than the Long Island Railroad. It's like the lap of luxury. I've never sat in a seat this comfortable in my entire life. This guy knows how to live.

It's quiet in the car and he doesn't reach to turn on the radio. Which means we're basically sitting in awkward silence. I feel compelled to fill the silence.

"So... what was Victoria like?" I realize too late I've used the past tense to refer to a woman who is still very much alive. "I mean, before she..."

He doesn't seem angry about my slip. "She's really smart. I mean, *really* smart. She's a nurse practitioner and she used to work in an ER—that's actually how we met."

"Oh, wow." I try to imagine the woman staring vacantly out her bedroom window, taking care of patients in a busy ER. I can't do it. "That's amazing. Where did she work?"

"Mercy Hospital." He pauses. "In Manhattan. She was taking some time off after we moved. She always wanted to have a break from working, and I wanted to give that to her. She deserved it."

"Were you working in the ER too then?"

Adam gives me a shocked look. "Are you kidding? I was a *patient*. I had been waiting in there for hours and I was getting kind of pissed off, but when she walked into the room, I just... I forgot all about it. It was..."

I raise my eyebrows at him. "What?"

"Love at first sight. Shot by an arrow. Angels playing harps. That kind of thing." His ears turn pink. "I know it sounds dumb, but that's what it was. I just saw her and I knew right away. She was the one I was going to marry."

He's silent then, lost in his own thoughts. I can sympathize with how he's feeling. I thought I met the love of my life once upon a time too. And then that went... well, really badly. At least Victoria isn't stalking him outside his apartment building, playing Peter Gabriel on a cell phone.

"How about some music?" Adam asks after he merges onto the Long Island Expressway.

"Sure." It beats making awkward conversation for three hours. I'm definitely done asking about Victoria.

He fumbles around in a compartment between the seats. "I have my driving mix CD. I'll put that on."

"What's a CD?"

Adam gives me a look out of the corner of his eye. "Oh God. You're joking, right?"

"Yes, I'm joking. I know what a CD is. Although I have to admit, I've never actually seen one up close."

"Christ, you're making me feel ancient." I had estimated Adam's age at mid-thirties, about ten years older than I am. But there's something youthful about him. I don't feel like I'm around a much older man. Anyway, women mature faster than men—it's a biological fact. That's definitely true about Freddy, who is the same age as me.

"Anyway, you're in for a treat," he says. He yanks a compact disk from the compartment. "Ta da!"

"Ooh!" I take it from him and hold it up in mock wonder. I had been joking about never having seen a CD— my parents had stacks of them. "It's like a tiny record. Amazing."

Adam laughs. "Hey, when I was younger, this was all we had. Well, and tapes."

"What are tapes? You mean like scotch tape?"

He gives me a dirty look. "I made this CD probably back when you were in kindergarten. The ultimate driving mix. I made sure to buy a car with a CD player just so I could play this CD."

"I feel like you're raising my expectations too much though." I insert the CD into the player. "Now if this isn't the best album I've ever heard, I'm going to end up being disappointed."

"Luckily, it *will* be the best album you've ever heard."

A second later, the first song starts playing. Life is a Highway. Adam turns the volume way up, and he starts singing along in a hilariously off-key voice, to the point where it's endearing. I can't help but laugh, and a minute later, I'm singing too. Even though I am very far from the kind of girl who sings along with country anthems while cruising along the Long Island Expressway in a BMW. This is definitely not my bag.

But somehow, I'm having a really good time.

Somewhere along track number ten, when my voice is

getting hoarse, I start to think to myself that this is the most fun I've had in… maybe in years. And it's with a man who is very much married. To a woman I am about to start working for, who is seriously ill. I would be the absolute worst person in the world if anything happened between him and me. I have to keep reminding myself of that. Over and over.

Adam is married. He's married dammit.

We listen to the driving CD three times before we make it out to Montauk. By the time we pull up in front of Adam's house, I'm feeling regretful that the trip wasn't even longer. But it's nice to finally get out of the car and be able to stretch. And as I look up at the large house, I still get that sense of dread, but it's not quite as strong as the first day. Maybe this will all be okay.

I go around to the trunk to grab my luggage, but Adam is too quick for me. He pulls both my bags out of the trunk and sprints for the front door.

"You know," I say, "I can carry one of those bags."

"You've got your backpack."

I want to point out that I am his employee—not the other way around—and he doesn't have to rush around to please me. But he's already reached the front door with my bags. It's fine. If he wants to be a gentleman, I'm not going to complain.

"Our cleaning woman, Maggie, was keeping an eye on Victoria while I was getting you," Adam explains as he fumbles with his keys. "She's been pitching in a little bit, but it's really not her job. It'll be nice to have you around."

He gets the door open and then snatches another set of keys off a bookshelf. He tosses the keys to me and I catch them expertly. "Your set," he says.

There are, I swear to God, thirteen keys on this ring. How many doors does this place have?

As Adam brings my bags upstairs to my bedroom, I linger awkwardly in the living room. I realize too late that I should have followed him up there. I grab my backpack off the floor and start towards the stairs, just as a woman in skinny jeans and a tank top comes out of the kitchen. She's a few years older than me with a shock of red hair and freckles all over her face. When she sees me, she narrows her eyes and takes a step back.

"Hi!" I curse the fact that I'm not more outgoing. I don't have the sort of face that makes people like me instantly—like Victoria did. "I'm Sylvia. I'm... um, new here. I'm supposed to be helping out Victoria..."

After the warm welcome I got from Eva, I'm not expecting much. But to my total shock, she throws her arms around me and squashes me in a hug. "Sylvia!" she cries. "I'm so glad to meet you!"

"Oh." I feel oddly flattered by her ultra-enthusiastic greeting. "Thank you."

She laughs and pulls away. "Sorry. That was weird. My name is Maggie—I clean around here."

"Yes, Adam mentioned it."

She tucks a few strands of red hair that had come

loose from her ponytail behind her ear. Her hair is so red that it doesn't seem like a color that could occur in nature. But I don't see any dark roots. "It's just... It gets really lonely out here and it's nice to have somebody around who's... you know, my age. I was scared when I heard your name that you might be an old woman."

I can't help but laugh. I've heard that before. "The name Sylvia is making a comeback. A lot of people call me Sylvie."

She nods eagerly. "I can't tell you how great it is to have a young, normal person working here."

I'm guessing that the older, strange person she's referring to has to be Eva. In which case, I can't blame her. "Do you live here too?"

Maggie shakes her head. "I live about ten minutes away, with my boyfriend. He works around here, so I wanted a job that was local. It was supposed to be temporary, but I've been here like a year and a half."

"So you were around before Victoria's... accident?"

She picks up a washcloth from the kitchen counter as she drops her eyes. "Yes. I was here from the beginning."

I glance up the long, curved flight of stairs that nearly did Victoria in. "What was she like?"

She frowns. "What do you mean?"

"Victoria. What was she like?"

Maggie suddenly becomes very busy with her washcloth. She doesn't look up at me. "She was nice. Very pretty. You know. The usual."

I get the sense Maggie is reluctant to talk about Victoria Barnett. Which is frustrating, because I get the feeling she's the only one in this house who might be capable of telling me the truth.

Before I can press her any harder, I hear Adam calling me from upstairs. Time to unpack in my new room. And anyway, it doesn't look like Maggie is going to tell me anything more. At least not right now.

CHAPTER 7

One of my jobs is helping Victoria with meals.

I meet Adam in the kitchen to discuss meal planning. I'm not exactly a gourmet chef, but I can do the basics. Spaghetti. Macaroni and cheese. I can put together a sandwich. It's not rocket science. Unfortunately, Adam explains it won't be that easy.

"Vicky chokes on regular consistency foods," he says. "So anything you give her has to be ground up." He gestures at an expensive-looking device on the kitchen counter. "I got this food processor to turn everything into a purée. Everything she eats has to go in there first."

I cringe, imagining what it would be like to have all my meals puréed for me. Puréed steak would get old fast.

"And in a pinch…" He taps open a cabinet above the sink. "She could eat any of these."

It's baby food. Rows and rows of baby food. Puréed carrots. Sweet potato. Mashed peas. Stuff no adult should ever be consuming.

I swallow a lump in my throat. "I'd hate to have to feed her baby food…"

His cheeks color slightly. "I don't use the baby food much, but sometimes there just isn't time to cook something that tastes reasonable as a purée. Believe me, this stuff is a lifesaver." He lets the cabinet door swing closed. "You can let her have water, but only if she drinks it very slowly. Keep a close eye on her."

I nod. "What if she doesn't want to eat?"

He lifts a shoulder. "It's not a big deal. She's got a feeding tube in her belly, so if you give me a sense of how much she eats, we can give her extra nutrition through the tube."

Poor Victoria. She looked so happy in that photograph on the mantle. Happy and beautiful and young and alive. And now her life is puréed baby food and a tube stuck in her belly. "Adam?"

He raises his green eyes, although I can tell he's still focused on the task of teaching me food preparation. "Yes?"

"Is… Is Victoria ever going to recover?"

Of all the hard questions I've had to ask him, this is the worst. He inhales sharply and rakes a hand through his hair. I want to take the question back, but I also don't. I want to know the answer. I want him to tell me that, yes, she looks bad right now, but she's going to get better. Someday, she'll be that pretty girl in the photograph again.

"The doctor said…" He clears his throat. "They said

she's recovered all she's going to at this point." He drops his eyes. "We had her in rehab for a while, but she wasn't making any progress. She was there for three months and was still completely dependent for everything. She still couldn't move her right side at all and that was really limiting her progress. And the speech just wasn't getting better. So... I took her home, figuring she might do better in her own environment. But..." He squeezes his eyes shut for a moment. "It looks like this is it. This is the best she's going to get."

Wow. So that's that.

I want to reach out and put a hand on his shoulder, but it seems like it would be somehow inappropriate. "I... I'm sorry."

He lets out a sigh. "Yeah. Well, she's my wife and I'm going to take care of her. I made a vow. I'm not going to let her end up in a nursing home. No way."

I admire this man. Adam is young and attractive—he could have any woman he wants. But instead, he's honoring his marriage vows and staying loyal to a woman who barely seems capable of acknowledging his existence. He promised to love her in sickness and in health, and by golly, he's doing it.

I feel terrible that my next thought is: this guy is never going to have sex again for the rest of his life.

It's true though. And it seems unfair. Adam is young. Victoria, as she is now, can't be a partner to him in any sense of the word. She can't give him children. Is he simply going to dedicate the rest of his life to a woman who can give him nothing back?

Of course, I can't say any of that. I barely know the guy, and he's my boss. So I just smile and say, "I think that's really romantic."

Which is partially true.

He rubs at the back of his neck. "Here, let me show you how to make mashed potatoes the way she likes them."

Ultimately, Victoria's dinner consists of a mound of mashed potatoes, seasoned with butter and salt ("nothing spicy—it will upset her stomach") and a mound of puréed meat. The meat is ground beef at least, so it could be worse. It could be puréed lobster. But the food on the plate seems very unappetizing. I certainly wouldn't want to eat it.

But Victoria will have to.

I climb the stairs carefully, holding the plate in one hand and the railing with the other. I'm terrified of this staircase. With every step, I wonder if this is the one where Victoria tripped and fell down the stairs, ruining her entire life.

When I get to Victoria's room, I find her exactly as she was the first time I met her. She's sitting in her wheelchair, staring vacantly out the window. She does not react at all when I rap my fist against her open door. I know she won't answer, but it's force of habit.

"Hi, Victoria!" I say cheerfully. "It's dinner time!"

She still doesn't look up at me. Well, fine.

I walk across the room with her food and place it on the tray that Adam snapped onto her wheelchair. There's a glass of water on her dresser and I put that on the tray as well. Then I pull up a seat next to her and sit down.

"Do you want to give eating a try, Victoria?" I ask her.

She doesn't turn her head. Her restless left hand reaches for her face. Her fingers run along that painful-looking scar on her cheek.

I clear my throat. I remember the nickname Adam always calls her by. "Vicky?"

Finally, she tears her eyes away from the window. But she doesn't look pleased. She frowns at me. Maybe I shouldn't have called her Vicky. I don't know her well enough to call her by a nickname. I'm going to start over.

"My name is Sylvia." I already told her that once, but I'm assuming it's now new information to her. "But a lot of people call me Sylvie. You can call me that if you like."

Victoria doesn't have anything to say to that.

"Can you say my name? Sylvie?"

I don't know what I was thinking. That maybe I could teach Victoria to say my name? That I would perform some sort of miracle on this poor woman? Well, that doesn't happen. She just stares at me with her one good eye with the other one still pointed at the window.

I pick up her spoon from the plate and hold it out to her. "Do you want to take a bite? It's pretty good."

Well, the mashed potatoes are pretty good. I can't say the same for the puréed meat. To be honest, the sight of it is making me queasy.

Victoria obediently takes the spoon with her left hand. Her right remains motionless in the armrest. But she doesn't make any motion to scoop up any potatoes. She doesn't have the slightest bit of interest.

Well, Adam had said that most days, he has to feed her. It looks like that's going to be the case today.

"Would you like me to feed you?" I ask her. "Or... would you like something else to eat?"

Victoria's eyes widen. All of a sudden, there's a clarity there that I hadn't seen before. The blank expression is gone and I catch a glimpse of the girl from the photo. "Dorn," she says.

Dorn? What the hell is a dorn?

I look around the room, trying to figure it out. "Door?" I try. "Do you want me to close the door?"

"No. *No.*" Victoria shakes her head. A little bit of drool leaks from the right side of her mouth, and that's when I realize the entire right side of her face droops. She can only lift her lips on the left. I hadn't noticed it before because her expression was always so blank. "Dorn. It's... *dorn.*"

"Dorm?" I guess. Whatever that means.

She's getting frustrated. She throws the spoon down on her tray and starts gesturing with her left hand. "Dorn! In... dorn!"

Oh God. She's getting really agitated. "Listen..." I rise to my feet. "Let me get Adam. He'll know—"

"No!" The expression on her face is almost wild. "Dorn! For... dorn!"

Her left hand is shaking, but she manages to extend her index finger. She's pointing at something. I turn around and realize she's pointing at her dresser. "Drawer? Do you mean drawer?"

Victoria's shoulders finally go limp. She nods slowly.

Okay then.

I walk over to the drawer she was pointing at. I pull it open. It's filled with... sweatpants. So.

I lift one of the pairs of pants from the drawer. "Do you want new pants?"

She looks at me like I'm the biggest moron on the planet. She shakes her head and puffs with frustration. Her left hand is very shaky but she manages to point more vigorously. "Dorn. In..."

I don't know what else to do. So I start pulling pairs of sweatpants out of the drawer and holding each one up for her. They all look about the same. I get that she's frustrated, but so am I. It seems like there's something very specific she wants, and I have no clue what it is.

Until I pull a pair of gray sweats from the drawer and a notebook falls out.

Victoria's shoulders finally relax. "Dorn," she says softly. "You..."

I pick up the notebook which is bound in leather and about an inch thick. I flip through it and see pages of handwritten words. I can tell from the tiny, careful lettering that a woman wrote it. (What can I say—men have terrible penmanship.) I flip to the first page and see the date from three years ago.

Today I met the man I am going to marry.

I realize what I'm looking at. This is a diary.

I lift my eyes from the book. Victoria is watching me. Her one good eye is clear as day. The other is still looking in the other direction. This is the most alert I've ever seen her.

"You," she says again.

I nearly jump when I hear loud footsteps outside the door. I shove the notebook back into the drawer and slam it shut, barely missing the tips of my fingers. Adam is standing in the doorway, a large syringe in his hand that looks more appropriate for basting a turkey than giving an injection.

"Hey," he says. "I want to give Victoria her medications. Is this a bad time?"

Oh my God. Is he going to inject her with that? It looks like a syringe you'd use to give elephants their medications. "You're going to inject her with *that*?"

He looks down at the syringe then his face breaks out in a smile. "No. God, no. It goes into her feeding tube."

He mentioned earlier that he would train me to give her food through the tube, but this is the first time I've ever seen a feeding tube up close and personal. He lifts the hem of her T-shirt and I see the tube jutting out of her belly. He reaches for the end of the tube, and while he's trying to uncork it, Victoria grabs at his wrist with her left hand. It takes me a moment to realize she's trying to keep him from giving her the medications. She's fumbling for his wrist, trying to scratch him and shove him away, but he ignores her. He sticks the syringe into the end of the tube and injects the contents.

"She doesn't seem to like that very much," I comment.

"No, she doesn't," he agrees. He puts the stopper back on her tube and lowers the hem of her shirt. "I'm sure it doesn't feel good when it goes in. But she needs her medications. That reminds me..." He taps on her right hand. "One thing I need you to do is keep her fingernails trimmed. I don't need to get scratched when I'm trying to do this. There's a nail clipper in the bathroom."

It makes me think of when I used to trim my cat's fingernails when I was a child, so she wouldn't scratch up our furniture. "Okay," I agree.

Now that she's had her medications, the fight seems to have gone out of Victoria. She's slumped in her wheelchair, her blue eyes cloudy. Adam touches her cheek gently. "I'm sorry we had to do that, Vicky baby," he murmurs.

She doesn't say anything. She doesn't even look at him.

I want to tell him about the notebook I found, but when I look over at Victoria, she slowly shakes her head. I have no idea why, but if she doesn't want him to have her notebook, I have to respect that. It's obvious she wants me to have it. *You*, she said.

He lets out a sigh as he looks down at the plate of food she hasn't even touched. "Sylvia, see if you can get her to eat… something. But I'll come back in half an hour and we'll give her food through the tube if she won't."

"Does she eat most nights?"

He shakes his head. "No. Not really."

The first thing I do when Adam leaves the room is take the notebook back out of the drawer and tuck it inside my sweater.

CHAPTER 8

I don't take the diary out of my sweater until I'm back in my room.

The questions are swirling around my brain. How long was the diary sitting in there? Why was I the first person to notice its existence? And why did Victoria want me to find it? She doesn't even *know* me.

I turn the book around in my hand, testing its weight. When I flip through the pages, I see Victoria's careful writing in black ink filling page after page. The dates seem to span the course of the last two years. I notice the name "Adam" repeatedly in those pages. Which makes sense. If Victoria was keeping a diary, of course she'd write about her husband.

One thing is clear to me. Victoria wanted me to have this book. She wants me to read it.

I've wanted to learn more about Victoria, and it's obvious she's not going to be able to tell me her life story. This is my only chance to learn more about her.

So I lie down on my bed, crack open the book, and start reading.

CHAPTER 9

Victoria's Diary

June 20, 2016

Today I met the man I am going to marry.

I know, I know. I sound like a teenage girl who is all googly-eyed over a hot guy she just met. I swear, I'm not usually like that! I am one of those people who is maddeningly sensible. I do my taxes in January. I went to nursing school when my real passion was writing, because I knew the former would lead to a good, stable career, and the latter would leave me poor and starving.

But when it comes to men, I have a bit of a tendency to… well, get ahead of myself. Sometimes. Occasionally. So I've been told anyway. I admit, there have been other men I thought were the one. Bradley, in college. Noah, right after college. And Evan. I'm still not sure how I misread that one so badly…

But this is totally different. This one is it. And by that, I mean, this is It. *It.*

So of course, the first thing I wanted to do when I got home was write about it. I may be a sensible nurse practitioner rather than a writer, but I can at least use my skills to keep beautiful notes of every detail, so that someday when my children ask how I met their father, I can hand them this book and say: *Here!*

So this is for you, Future Children.

The day started out absolutely normal. Actually, worse than normal. Right before *It* happened, Mack had just brought in a couple of drunk frat boys to the ER. One was passed out cold with concern for alcohol poisoning. Another had a big bloody laceration on his forehead. And it was only eight o'clock at night, for goodness sake! How did things get so out of hand at the fraternity?

"Our best and brightest," Mack remarked after giving report on the kids.

Mack is a paramedic who brings patients in here a couple of times a night. I suspect at the point that you are reading this, he won't be a part of my life anymore. But I've gotten to know him fairly well in the last two years during his frequent drop-offs here. Sometimes he tags along with us for coffee or something stronger after the shift is done.

Mack is a good guy. He's smart—I can tell from the insightful reports he gives to the nurses. He always keeps cool under pressure. And he's big and strong enough that he can lift the two-hundred-pound drunk college kids without skipping a beat. He's also… well, he's undeniably cute. Sorry, Future Children, but it's true. He's tall, muscular without looking like he spends his days at a gym, and he's got a shock of adorably messy black hair. There was a time when I thought he might be a future husband, but then I found out he had a serious girlfriend. It was such a bummer.

Not that I care anymore about Mack having a girlfriend. But it's something that used to bother me. Yesterday.

"Are you busy tonight?" Mack asked me. He didn't mean me specifically, of course. He meant the ER—the general "you."

And yes, we were packed. It was a mix of people who started drinking early and did stupid things and people who had been sitting on that abdominal pain all week until work finally ended on Friday afternoon. Tonight seemed particularly bad. The waiting room was so full, soon people would have to start sitting on other people's laps. Every examining room was full and there were patients on stretchers in the hallway. Never a good sign.

"It's a little crazy." I shrugged. "Full moon maybe?"

Mack winked at me. "I'll try to divert patients uptown then."

"Much appreciated."

I looked over at the bloody laceration guy, who vomited all over the side of his stretcher. My own stomach turned.

"Shoot," I muttered. Technically, it wasn't my job to clean that up, but I had a feeling I was going to end up doing it somehow anyway. You can't just leave a pile of vomit in the hallway.

"I know," Mack remarked. "That kid is really fudged up."

Mack was grinning at me. He finds it hilarious that I never, ever curse. Especially since a lot of the people who work in the ER curse like sailors. What can I say—my parents taught me not to say any naughty words. Or take the name of the Lord in vain. And now that they're both gone, I'm even more dedicated to keeping it clean. There's nothing wrong with that, is there? I don't go to church on Sunday anymore, but this is a habit I'll never be able to break.

The queue of patients left to be seen was endless. The pending patient list popped up in a spreadsheet on the computer, ordered by acuity and then by the amount of time they had been waiting, and the list easily spanned three pages. That list wouldn't be completed until the sun came up. But my shift ended at ten p.m., thank heavens. I just had to make it through my shift.

So I chose the next patient in the queue.

Based on the report from the triage nurse, the patient, Adam Barnett, was a thirty-two-year-old male who had been cooking dinner, and while chopping a yellow onion—I appreciated this bit of absolutely extraneous detail from the triage report—he sliced his finger open. Anyway, the point is, he needed stitches.

I like suturing lacerations—a lot of the times when people come into the ER, we don't have an answer or an easy cure for their malady. If you come into the ER with chest pain and huge ST elevations on your EKG, we can send you up to cardiology, but it's not going to be a quick stay. If you come in with a fever and coughing up green phlegm, you're probably still going to be coughing when you leave the ER. But if you've got a laceration, I can sew you up and send you on your way. You're cured! Well, more or less.

So I headed into the room where Adam Barnett was waiting, expecting to heal him and send him on his way. But that isn't exactly what happened.

I have been a nurse practitioner for four years, and I've been working in this ER for three of those years. I've seen a lot of patients during that time. A *lot*. And of course, some reasonable percentage of them happen to be cute guys. It's just odds. I mean, yes, most of them are elderly and dripping phlegm or possibly blood, but every once in a while, the ER Gods take pity on me and there's a cute guy thrown in. And mostly, I take it in stride. Dating patients is frowned upon, so basically, they're just eye candy.

But this guy.

This guy was different.

I can't explain it. I'm a sucker for chick flicks—I've seen them all—and often when the girl meets the guy, she says it's like she got "struck by lightning." And you roll your eyes because it's such a clichéd, ridiculous thing to say. Except, somehow it was actually like that.

I feel so silly writing it down. But it really was! I walked into the room, looked at your father, and something just hit me. Like a slap in the face. Or a dose of smelling salts. (Smelling salts are surprisingly unpleasant. Don't try it at home, Future Children!)

I don't know why exactly. Yes, he was quite handsome, but there have been other handsome patients I've treated. I once treated this guy who was a vet from Afghanistan and he had muscles up the wazoo when he took off his shirt. But he didn't give me the lightning bolt like Adam did.

Maybe it was his green eyes. They were the exact color of freshly cut grass.

So instead of giving my usual spiel about how I am Victoria Benson and I will be his nurse practitioner, blah blah blah, I just stood there, my mouth hanging open. Possibly with a little bit of drool coming out.

To be totally fair though, he was doing the same thing. Well, he was sitting on the examining table, holding a hand wrapped in bloody gauze. But other than that, his expression looked a lot like mine. His mouth was hanging open and he was blinking at me. We were staring at each other like a couple of idiots, and I swear I could hear harps playing in the background.

So this is love. La la la la.

"Hi." I was the one who finally broke the silence. After all, *I* was the professional here. "I… I'm Victoria. I'm here to, you know, I'm going to hand you a suture."

He frowned at me.

"I *mean*," I corrected myself, "I'm here to *suture your hand*."

At least I got the words out. That's just what your father did to me, kids.

"Right," he said. A smile slowly crept across his face. And oh my, he was so much more gorgeous when he smiled. There was just something about him that was so *sexy*. Hmm… if my children are reading this, maybe I shouldn't use words like "sexy." I'll have to wait until you're at least twenty to let you look at this. Anyway, you're not even conceived yet, so I'm not going to worry about it.

"Is that okay?" I asked.

He nodded. "Sure. Uh, have at it."

I carefully unwrapped the crimson-stained gauze that was around his left hand. As I did so, I took note of the fact that there was no ring on his fourth finger.

Interesting. Very interesting.

The laceration was on his index finger, about three centimeters, without signs of any deep tissue damage. I could sew it up myself without having to involve the attending. I'm going to attempt to re-create our flirtatious banter:

"How did you cut yourself, Mr. Barnett?" (Barnett—

same last initial as mine. I'll still have the same initials!)

"Adam." He cleared his throat. "So... I decided to learn how to cook. I bought this book by Julia Child with all these recipes. I figured... well, anyway... it's not... it's not going that great. I think my knives are too sharp. Or not sharp enough. Or I'm just not a good cook."

I laughed, and he smiled wider. "Why did you suddenly decide to learn how to cook?" I paused. "To impress your girlfriend?"

Did you know your mother could be so smooth???

He shook his head. "No, I don't have a girlfriend. I just felt like it was an important life skill. But clearly, it's not for everyone. Maybe I should stick to things I'm good at."

No girlfriend. Even more interesting. "What are you good at?"

"Well, writing books, I guess."

And then something clicked in my brain.

The name Adam Barnett had sounded familiar when I first heard it. But now it came to me. This wasn't just some random guy. This guy was a *New York Times* best-selling author. He was a freaking *celebrity*. I had picked his latest book off the shelf at Barnes and Noble a couple of months ago and read the whole entire thing in a day. And now he was sitting in front of me!

Of course, you already know your father is a celebrity. I bet at the point you're reading this, he has written ten more number one bestselling novels. But it was a revelation for me. I had always enjoyed my writing workshop classes in college, but I went a more practical route, as you know. I admired that this guy had gone for it. And what's more, he *succeeded*. Of course, he had talent coming out of his eyeballs.

"Oh my goodness!" At this point, I had completely abandoned any attempt to be cool and sounded like a lame fangirl. All my sentences had multiple exclamation points at the end of them. "You're Adam Barnett! The writer! I love your books! I'm such a huge fan!!!"

To his credit, his ears turned slightly pink. "Well, thanks."

"Your books are so thrilling and suspenseful." Now I was gushing. How embarrassing. "How do you think of all that? I just... I mean, *The Edge of Town* was one of the best books I've read this year. I guess I always thought that the person who wrote it would be..."

There was no photo on the book jacket of Adam Barnett's bestselling suspense thriller. I remember that much, because I always check for things like that. When I'm reading a story, I like to know who is telling it. So when there was no photo, my mind came up with a picture on its own. I imagined a distinguished man with flowing silver hair who always wore a suit. It was a far cry from the guy in jeans and a T-shirt with thick chestnut hair, and lines around his eyes only when he smiled.

He raised an eyebrow. "Would be what?"

"Uh..." I searched for a word that would be the least

offensive. "Older?"

"So… I write like an old man?"

I started to correct myself but then I realized he was smiling. He was teasing me. Flirting with me. This sexy guy (sorry again, kids!) who had written one of the best books I've ever experienced was *flirting* with me. My head was starting to spin.

"Let me get you sewn up," I said.

I will confess that after I left the room, instead of grabbing the suture material, I ran straight for the bathroom to do an inventory of my appearance. Thank heavens I chose to wear my fitted scrubs today, instead of one of the baggy pairs that I wear when I'm bloated from PMS or I just don't feel like being hit on by drunk guys. My blond hair was pulled back into a messy bun in the back of my head, and I spent a good minute trying to decide if it was messy in a sexy way or messy in a sloppy way. Ultimately, I left my hair alone and just did a quick touchup of my mascara and lipstick.

I had to hand it to him—Adam was stoic when I sewed him up. An hour later, when I sewed up one of the frat guys, he cried like a baby. But your father took it like a man. He didn't even flinch when I injected the lidocaine, and we joked around as I took way too long to pop a few stitches in place. Given how busy the ER was, I really should have done it as quickly as possible and gotten him out the door. But I was selfish. I didn't want him to leave.

"I hope you're not stuck here all night," he said as I

wrapped his sutured finger in a Kerlix bandage.

"My shift ends at ten," I said.

Aaaaand… this was his chance. Hint, hint! I stood there, waiting for him to suggest going out for a drink. Okay, I'm technically not supposed to date patients, but I was willing to risk getting in trouble for a date with this guy. You don't get lightning bolts every day. Right???

But he didn't ask me out. He didn't suggest drinks or a walk around the neighborhood or a late dinner or even going back to his place. (Which I absolutely would have said no to, and you kids should do the same. Don't go back to a strange guy's apartment, no matter how gorgeous or sexy or certain you are that he's going to be the father of your children.)

After we got Adam's discharge paperwork ready and I sent him on his way, I was in a bad mood. I'm usually right when I think a guy is into me. How could you get a lightning bolt and then nothing happens, for goodness sake?

But the answer seemed obvious at the time. *I* felt the lightning bolt. He didn't. The lightning bolt was entirely one-sided.

The remainder of my shift dragged on for what felt like an eternity. All I wanted was to go home, take a nice hot shower to wash off the various smells of the emergency room, and try not to think about Adam Barnett. After a glass of wine, it wouldn't hurt quite as bad. In a week, he would be a distant memory.

By the time my shift was coming to a close, the pain was slightly dulled. Mack rolled into the ER with yet another patient, and I managed to almost return his smile.

"Hey, Vicky." Mack nudged me in the shoulder as he waited for a nurse to sign off on his paperwork. "You look wiped. Almost done?"

I winced. "Just about. But then I've got a ton of documentation to finish up."

Mack looked wiped too. His black hair was even more mussed than usual and he had beads of sweat on his forehead from his recent efforts lifting a morbidly obese patient off a stretcher into a bed. He's been taking post-bacc classes, because he says he needs to train for another job before his back goes out on him. He's been considering medical school. He thinks he's too old, but I keep telling him he should go for it. He would be a great doctor. And he's not *that* old—not even thirty.

Mack glanced down at his watch sticking out of the sleeve of the navy blue uniform all the EMTs wear. "I'm done at midnight. If you're still around by then, you want to grab a drink?"

I shrugged. "Sure. Why not?"

Of course, since Mack has a girlfriend, we would just be two friends hanging out and sharing the war stories from an exhausting shift. But I figured it would help me forget about Adam even better than a hot shower. And there would be alcohol—a key ingredient in forgetting anything painful.

Hmm. Maybe I shouldn't have said that. Don't drink, kids! Except at weddings and a glass of champagne on New Year's Eve.

But for once, I managed to finish up my documentation quickly and I was done before eleven. At that point, I didn't feel like sticking around for another hour for drinks with a cute guy who was already taken. Mack would understand.

The waiting room of the ER was still packed. A couple of hours ago, the sight of that waiting room would have given me a throbbing headache, but now I was just relieved to be done. I love my job, but at the end of a twelve-hour shift, I've got nothing left to give. But the nice thing about shiftwork is that when you're done, you're done. I could go home and not think about what I saw today.

But then when I got outside the ER, I saw him. Your father. Sitting on the bench right outside the door.

And get this: he was holding a rose!

"Victoria?" He scrambled to his feet. "Hey..."

"Hey," I said.

He later told me he had been sitting there for nearly an hour, ever since my shift ended. He walked around for an hour trying to find an open florist, even though the lidocaine had worn off and his hand was throbbing.

"Don't think I'm crazy," he said. "But as soon as I left the ER, I couldn't stop thinking about you. I'm sure there's some rule about not being able to date patients, but I would be kicking myself for the rest of my life if I didn't at least give it a shot."

"Well…" I cleared my throat. "It's not so much a rule as it is a guideline…"

He raised his eyebrows. "So… does that mean you'll come have a drink with me?"

That's right, Future Children: At the end of an exhausting ER shift, your father was waiting for me. And he gave me a rose and we got a drink that turned into a late dinner. And then we walked around the city talking until the sun came up.

He told me about how he backpacked through Europe the year after college and stayed at youth hostels until he ran out of money and then would sleep on the street because he didn't want to go home. He told me how in high school he used to sing in a country music a cappella group, but got kicked out because he couldn't carry a tune. He said his favorite movie is *Pulp Fiction*, and teased me when I said mine is *Sweet Home Alabama*, but promised to watch it. He told me that he's never cold, but he wears coats during the winter because everyone looks at him funny if he's got a T-shirt on in thirty-degree weather. I told him that I'm always cold, and he said he would keep me warm and wrapped his arms around me.

Then just as the sun was peeking out from the horizon, he leaned in and kissed me for the first time.

And oh my…

I've never met anyone like him. He is such a great guy. I've only known him less than twenty-four hours, but it's long enough to know that I'm in love. This is It. *It.*

I never believed in love at first sight until I met your father.

Chapter 10

It's so sweet, I almost want to vomit.

She sewed up his hand. He walked all over Manhattan to find her roses. They stayed up all night talking. Then they had their first kiss. It's like something out of one of those corny chick flicks that Victoria apparently liked. I wanted to roll my eyes. Multiple times.

I know Victoria wanted me to have this book, but I'm not sure how much I can read. It's painful to hear how happy she used to be, knowing how she ends up. I'll read it, but no more tonight. I can't handle it.

My stomach lets out an embarrassingly loud growl. I was so focused on Victoria's dinner that I completely forgot to eat myself. Adam told me to help myself to anything in the fridge, but I'm too tired to do any serious cooking. Maybe I'll make myself a sandwich.

When I get out of my room, I catch Adam coming out of Victoria's bedroom. His brown hair is mussed and there are slight purple circles under his eyes. He lets out a yawn, but covers his mouth when he sees me standing there.

"Sorry," he says. "I know yawns are contagious."

"Everything okay with Victoria?"

He nods. "Just getting her into bed. Her routine takes a while, so…" He yawns again. "Sorry. I'm actually more hungry than tired."

My empty stomach lets out a little roar. "Me too. I'm starving…"

He offers me a sleepy smile. "How about some fettuccini alfredo?"

Yum. That sounds amazing. I follow Adam down to the kitchen, but my excitement is somewhat dampened when he pulls two boxes out of the freezer featuring a photograph of a plastic container of fettuccine Alfredo. He shoves one of them into the microwave and hits a button.

He raises an eyebrow at me. "You look disappointed."

"I thought you were cooking them from scratch," I admit.

He laughs. "Well, sorry. I used to cook a little, but not much these days."

I cock my head to the side. "It's just sort of funny. I mean, you live in this giant house and you've got a BMW, but you eat TV dinners. I would expect you to have a personal chef or something."

He laughs harder. "You make me sound so bourgeoisie. I'm not like that." He reaches into one of the cupboards and pulls out a bottle of red wine. In spite of his protests about not being bourgeoisie, the wine looks really expensive. "Want a glass?"

"Sure." I could use a drink after the day I've had. "I've always wondered what a thousand-dollar bottle of wine tastes like."

"Thousand-dollar bottle of wine?"

"Admit it—that's how much you paid for this. At *least*."

Adam holds up the bottle and studies the drawing on the label. "Actually, I have no idea how much we paid. Victoria bought it."

Of course she did. This is Victoria's home, after all. She bought the wine, and she probably bought the corkscrew he's using to open the bottle, and the microwave he's using to heat our magnificent TV dinners. This woman had very expensive taste.

"It's okay if you spend a lot of money." I accept a heaping glass of wine from his hand—I respect that he didn't fill it up halfway. "I mean, you're a celebrity. Right?"

He snorts and looks down at his own wine glass. He filled his up to the brim too. "Not really. I wrote a few books that were a little popular."

"More than a little."

"Okay. Very. But still. I'm not exactly Hugh Jackman."

Actually, he's way better looking than Hugh Jackman. And I was a big Wolverine fan. "I feel bad that I haven't read any of your books. I'm not much of a reader, to be honest."

I bite my lip to keep from mentioning I was always a solid C student—and that was in a good year. I dropped out of high school, and although I did eventually get my GED, I never would have considered college, even if it were an option with everything else going on in my life. Adam looks like one of those guys for whom college was a given. And Victoria has an advanced degree.

"I'm glad you haven't read them," he says. The microwave dings and he swaps out one box of fettuccini alfredo for the second. "You're not going to believe me, but I hate it when people start gushing to me about my books."

"You're right. I don't believe it."

He smiles crookedly. "Fine. I like it sometimes. But I never know if they mean it or if they're just kissing my ass."

I lean against the wall of the kitchen and something jabs me in the back. I turn around and notice a large dent in the wall. I run my fingers along it.

"The wall got dented when we were moving the refrigerator in." Adam drains the rest of the wine in his glass in one swig. "I meant to get it fixed, but…"

He doesn't have to finish that sentence.

He picks up the bottle of wine and pours himself another heaping glass. He tilts the bottle toward me. "Another?"

I look down at my glass of wine, which I now realize is almost empty. Damn, I finished that quick. I look at the bottle and then at my handsome boss. I'm sorely tempted to say yes. But there's something about this place that makes me feel like I need to stay sober.

"No, thanks."

Adam nods and sticks the cork back in the bottle. "This is my last one." He glances up the stairwell, at his wife's bedroom door at the top of the stairs. "It's just been… it's been rough this year."

"I can imagine."

His eyes become cloudy and distant, the same way Victoria's were when she was gazing out the window. He runs a finger carelessly along the rim of the wine glass. "She was pregnant, you know."

I suck in a breath. "Victoria?"

He drops his eyes. "It was very early. We hadn't even told anyone yet. And obviously, she lost it when she…"

I clasp my hand over my mouth. Jesus Christ, just when I think Adam and Victoria's story can't get any sadder, he throws in another little nugget. "I'm so sorry, Adam. That must have been so hard."

He nods wordlessly. No wonder he looks so defeated. He lost his wife and his unborn child in one swoop.

After all, the only time I've ever seen Freddy cry was when he was sitting by my bed moments after the doctors told us I had miscarried our baby. But at least we had each other.

I almost tell Adam all that, but I keep my mouth shut. I don't want this to be a competition of tragedies. If it is, he would win. Mine is bad—really bad—but his is worse. Not only did he lose the baby, but there will never be another one. Even if Victoria could still get pregnant biologically, it's an ethical gray area. He'll never be a father now, whereas I still have a chance to move on. Just not with Freddy.

Adam downs about half the second glass of wine in one gulp. "It's okay," he says. "It just wasn't meant to be."

I nod, not sure what else to say.

He manages a tiny smile. "I'm glad you're here, Sylvia. The truth is, it's a lot to manage. It's nice having help. And…" He glances around the vast expanse of space that makes up the living room and kitchen. "And some company."

"Right, well…" I return his smile. "I'm glad to be able to help."

We just stare at each other for a moment. When the microwave beeps, I practically jump out of my skin. The truth is, I have no idea how Adam was living all alone in this massive house. It's so isolated here. If he wasn't in the room with me, I'd feel terrified. Even with him here, this place gives me the creeps.

"Tell you what," he says as he carefully pulls the plate from the microwave. "Let's bring our delicious dinners out to the living room and watch some TV while we eat."

I nod vigorously. "Well, they *are* TV dinners."

"My thought exactly."

So we eat our TV dinners in front of the television. We end up just watching whatever reruns are on network

TV, and even though we don't talk, we laugh at all the same places. But even as we are watching and laughing, my mind wanders.

Did Victoria and Adam sit together on this very couch, watching television while eating TV dinners?

Did Victoria have any inkling of what was about to happen to her?

And how would she feel if she knew another woman was sitting here with her husband right now?

But I don't have to wonder about that last one. I know the answer.

CHAPTER 11

Adam told me Victoria always wakes up early, so I set an alarm to get me up at seven. If I were back in my crappy neighborhood in Brooklyn, there would be some siren or explosion on the street that would get me up before any alarm, but it's absolutely silent out here. I have the best sleep of my life on this super comfortable mattress. I feel like I'm living in the lap of luxury.

I take a quick shower and then dress in simple jeans and a T-shirt. I tie my hair back in a ponytail and head over to Victoria's bedroom. I stop short when I see Eva inside the room, loading Victoria into some sort of sling. Victoria looks about as thrilled as I would be in the same situation.

"You come back later," Eva barks at me. "I get Victoria out of bed, then you come back."

"Oh, okay." I tug at my jeans. "Should I... feed her breakfast?"

Eva turns away from the sling to shoot me a look.

"That is what Mr. Adam pays you for, yes?"

Yes.

I want to ask her what sort of food I should make, but I don't feel like being yelled at again. Eva hates me. I don't understand why because I'm not *that* detestable, but it's clear she does. I'm going to have to find a strategy to stay out of her way. But in the meantime, I'll go downstairs and make Victoria some breakfast.

When I get to the first floor of the house, Maggie is down there with her red curls pulled back, vacuuming the carpet with earbuds stuffed in her ears. Before she sees me, I hear her belt out, "Girls just wanna have fu-un!"

When she sees me, she pauses her solo and pulls the earbuds out, although she doesn't look as embarrassed as I would feel if caught in a similar situation. She offers me another of her infectious, toothy grins. "Sylvie! Hi!"

I can't help but return it. "Cyndi Lauper fan?"

"Who isn't?" She kills the motor on the vacuum. "So what brings you down here?"

"Um…" I glance over at the kitchen. "I was going to make some breakfast for Victoria, but…"

Maggie gets it immediately. "Oatmeal. That's the best thing for her to eat for breakfast. I'll show you where they keep it."

"Thanks." My shoulders sag in relief. At least one person here is willing to help me. "I was going to ask Eva, but she's…"

She winks at me. "Terrifying?"

"Yes! Oh my God, I'm *so* scared of her. What's her deal?"

"I have no idea." She shrugs. "If I'm going to be charitable, I think she's just being overly protective of Victoria. Worst case: she's going to eventually murder us all with a kitchen knife."

She laughs like she's joking, but there's a part of me that's worried Eva really might murder us all at some point. She looks like the kind of person who feels the need to exact some sort of vigilante justice. And I'm fairly sure she'll murder me first.

In one of the cupboards, there are packs of instant oatmeal in every flavor you could imagine. It makes me think that oatmeal is a frequent breakfast for Victoria. I pick out a pack of apple sugar and grab a bowl to cook it in the microwave.

"Will this be enough food for her?" I ask Maggie.

She opens up the cupboard with all the baby food and pulls out a container of puréed apples. "You can serve it to her with this."

I hesitate before taking the jar. I don't want to feed Victoria baby food. It doesn't seem right.

"It's the right consistency," Maggie says. "And it doesn't taste bad. I've had it."

"You have?"

"Sure. It's like bland applesauce. What's not to like?"

The microwave dings and I remove the bowl of oatmeal. I stir it before putting it back in for another minute. It smells good at least, but the consistency is gummy. I'm not certain how it's going to taste, but it's not like Victoria eats much anyway. She only ate about a quarter of her dinner last night after I so lovingly puréed those potatoes.

The front door slams, and a second later, Adam jogs into the kitchen, wearing a T-shirt, shorts, and running shoes. He's got a vee of sweat on his T-shirt, and he pulls his earbuds out from his ears as he waves hello to us. His shirt is slightly stuck to his muscular chest—holy crap, he looks *hot*. I certainly get what Victoria saw in him that day in the ER.

"Everything going okay, Sylvia?" He leans over the counter, his green eyes focused on my face. "Do you have any questions?"

"Maggie was just helping me." I flash her a grateful smile. She has an amused expression on her face. "I'm making some oatmeal for Victoria."

"Excellent." He gives me a thumbs up. "Strong work, Sylvia. Maggie." He backs away from the counter. "I'm going to hit the shower—I'm really sweaty. I'll be up in the attic working if you need anything."

I forget about the oatmeal for a moment as I watch Adam climb the stairs. Not only does he have a nice chest, but it looks like he also has a pretty nice butt. I should probably stop staring at it though before Maggie notices.

"My boss is ever so dreamy."

I snap my head around to look at Maggie, who still

has an amused expression on her face. She's got her freckled arms folded across her chest. "What?" I say.

She laughs. "He's hot. I get it. I may have a boyfriend but I'm not blind."

I play with a lock of my hair. "He's okay."

"Suuuuure…"

"Fine." I roll my eyes. "He's hot. Obviously he's hot. But…" My eyes drift up the stairwell. "It's not like I'm going to do anything about it. He's married. And I'm…" Celibate, apparently. "I work for him. I work for his *wife*, actually." I avoid her eyes. "And even if I was going to do something about it, he wouldn't be interested. He's completely devoted to his wife."

"Well, that's true." She pulls out a large garbage bag from the pantry closet and shakes it open. "But… I mean, he's a young guy. He's got to be pretty lonely. He's a good guy and he's got good intentions, but this can't go on indefinitely. Eventually, he's going to move on."

"Well." I pull the oatmeal out of the microwave. It doesn't look appetizing. "It's not going to be with me."

Maggie grins. "Well, it's nice that you've got good intentions too."

She gives me a wink, then stuffs her earbuds back in her ears. A few moments later, she is replacing the garbage and singing Cyndi Lauper again. I grab the oatmeal and the container of apple sauce and go upstairs to Victoria's bedroom.

Eva is leaving the room just as I arrive. She glares

down at the offerings in my hands and gives me a look of disgust. I suppose instant microwave oatmeal and a jar of apple baby food isn't all that impressive. Maybe I can make her something better in the future. I wonder if I could cook some eggs and chop it up? Or throw it in the food processor. My goal is to get Victoria to eat an entire meal instead of three bites like last night.

But when I see Victoria, I have a feeling any effort I make will be a lost cause.

She looks really out of it. Much more so than at dinner last night. Her head is lolling against the headrest of her chair, and there's drool dripping out of her mouth. When I say her name loudly, she briefly opens her eyes, then shuts them again.

"VICTORIA!" I am nearly shouting now. "It's me. It's Sylvie. SYLVIE!"

Her eyes have a glazed look that's a stark contrast from the vivid blue in the photographs of her peppered all over the house. She's only able to get them open about two millimeters, then she closes them again. There's no chance of getting her to hold the spoon. I'm glad I didn't spend a lot of time making a fancy breakfast, because I'll be lucky if I can get her to take one bite.

I make an effort though. I scoop up the oatmeal and hold it to her lips. "Come on," I plead with her. "Just one bite. One little bite."

Her lips finally part about half an inch. Before they can close again, I shove the spoonful of oatmeal between her lips. She makes no effort to chew or swallow. Most of it comes right back out and I need to wipe it off with a napkin.

Goddamn it.

"It's always difficult in the morning."

I lift my eyes and see Adam standing in the doorway to the room. He's showered and changed into jeans and a T-shirt. He looks great, as usual. If I spend much more time with him, I'm going to have to start taking cold showers.

"I can't seem to wake her up enough to eat," I mumble.

He runs a hand through his damp hair. "That's typical. She's always really groggy when she first gets up. It takes at least until lunch for her to be able to keep her eyes open. Usually, after breakfast, I let her take a nap."

"Oh." I look over at Victoria, whose head is now sagging to the left in the headrest. "She does look like she could use a nap."

In fact, she looks like she's already started on that nap.

Adam shows me how to tilt the seat of the wheelchair all the way back so that Victoria is in a reclined position. I hear air whistling between her lips—she's fast asleep.

"Feel free to do whatever you need to do for the next couple of hours," he says. "She'll probably wake up around lunchtime." He nods at the window. "Why don't you go for a run? The weather is perfect for it."

I don't own a decent pair of sneakers, but I don't want

to admit that to Adam. Instead, I just smile. "Maybe."

I have no interest in going for a run. But at least I've got some time now to read more of Victoria's diary.

CHAPTER 12

Victoria's Diary

September 29, 2016

I'll be honest with you. Before I met your father I had several other relationships with men. But I want you to know that none of them meant anything to me. Well, at the time, I thought they did. Each time, I thought I was dating The One. But now I realize that they were all just practice. I was waiting for the real thing.

You'll get it someday. One day, you'll have a kind of love that you want to sing about from treetops. The kind of love where you want to use obnoxious hashtags like #Blessed or #BestBoyfriendEver. Or maybe by the time you read this, hashtags won't be a thing anymore. Maybe instead of hashtags, you'll use zebratags. Or I don't know what.

Last night, Adam took me to see *Hamilton*. That's a

show that's really big right now, based on the life of Alexander Hamilton, the first secretary of the treasury. I know, it's hard to believe that could be a hit Broadway show, but it really is. I can't even imagine what he must have paid for the tickets. Granted, he is a number one *New York Times* bestselling author (as you know), but sometimes I worry he spends too much money on me. All the guys I've dated in the past have been in student loan debt like I am or working some blue-collar job, so this is the first time I've been with a guy who spoiled me. And... well, I have to be honest here... I don't hate it.

I mean, dinner at expensive French restaurants? Flowers every time we see each other? Tickets to the hottest Broadway shows? Who wouldn't like that???

But I don't need any of that stuff! I would like Adam just as much if he took me out to McDonald's every night. I could be happy with a Big Mac and a large french fries if I had him with me.

Adam always picks me up at my apartment, even though his is much closer to Broadway. Your father is a gentleman—you can't argue with that. He holds doors open for me. I've never had a man hold doors open for me before. I just assumed that was something people only did back in the olden days, back when men wore cummerbunds and women wore hoop skirts.

When Adam showed up tonight, he was holding a bouquet of roses. "*Pour vous.*"

It's a biological fact that women love flowers. There's

so much to love about them. They smell nice. They look beautiful. And oh, the colors! I would be just as happy with a handful of daisies, but Adam always gets me roses. It's so sweet.

"You don't have to bring me roses every time we go out."

"But you love it," he pointed out. "And I *can*. So..."

"I know, but..."

It was silly to argue about it. Why would I try to dissuade him from buying me flowers? I have this fantasy that at the time you are reading this, your father is still bringing me roses... Maybe not every day, but maybe once a week. Every Friday evening. For the last forty years.

"Also," he said, "I've got something else for you."

And then he reached into his coat pocket and pulled out a rectangular box. I gasped when I saw a white gold chain with a diamond-studded snowflake pendant. It was so beautiful, I wanted to cry. I stared at the necklace, giddy with pleasure. "This must have cost a fortune," I murmured.

"You're worth it," he murmured back.

And then I pulled him inside because we honestly can't keep our hands off each other. Sorry to tell you something so unsettling about your parents, but it's true. But last night, it just ended up being kind of frustrating, because, you know, we had our tickets.

"I love you so much, Vicky," he breathed in my ear.

"I love you too," I whispered back.

And I do. I *so* do! Yes, I know we've only been together for a few months, but that's long enough to know I'm absolutely head over heels for this guy. I love him! I love him so much that I feel like I need to make up a new word to express the extent of my feelings. I *lurve* him. I *louve* him. I looooooove him.

"Hamilton," I managed as his hands slid up my back.

He kissed my neck. "I'm willing to blow it off if you are."

"Didn't the tickets cost you like a thousand bucks?"

"It's just money."

And that's your father. He loves me more than he cares about some money or some theater tickets.

Of course, good sense finally took over and we decided that we could do this just as well after the show. Adam looked a little disappointed, but he couldn't really argue. And I got to wear my snowflake necklace, which complemented my dress perfectly.

The show was, of course, amazing. I mean, it's freaking *Hamilton*. But Adam had his hand on my knee or elsewhere through the entire production, and there were moments when I was worried we might get kicked out of *Hamilton*. But then again, that would've been a story to tell, wouldn't it? Not that I would tell *you* that story. There are some things I'm sure you don't need to know about your parents!

After the show was over, we got into an argument over whose apartment we were going to go to. Well, I wouldn't exactly call it an *argument*. It was a spirited discussion. Adam is often reluctant to spend the night at my place. Which is understandable, since his place is about a million times nicer than mine, as you would expect. He's got lots of money so he's got a gorgeous two-bedroom apartment with a spectacular view of the Manhattan skyline. Whereas I've got a studio apartment with a great view of a brick wall six feet away.

I also have a slight roach problem, in spite of my diligent use of Combat. I don't understand why I can't get rid of those little buggers. That's evolution at work.

"I have a shift at work tomorrow," I explained. "I don't have time to get home and shower and get ready if we go back to your place."

"Hmm." He tapped his finger against his chin, which was sporting a rather sexy five o'clock shadow. "Well, maybe you should start leaving more of your stuff at my place so you can go to work from there."

"That's an idea…"

"Or… you could just move in with me."

All the air suddenly left my lungs. I stared into Adam's green eyes, my heart slamming in my chest. There was a smile playing on his lips, but it wasn't a jokey smile.

"Are… are you serious?" I managed.

"Well, why not?" He reached out to toy with a lock of my blond hair. He loves my hair. He says it reminds him of golden straw, which makes me feel like I'm a princess in a fairytale. "I'm crazy about you. Every night we don't spend together is just... frustrating."

Of course, I agreed instantly. As you know, I was certain from the moment I laid eyes on this man that we were going to end up together. So moving in together was just a step on the path toward spending our lives together. I can see my whole future with him. Marriage. Kids. Retirement home with matching rocking chairs, holding hands.

No, I'm not advocating that everybody should move in with her boyfriend of only three months. In many cases, it's probably not a wise idea. But in this particular case, I'm sure you would agree with me that it worked out for the best.

It was such an absolutely magical evening. *Hamilton*. Deciding to move in together. It was a night I will remember always.

There was only one tiny little incident that kind of put a damper on it.

While we were walking down the street, hurrying to get a taxi so we could get home (my new home!), a man nearly knocked into me, jostling my shoulder roughly.

I have lived in the city for a long time, so I'm used to getting jostled or pushed or shoved and once peed on (my shoe—it was a dog). And Adam has lived here for a long time too. So I was surprised at how furious he seemed at what was clearly an accident.

"Hey!" Adam snapped at the overweight man in his mid-fifties who had knocked into me. "Why don't you watch where you're going?"

The man gestured down at the cane he was holding in his left hand. "Hey, buddy, you and your girlfriend were taking up the whole street. I needed space."

Adam took a step forward. There was a dark look in his eyes that was unfamiliar to me… and a bit scary, if I'm being honest. "So you decided you wanted to feel her up?"

I blinked a few times. It's not like I've never been felt up before by a stranger in the city—the subway during rush hour can be treacherous—but this man did *not* feel me up. He just bumped into me. Why was Adam so angry over this? "Adam…" I started to say.

"Listen, buddy," the man said. "I didn't…"

"What?" Adam took another step forward, sticking his finger in the man's face. "Since you know you can't get a girl as pretty as mine, you decided to cop a feel?"

The man's eyes widened. He looked between me and Adam, and he raised his hand not holding the cane up in the air. "Look, I don't want any trouble. I wasn't doing anything."

"Yeah, right. Maybe you should apologize."

The man looked at me, a strange expression on his face. "Sorry," he finally said. Then he limped off down the street, leaning heavily on his cane.

The whole episode left me shaking a bit. I had never been in a confrontation like that with anyone before. I knew that the man hadn't felt me up, but I was oddly touched that Adam had defended my honor that way. I mean, that is real gallantry. It left no doubt in my mind that he'll be a good provider and husband.

"That probably wouldn't have happened if you didn't wear such a short skirt," Adam said.

At first, I thought I had heard him wrong. I wasn't wearing a short skirt. At all. Girls who haven't uttered a curse word in their entire lives don't walk around in itty bitty skirts—the skirt I wore tonight fell just above my knees. That's not too short.

Is it??

I blinked at him. "I thought you liked this skirt."

"I *do*." He winked at me. "I'm just saying. A skirt like that makes guys want to grab you."

He had a point, I suppose. It's unfortunate that in this day and age, a woman can't walk down the street wearing even a modestly short skirt without getting whistled at or grabbed! I hope things are better for women at the time you're reading this. Thank goodness there are men like your father to look out for women like me.

CHAPTER 13

I've spent the last hour reading Victoria's diary.

She described in detail her earliest dates with Adam. How romantic he was. How totally in love they were. When I finally read the entry about how he gave her the necklace with the snowflake and they decided to move in together, I had to stop. It's too hard to read, knowing how it ended in tragedy.

At the very least, I need a break.

Fortunately, Victoria is awake by then and is even willing to eat about a third of the lunch I prepared for her. She has tremendous trouble keeping food in her mouth. I finally have to stuff a napkin into her shirt, because about half of the stuff I put in her mouth comes right out and stains her clothing.

"Is there anything you'd like to do this afternoon?" I ask Victoria as I mop off the food that got on her chin.

She doesn't answer me. But at least her eyes are open and she's looking right at me.

"What if we style your hair?" I picture the photograph of her with the shiny golden locks. It's a far cry from her current limp colorless hair. "I can brush it out for you. And… French braid it? What do you say?"

She blinks at me. I take it as a yes.

Victoria's stash of hair care products is located in one of her bathroom drawers. There's a layer of dust covering them, which explains the condition of her hair. I find a bottle of Moroccan oil infused with antioxidant Argan oil and flaxseed extract that supposedly nourishes and helps strengthen hair. It looks incredibly expensive, and it smells nice. I also pick out a brush and one of her many combs. God, she had a lot of hair care products. All I've got is a brush and a shampoo/conditioner-in-one. I can't even afford separate shampoo and conditioner.

When I return to the bedroom, Victoria isn't looking out the window for a change. Her eyes are pinned on the door. She's been waiting for me.

Maybe she's getting to like me.

"I'm back!" I hold up the bottle. "I got you some of this great Moroccan oil. It's going to make your hair look so beautiful."

I watch her face, hoping for a tiny smile. Nope. Oh well. At some point during my time working here, I'm going to coax a smile out of this woman.

I spend the next hour working the oil through her hair. Presumably, somebody has been brushing out her hair because it didn't look tangled, but there are tiny matted areas that I need to work through carefully. Also, the last person who cut her hair obviously didn't care about doing a good job. The ends are all uneven, so I have to grab scissors from the bathroom and I spend some time trying to give her a decent haircut. I even give her a little bit of layering, but I don't want to go to crazy. I'm not exactly a master hairstylist.

"Adam is going to love your hair like this." Even though she doesn't acknowledge what I'm saying, I feel a need to keep talking. On some level, she must understand. "Men are obsessed with hair. I mean, they like boobs and butts and legs, but you can't underestimate the importance of nice hair." I pause as I snip at an uneven strand in the back of her head. "Freddy—he was my first boyfriend—he always really loved my hair."

When I come around to cut the front of Victoria's hair, I realize how intently she's watching me. She likes it when I talk to her. And for some reason, there's something therapeutic about it for me too. I've never really talked about the whole Freddy thing with anyone. Not really.

"I met Freddy in high school," I tell her. "He was a year ahead of me. He was a senior and I was a junior. He just seemed so… cool and sophisticated. And cute." I smile at the memory of watching Freddy smoking with his friends behind the school. I used to let my hair fall in my eyes as I walked past because I was embarrassed to let him catch me looking at him. "Not as cute as Adam, I guess. But he had this adorably tousled dark hair and these smoldering dark eyes… and a cleft in his chin. Jesus, he was *so* hot. I used to fantasize about him late at night. I couldn't believe it when he liked me back. I mean, *me*."

I wasn't cool when I was in high school. I was quiet and not particularly good at writing or math or sports or anything. I wore way too much eye make up, at least according to my mother, and in retrospect, she may have been right about that one. Freddy was a guy who everybody liked, a bit of a class clown, but decidedly cool. The first time he talked to me, I could barely string two words together. I didn't even realize at the time that he was shy and awkward around me too.

"So we started dating." I snip a lock of hair on the right side to even it out. "And this is the crazy part: he was a really good boyfriend. I mean, I didn't have much to compare to. I only kissed a boy once before him. But… he was sweet. He used to call me every night and we would talk for hours. Like, about *everything*. My friends said when we started going out that he just wanted to get in my pants, but that wasn't true at all. We *connected*. I thought he was…"

I thought Freddy was the love of my life. But I feel silly saying it now. *The love of my life.* What does that even mean? "I really liked him a lot," I finally say.

I tie her hair back in a French braid. I remember when I was a kid, how I used to practice French braids on my dolls. And then later, my friends. I haven't tied a French braid in years, but my fingers haven't forgotten how. Unfortunately, the braid makes the scar on her scalp more prominent. So I pull apart my handiwork and start combing it out again.

"Anyway, Freddy loved running his hands through my hair." I run my hand through Victoria's now silky hair. "We would lie together in his bed and he would just run his hand through my hair for hours."

Victoria looks up at me, a question in her eyes. *What happened next?*

What happened next was Freddy got me pregnant. Obviously, we did a little bit more in bed than just hair touching. I mean, we were a couple of teenagers.

But I don't think I should tell her that story. I should stick with happy stories. Too bad I don't know any real ones. But she doesn't know that.

"Your hair looks gorgeous," I tell her. "I'll show you. Let me get a mirror."

I run to the bathroom and grab the handheld mirror. I bring it over to Victoria and hold it up to her face. She looks at herself for a long time. Well, she looks with her right eye. The other eye still is looking off somewhere entirely different.

"You look beautiful," I say. "Adam is going to *love* it."

She frowns at herself. Then she reaches out and touches the jagged scar on her left cheek. She shakes her head.

"You know," I say. "I bet you could cover that up with makeup."

Well, not cover it up. There's *no* chance of covering up that scar. But we could make it less prominent, at least.

She shakes her head. "No," she says.

Despite everything, I have to smile. "That's the first thing you've said to me all day."

Victoria blinks at me silently. Apparently, it's going to be the last.

I clap my hands together. "I've got a great idea. How about a manicure?"

Unsurprisingly, Victoria does not seem enthusiastic about the idea of a manicure. But I look around the bathroom again and find a stash of nail polish, as well as an emery board and nail clipper. I select a vivid color called Big Apple Red.

While I give Victoria a manicure, I tell her more about Freddy. I tell her about our courtship, about how we got married in this beautiful church with our family and friends watching, and about how he completed college and got a great job as a salesman. About how we wanted to have children, but we were waiting for the right time. Saving up our money so we had a nice little nest egg.

It's all fiction, of course. It's the life I had imagined with Freddy a long time ago. It's the happy ending I always wanted to have.

Victoria's nails have been clipped down to the quick. I brought the nail clipper, but I'm hesitant to use it. Her nails are never going to look pretty if they're cut so short.

Then again, Adam told me I need to cut them short.

She scratches at him when he tries to give her the medications she needs, and I don't want her to scratch his eyes out. So the nails need to go.

Victoria watches me clip the nails on her immobile right hand. When I try to clip the left, she attempts to pull away from me.

"Just hold still," I tell her. "I'm almost done. Then your nails are going to look pretty for Adam. You'll see."

She shakes her head. "Nub," she says.

Well, at least she's talking again. "They're not completely nubs. They're just short."

"No." She grips my right hand in her left. "Nub. Adam nub."

"Do…" I search her face, trying to figure out what she wants to say. "Do you want Adam to cut your fingernails?"

"No." She shakes her head again, her eyes filled with frustration. I can't even imagine what it's like to not be able to get out the words you need to say to express what you want. "No. *No*. Adam nub. In the… nub."

Uh…

"I'm sorry," I finally say. "I just don't… understand."

It's at that moment Adam peeks in the doorway to Victoria's room. It's sweet that he's always coming to check on her. Although once I get my footing, he probably won't feel the need to do it anymore. He offers a crooked smile. "Everything okay in here?"

I look over at Victoria, who has given up on what she wanted to say. She's now staring vacantly out the window.

"She keeps asking for something," I say. "But I don't know what it is. She keeps saying 'nub.' Do you have any idea what that means?"

He cocks his head to the side. "I don't know. I've never heard her say that before."

Oh well. "Anyway, we did her hair and her nails. Doesn't she look great?"

"She looks beautiful," Adam says, although there is a definite lack of sincerity in his voice. He is telling Victoria she looks beautiful the same way you tell a small child that their scribble in crayon is beautiful. "You cut her hair. It looks good."

"Yeah, whoever did it last time did a terrible job. You shouldn't hire them again."

Adam snorts. "I think it was the surgeons, right before they operated on her skull."

"Well, they should stick to emergency surgeries then."

"I'll pass on the feedback." He crosses the room and spends a moment looking at his wife. He lifts her right hand out of the armrest. "Did you cut her nails?"

"Yes. But she didn't like it."

"Unfortunately, it's not her decision."

Victoria won't turn her head to look at him. It's like she has completely turned herself off the moment he walked into the room. Given they were married before and he has dedicated his life to taking care of her, it's strange that she won't even acknowledge him. Strange and sad.

"Why don't you take a break, Sylvia?" Adam says. "I

need to help Victoria with some personal stuff."

"Personal stuff?"

His eyes flick downward. "Change her diaper."

Oh God. Of course, it makes sense. But I'm suddenly mortified for this beautiful, intelligent woman who is now so dependent for her most basic needs.

I wonder what a nub is. I wonder what she was trying to tell me.

I just want to understand her better. And the only way to do that at this point is to keep reading her diary. After all, she wanted me to have it. And I've got nothing but time out here.

CHAPTER 14

Victoria's Diary

October 10, 2016

You know what's a bummer? When you're happy, but somehow, your friends can't be happy for you.

I was nearly at the end of my shift today in the ER when Carol suggested getting drinks. Carol is my closest work friend, and because of how often I work, she's quickly becoming my closest friend—especially because of her proclivity to want to hang out after work to unwind. Mack was finishing his ambulance shift, so he jumped in and said he wanted to go also. Of course, Carol is fine with that because everybody likes Mack. Then Mack asked me if I was going.

"Sorry," I said. "I've got to pack."

Mack wrinkled his nose. Before Adam came into my life, I used to find it very cute when he did that. "Pack?

Where are you going?"

Carol giggled. "Didn't you hear? Vicky is moving in with Mr. Perfect."

Yes, Mr. Perfect is Carol's nickname for Adam. He *is* rather perfect.

Mack blinked at me and took a step back. "You mean that big shot author guy? You're *moving in* with him?"

He seemed upset, which I didn't understand. Mack had never been interested in my personal life before. "His name is Adam, you guys," I said. "And yes. We're moving in together."

I still have a hard time saying those words without smiling like a fool.

Mack frowned. "Don't you have a lease?"

"Well, yes," I admitted. "But Adam is buying me out of it."

"Wow." Carol patted her pixie cut. "I wish I had a rich boyfriend…"

"He's not rich…"

The truth is, I'm not sure how much money Adam has. He certainly spends like he has a lot of money. Not that it matters to me either way. I'd like him just as much whether he's rich or poor.

Weirdly, Mack didn't end up going out with Carol, even though he was done with his shift. He kept hanging around the nursing station and casting looks in my direction. About five times, he opened his mouth like he wanted to say something. Finally, I couldn't take it anymore.

"Is everything okay?" I asked him.

He frowned. "Can I talk to you for a minute?"

"Sure. What's up?"

"Not here."

And then without warning, he grabbed me by the arm and pulled me down the hallway. I had no idea what he was doing until he opened the door to the linen closet and pulled me inside. Good thing I'm not claustrophobic, because it was a tiny space surrounded by piles of towels, sheets, and blankets.

"Um, excuse me!" I said. "Can you please tell me what's going on here?"

Mack's eyebrows knitted together. "Vicky, don't you think things are moving a little fast between you and that guy?"

I feel like there is an unspoken understanding between friends that you don't say bad things about your friends' significant others. I mean, after the breakup, you can say whatever horrible thing you want. But when you're dating, you keep your fool mouth shut! Unless the other person is doing something really horrible, like cheating on you with hookers.

Mack was breaking the unspoken rule.

"Honestly, Mack?" I lifted my chin to look him in the eyes. "It's none of your business."

He lowered his eyes. At least he had the sense to look embarrassed about what he had just said.

"I'm sorry." He rubbed at his black hair until it stood up straight. "I just get a really bad vibe from that guy. I feel like you don't know him well enough."

That's what I get for inviting Adam to come out for drinks with my friends from work. Now all they do is judge him. But at least when Carol judges him, she calls him Mr. Perfect. But now Mack is saying Adam gives off a bad vibe. What does that even mean? Adam is a successful author, he's handsome, he's smart, he's considerate, he's romantic... I could go on for a while like this.

A bad *vibe*? Really???

"Look," I said. "Adam is a great guy. You only met him one time."

"And that's enough to know."

"Well, I've been dating him for three months. So if one night is enough, three months has to be enough, right?"

Mack took a deep breath as he leaned against a precarious cart of towels. Mack is a big guy and I was a little bit worried the rack might tip over. "Please, Vicky. Just think about it. I don't want you to make a mistake."

I snorted. "You know, this is *really* inappropriate. I never told you I didn't approve of Kaitlyn. I never said a word about her."

He was quiet for a moment, just staring at me. "Kaitlyn and I broke up."

What?

So Mack's girlfriend Kaitlin was one of those girls.

One of those girls who is just so pretty and funny and clever that you want to hate her, but you can't because she's actually really nice. Kaitlyn had no flaws. After I met her, I knew I had zero shot with Mack, because there was no way anyone would ever break up with a girl like Kaitlyn.

"I... I'm sorry to hear that."

He shrugged.

"What happened?"

"It's a long story." He glanced over at the door to the closet. "Maybe another time..."

That is *such* a typical guy thing. He thinks he can tell me what to do in my relationship. But at the same time, he won't even tell me why he broke up with his girlfriend!

"Listen." He lowered his voice a few notches. "Just... please think about it before you do anything. Promise me you'll think about it."

"Fine. I promise."

But I didn't mean it. Goodness, what is there to think about? Right now, I live all alone in a tiny, roach-infested apartment. The man of my dreams is asking me to move in with him. What on earth is there to think about? It's terribly sweet that Mack is worried, but there's nothing to worry about. Carol is the one who's got it right—your father really is Mr. Perfect.

October 18, 2016

Today was moving day! I am currently writing this from my... drum roll please... new apartment! That I share with my wonderful, handsome, multitalented boyfriend!!!

The day started out absolutely insane. I had everything stashed away in boxes and Adam hired a moving company to help me. A moving company! I felt so bourgeoisie. Every time I have ever moved in the past, I had to beg a bunch of friends to help me in exchange for pizza and beer. It did seem a bit like overkill to hire a moving company considering I only had a studio apartment's worth of stuff, but Adam was insistent.

He likes to spoil me. It's so sweet.

About an hour before the movers were supposed to arrive, I was packing up the last of my stuff when my phone started to ring. I glanced at the screen and saw Mack's name. My fingers hovered over the green button, but I wasn't sure if I should press it.

I was still miffed about the way Mack spoke to me a few days earlier. And I had no delusion he had changed his mind. I didn't want to have yet another discussion about how I was making a giant mistake. He just didn't get it.

But finally, curiosity got the best of me and I picked up the phone.

"Hey, Vicky." His voice sounded upbeat on the other line. He didn't sound like a guy who was about to give me another lecture. "I heard today is moving day."

I smiled. "Who told you?"

"Carol."

I gripped the phone in my right hand. "So… is this one last phone call to talk me out of it?"

He was silent for a beat. "No. Actually, I… I want to apologize. What I said to you the other day… That was out of line."

My eyebrows shot up. One lesson I've learned in life is that people don't apologize much. At least, not as much as they should. Even if they are wrong wrong wrong.

"Well… yes. It was. Sort of."

"Well, I'm sorry." He cleared his throat. "And if you say Adam is a good guy, I'm sure he is."

"He's a good guy, Mack."

"Then fine. That's good enough for me." I could hear him take a deep breath on the other line. "Also, as penance, I want to offer to help you move. I'm pretty good at lifting heavy things like boxes. Or if you have some patients in your room that need to be moved onto or off a stretcher, I can do that too."

I laughed. "No, I don't need help. Adam hired a moving company for me."

"A moving company? Wow. That's too rich for my blood."

Me too, I wanted to say. But I couldn't say it, considering my boyfriend was the one paying for all this.

"Anyway," he said, "I just wanted to offer. And, like I said, to apologize. So… good luck. With the move, that is."

"Right. Thank you."

Mack was quiet again on the other line. I got the sense there was more he wanted to say, but he wasn't saying it. And I also got the sense that whatever he wanted to say, I probably didn't want to hear. So it was better to just say goodbye.

The moving guys were amazing. They came to my door and lifted all my heavy furniture like it weighed less than air. My bed wasn't coming with me—a nurse from work was taking it, so she didn't have to sleep on a futon anymore. I was also giving up my dresser because Adam said he had more than enough space in his own dressers. After the movers got everything packed up, I took a taxi over to Adam's apartment.

When I got to his apartment, I had to ring the doorbell because he hadn't gotten around to making me a key yet. It took him forever to answer the door—I started to get a little panicked he wasn't there! I didn't know what I was going to do if the movers showed up here with all my belongings and I couldn't even open the door to the apartment. But thank heavens, he materialized in boxers and an undershirt, and he let me inside. But he did not look happy, especially given that the love of his life (i.e., me) was about to move in with him.

"What are you doing here so early?" he snapped at me.

I frowned, not entirely certain what to say. "I told you the movers were coming at nine. It's ten o'clock now."

He shook his head. "*No*, I told you not to have them here before noon. I'm trying to *write*, Victoria."

"But I told you they were coming at nine."

"No. You never told me that." He ran a hand through his already messy brown hair. He hadn't shaved yet and he still had a day's growth of a beard on his face. "If you *had* told me that, I would've told you not to have them come so fucking early."

Adam does not share my feelings about never taking the name of the Lord in vain. I mean, he doesn't have a terrible potty mouth. I'm sure you know your father by now. I'm sure he lets out an F-bomb or S-bomb every once in a while. There are worse things.

But this was the very first time he ever cursed *at* me. Although to be fair, he wasn't cursing at me *exactly*. He was cursing about the earliness of the day. But I did feel like it was directed at me. Like the earliness was my fault.

I blinked and took a step back. "Adam…"

His lips formed a straight line. "I've got a deadline, Victoria. Do you think I'm going to be able to concentrate with moving guys tromping all over the apartment the whole goddamn morning?"

Again with the swearing.

"Um…" I squeezed my fists together. "I'll tell them to be quiet."

"You'll tell the moving guys to be quiet? You've got to be kidding me." He let out a long sigh. "This is really inconsiderate. You *knew* I had to get this draft done by

Friday."

I'm not the kind of person who gets things wrong a lot. I am the careful, responsible one. And I told him the movers were coming at nine. I am 110% sure. I bet if I took out my phone, I would find at least half a dozen exchanges where I reminded him the movers were coming at nine. I was tempted to do it just for the joy of saying I told you so, but I could see how stressed out he was. My job is stressful too, but in a different way. I can't imagine what it's like to have to be creative on command.

When you're in a mature, adult relationship, you realize that the most important thing isn't always proving you're right. I knew proving him wrong wasn't going to make the situation better, so there was no point.

"I'm sorry," I said. "It's my fault. But I promise it will be very quick. And I'll try not to bother you at all."

And guess what? The apology did the trick. Adam's shoulders relaxed. He wrapped his arms around me and pulled me close to him. "Thanks, Vicky," he said. His arms felt warm around me. "I'm sorry I snapped at you. I got this crazy deadline that's stressing me out. I just need to get this stuff done and then I'll be able to relax."

"I understand." I rested my head against his shoulder. "And I'm sure whatever you write will be brilliant."

"It's just all this pressure." He shook his head. "This is my third book, and people are expecting a lot from me. If it's not as good as the other two…"

"It will be."

"No offense, Vicky." Adam pulled away and rubbed at his temple. "But you don't know anything about this process."

I did admit to Adam that I had briefly considered becoming a writer in college. I even sent him a short story I had written, and he showered me with praise, although he didn't suggest I try to write a book or anything like that. He didn't say, *You absolutely must keep writing—you can't abandon your magnificent talent.* Which makes me think he didn't like the short story as much as he claimed to.

Anyway, he was right. I had a little experience with writing, but I had no experience with the process of writing a novel. But I was still confident anything Adam wrote would be brilliant.

The movers materialized within the hour and deposited all my belongings into Adam's much larger and vastly superior apartment. It was mostly boxes containing books and bags of clothing. The only pieces of furniture I had were a couple of lamps and a Papasan chair that I purchased when I first came to the city years ago. That chair is the comfiest piece of furniture I've ever owned. That chair has a 99% success rate for curing insomnia. Sometimes when I'm in my bed at night, I fantasize about that chair.

When I die, you're getting that chair. And you're going to thank me for it.

Adam proudly showed me all the space he had cleared away for me to store my clothes. He cleared out three drawers and about half his closet. I opened one of the drawers and ran my hand along the wood.

"You've never lived with a woman, have you?" I said.

He raised an eyebrow. "Why do you say that?"

"Because you clearly don't have any concept of how much drawer space we need."

That got a laugh out of him. "Sorry. I could probably fit everything I own in two of these drawers."

"Maybe I can still get my old dresser back…"

He made a face. "God no. We'll buy you a new one."

There was nothing wrong with my old dresser. I tried to tell him that, but he said something about how it didn't go with any of his furniture and it looked cheap, and I just gave up on arguing. If Adam wanted to waste his money on a new dresser, that was fine with me.

Adam led me into the kitchen. He threw open the refrigerator and I saw that the bottom shelf had been cleared out. "That shelf on the bottom will be yours and the top will be mine. We can split the middle one."

I stared down at the empty shelf. "Do we really need to have separate shelves in the refrigerator?"

He shrugged. "I think it's better this way. Don't you?"

I glanced down at a bottle of Pepsi in the middle shelf. Adam had scrawled his name on the bottle in permanent marker.

I opened my mouth to protest, but then I shut it. Adam was already stressed out. The last thing he needed was for me to give him a hard time over the refrigerator. I still haven't managed to bring it up with him, but we'll talk about it in the next few days.

When we went back into the living room, Adam's eyes immediately went to my comfy blue Papasan chair (your inheritance). His mouth fell open like I had brought a garbage bag filled with rotting eggs into his home. "What is *that*?"

"That's my Papasan chair!"

"It…" He frowned. "It looks like you got it from off the *curb*."

"It's old," I admitted. "But it's *super* comfortable. Give it a try. I promise—you're going to fall in love."

He took a step back like I had asked him to roll around in sewage. "It's probably infested with roaches."

"No, it's not!" Well, probably not. I guess I don't know for sure there are no roaches in that chair.

"Can't we just throw it out?" He looked up at me for permission. "I mean, I have a five-thousand-dollar leather sofa with a loveseat. Do we really need that piece of…"

For a moment, I considered giving in. I had already apologized for the moving people coming too early. I had not said a word about the division of the refrigerator. Why fight over a chair?

And if it were *any other chair*, I would've let it go. But this was my *favorite* chair. My comfy, irreplaceable Papasan chair! I was giving up everything else I owned. Why couldn't I keep this one thing?

"I really want to keep the chair," I said softly but

firmly. "It's important to me."

Adam opened his mouth as if to protest, but then his face softened. "Okay. If it's important to you, we'll keep the roach-infested chair."

And that's how it's done. That's how two adults in a loving relationship problem solve. I gave in on some of the issues that weren't that important to me, and he gave in on something that *was* important to me. It's funny because even though I had told Mack I was sure I was doing the right thing by moving in with Adam, I guess I did slightly have some doubts. There was this little nagging voice in the back of my head telling me it was too soon and I should wait. I feel guilty even writing it here.

But at that moment, I knew I was doing the right thing.

And guess what? Right now, Adam is brushing his teeth and we're going to go to bed together. In *our* bed.

I am so happy.

#Blessed

CHAPTER 15

Could "nub" be Victoria's Papasan chair?

No, probably not. But even so, it seems like she was very attached to that chair. What if I located Victoria's chair downstairs and brought it up to her? Obviously, she couldn't sit in it very long, especially since she seems to have trouble supporting her own head, but considering how much she loved that chair, it might be worth a shot.

I imagine the look of surprise and happiness on her face when she sees her old chair. I have to do this.

First I have to figure out what the hell a Papasan chair is.

I google what a Papasan chair looks like. It sort of looks like a bowl. It doesn't seem terribly comfortable, honestly, but I'm not going to doubt Victoria's word. In any case, I don't recall seeing it downstairs. But then again, I wasn't looking.

I head downstairs to the living room and find Maggie folding laundry on the sofa. She smiles brightly at me.

She's always eager to take a break from her housework. "How's it going?"

I scan the living room quickly. They've got an enormous sectional sofa, a lounge chair, a giant TV, and multiple bookcases... but no chairs shaped like a dish. "Do you know where Victoria's Papasan chair is?"

Maggie looks at me blankly. "Her what?"

"Papasan chair."

"What the hell is that?"

I'm relieved I'm not the only person who didn't know what a Papasan chair is. "It's a chair that kind of looks like a bowl. You sit in it." (Obviously. It's a chair.)

She folds up a pair of khaki slacks that look like they belong to Adam. "I haven't seen any chairs that look like bowls down here. Sorry."

"Is there a place where they store furniture?"

She frowns. "Maybe the attic? I'm not sure. You should ask Adam."

The last thing I want to do is bother Adam when he's helping Victoria with her hygiene. But it's been long enough now that I would hope he's done. He might be searching for me right now. So I carefully climb the stairs to Victoria's room, where sure enough, he's got her back in her wheelchair.

When he sees me standing in the doorway, he flashes a wide grin. "Hey. Perfect timing."

"I got a question for you."

"Shoot."

"Do you have a Papasan chair here?"

His brows scrunch together. "A what?"

I'm feeling less than optimistic that we're ever going to find this chair. "It's a chair that's sort of shaped like a bowl."

He blinks a few times. "Do you need an extra chair for your bedroom?"

"No, I…" This is hopeless. He has no idea what I'm talking about. Obviously, at some point, Victoria got rid of the chair. "Never mind."

Adam pulls off the latex gloves he was wearing. "Because if you need any furniture, I'd be happy to get it for you. Just let me know."

This man is exactly how Victoria described him. He's so generous. Anything she asked for, he would get her. And then some. He's so good-natured. He didn't deserve this to happen to him. And neither did she

Life is so unfair.

CHAPTER 16

It's my second week taking care of Victoria, and I feel like I'm finally getting the hang of things. I prepare all her meals, and I've managed to coax her into eating nearly half of her dinner most nights, although breakfast usually goes right in the garbage. Adam showed me how to do her tube feeds, so I give her a supplement if she doesn't eat at least half of the meal. She hates getting the tube feeds, so reminding her of this is usually enough to coax an extra bite or two out of her.

Victoria and I have bonded a bit. It's hard to tell because she doesn't talk much and she spends large quantities of time just staring out the window. I've yet to coax a smile out of her. But I talk nonstop while I'm doing her hair or helping her with meals, and she always looks like she's listening.

Unfortunately, Eva hasn't warmed up to me at all. I pass her in the kitchen this morning while I'm preparing breakfast for Victoria, and she doesn't even attempt to disguise the distaste on her face. I don't need to be liked by everyone, but I'm not used to the feeling of someone hating me for no reason at all.

"She is waiting for you," Eva says.

I force a smile. "I'm almost ready."

Eva tugs on her coat. "You always make her wait. I'm sure she is used to it by now."

"I don't—" I start to say, but then I wonder what's the point. Eva hates me. I don't know why, but I'm not sure I can change that fact. Instead, I try a different tact. "I like your hat, Eva."

Hey, compliments worked with Victoria. But Eva is not as easily charmed. She just glares at me and walks out the door without even thanking me for the compliment. It's just as well because I don't really like her hat.

Adam is returning from his jog just as she's leaving, and I notice she barely said a word to him either. Clearly, I'm not the only person in the house she dislikes. I wonder why he keeps her around when she's so outright hostile to him.

Adam looks adorably sweaty and tousled from his run outside. He looks so cute that I forget what I was trying to find in the fridge and just stand there like an idiot until he comes over to me and says, "Excuse me, Sylvia."

"Oh." I take a step back. "Sorry."

He reaches into the fridge and pulls out a water bottle. He takes a long swig that lasts at least a minute, then wipes his lips at the back of his hand. I wonder how far he ran. I can just imagine him pumping his legs as the muscles flex with each step.

Ugh, I need to stop fantasizing about my boss. This is the most pointless crush ever.

I clear my throat. "Nice weather out?"

He nods. "Beautiful. I'm going to keep running until there's snow on the ground."

I glance at the stairs. Victoria is supposedly waiting for me, but there hasn't been one day I've come to give her breakfast when she hasn't been sound asleep in her wheelchair. I don't know why she's always so tired in the morning.

"I thought maybe I could take Victoria out for a walk today," I say. "If you say the weather is nice, that is. I think she'd enjoy getting out of the house."

"Sure." He takes another swig from the water bottle. "Maybe after lunch, I'll help you bring her downstairs. But be careful." He glances out the window overlooking the front yard. "We haven't had a gardener in a while and the paths are overgrown."

"Yes…"

"I should have been on top of that." He hangs his head sheepishly. "It's just that Irina, our old gardener… well, she…" He lowers his eyes. "Anyway, I just didn't have time to think about it with Vicky's injury and getting the house ready and… all that."

"Of course," I say. "Don't worry. We'll be fine."

We arrange to have him help me get Victoria

downstairs at around two in the afternoon. I rush upstairs to tell Victoria, hoping she'll understand what I'm telling her enough to get a little excited about the whole thing. If I can wake her up enough to make her understand.

But when I get upstairs, her head is lolling to the side and she's sound asleep in her chair.

Eva must have turned on the television before she went. It's playing an episode of *Let's Make a Deal*. Everyone on the screen is cheering—the volume of the TV must be turned up to the highest number, but Victoria is sound asleep. Her lips are slightly parted as she blows air in and out, and there's a bit of drool coming out of the droopy right side of her mouth.

I sit down next to her and put the plate of food down on the tray Eva set up. I touch Victoria's shoulder. "Time to wake up."

Her eyes crack open briefly, then shut again.

"Come on, Victoria," I plead. "Just eat a little. Then we don't have to do the tube feeds."

Victoria hates anything going down her feeding tube. She hates the cans of nutrients we inject if she doesn't eat enough at meals. And she *really* hates the medications Adam injects every night. She fights him like a banshee to keep him from giving it to her, but it never works. She always gets her medications.

I scoop up a bit of oatmeal onto a spoon. I hold it out to her, pausing just before touching the spoon to her lips. "Come on. Take one bite."

I see a flash of her blue iris briefly, but then her eyes close again.

"Aren't you hungry?"

She groans and turns her head away so there will be no chance of getting any food in her mouth. Fine. Every day over the last week, I've tried to feed her breakfast for nearly an hour, then ended up having to do the tube feeds anyway. I'm wasting my time.

So I go to the bathroom, where we keep the cans of Jevity—a special formulation of nutrients that tastes horrible but it doesn't matter when it's bypassing the mouth. It's a tan color, and the sight of it makes my stomach turn. I retrieve a fresh syringe and a cup of water to help the tube feeds go down smoothly, then I return to Victoria's room.

Victoria cracks her eyes open again when I lift the hem of her T-shirt to get at the feeding tube. She watches me for a second, then lays her left hand against the curve of her belly.

"Bade," she says.

I lift my eyes and see a sad expression on her face. I wish I knew what was going on in her head. I have no idea what she's talking about. It's so frustrating not to be able to understand her speech. It's like taking care of a...

Oh.

"Baby?" I say.

Her abdomen bulges slightly, but not like there's a baby inside. It's more just from the gentle swell of her abdominal contents. But she's got her left hand on it, frowning. "Bade-bee."

I clear my throat. "I heard you were pregnant."

She lifts her eyes from her stomach, still frowning.

"I… I was once pregnant." I don't know what compelled me to tell her this. I haven't spoken about my pregnancy in a very, very long time. Maybe it's because I know Victoria is the one person I can guarantee won't ask a bunch of awkward questions or try to comfort me, and she definitely won't tell another soul.

"You." She points to my belly. "Bade…"

"It was an accident," I explain. So far, I've told her only happy stories about myself, but I suddenly feel compelled to tell her this one. No matter how painful. "I know you wanted yours, but… we didn't. We were too young. I was only seventeen and Freddy was eighteen. I still had a year left to go of high school, but…" I squeeze my eyes shut. "We wanted it. We were broke, but we wanted it."

I had expected Freddy to look horrified when I gave him the news, but instead, he danced around like an idiot. *I'm gonna be a father,* he kept saying. It was cute. I mean, we were terrified, but his excitement got me excited. I knew we were going to be broke, but we'd be broke and happy. And together.

I see the question in Victoria's eyes. "How…?"

"There was an accident and I lost the baby," I say. "Sort of like what happened to you."

But that's not true. Not really. Because what happened to me wasn't an accident.

Freddy walked me home from school that day. He held my hand like he always did, my smaller fingers laced into his bigger ones. When we got closer to my house, he pulled his hand away from mine and wrapped his arm around my shoulders protectively.

"You're going to tell your parents tonight?" he asked me.

I nodded. "I'll tell them after dinner. It's easier to give my father the news on a full stomach."

Freddy stopped walking and turned to me, a deep crease between his dark eyebrows. "Let me be there."

"It's better if you're not."

"I should be there. I want him to know I'm a standup guy. That I'm going to take care of you."

"It's a bad idea."

He chewed on his lower lip. "What if he gets really angry at you?"

"I can handle that."

I didn't want to tell him what I was thinking, which is that I *expected* my father to get really angry. He hated Freddy and was counting down the days till I went off to college and hopefully broke up with him. But none of that was going to happen now, and I was scared about his reaction. My father was a lot bigger than Freddy. I could imagine him beating my boyfriend to a bloody pulp.

Freddy tried to argue with me, but it was my decision.

So that night, after my father had eaten two large squares of Mom's homemade lasagna, I knew it was now or never. I had to tell him. Before I started to show and he figured it out for himself.

I watched him as he wiped tomato sauce off his ruddy face with the back of his hand. He loosened his belt buckle and undid the top button on his pants. Throughout my entire childhood, my father was always about ten pounds overweight, and lately, it had been edging towards twenty. But he was in good shape. Big and strong from years of construction work.

My mother was at the table too, finishing off a glass of wine. It was the second one I'd seen her drink that night, but I suspected it wasn't her second one of the night. I was worried my mother drank too much, but when I mentioned it to her, she brushed me off.

"Mom, Dad," I said. "I've got some news."

His blue eyes lit up. That was the very last time I ever saw my father look happy. "Did you get your SAT scores back?"

"No." I rubbed my palms against my jeans. I hadn't been able to eat more than two bites of lasagna tonight. I was too nervous. "It's something else."

"Oh?"

I took a deep breath. "It's about Freddy."

Any trace of a smile faded from his face. "What? I hope you're telling me you're breaking up with him."

"Dale…" Mom said. It was her warning voice, but I'd

never seen her successfully calm my father down. I don't know why she bothered.

"Did you?" Dad pressed me. "Did you finally toss that no good hoodlum to the curb?"

I looked down at my hands in my lap. "Not exactly."

"Not exactly?"

I couldn't bear to look at him. "Actually, we're getting married."

I could almost hear the steam shooting out of my father's ears. His voice became a roar. "*Married*? Are you out of your mind? You're only sixteen! Why would you get married unless—"

And then he got it.

I can still picture the way my father rose from his chair, his face slowly turning purple. Mom kept saying his name, but it did nothing. I had never seen him this angry in my entire life. I thought I'd seen him angry before, but this was something entirely different. It looked like he was possessed.

"You slut," he hissed. "How could you? How did you let yourself get knocked up by that little bastard?"

I didn't know what to say. It wasn't like I planned it.

"This is not going to happen." He pounded his fist against the table. "You are not going to marry him. You are not going to have his baby. I'm not going to let you destroy your future."

I looked up at him, my heart pounding. "What?"

A vein stuck out on the side of his temple. It throbbed

so violently, it looked like it might burst. "Tomorrow we're going to the doctor. We're going to take care of this."

"No!" Now it was my turn to jump out of my seat. "I don't want to do that! I want the baby!"

"You're just a stupid kid. You don't know what you want."

"I'm old enough to make this decision." I took a step back. "You can't make me do this!"

I started to walk away, but before I could, his fist wrapped around my wrist. He'd never laid a finger on me in my life, but he was making up for lost time. There was fire in his eyes and I knew I had made a terrible mistake when I told Freddy not to come with me. Freddy would have stopped this from happening.

"Let me go!" Tears were in my eyes but I refused to let them fall. I didn't want to give him the satisfaction.

"You're doing what I tell you to do." His eyes were like steel. "I spent my whole life working to give you a good life. And this is how you repay me? By getting knocked up by a loser like Freddy Ruggiero?"

I tried to kick at him, but it was no use. He was squeezing my wrist so hard, it felt like the bones might be crushed. My fingers started to tingle. And then, without warning, he shoved me so hard that I fell over my chair onto the ground. I landed hard, on my right wrist.

"You have some nerve!" As he spit the words at me, he kicked me hard in the side. Later, I found out he cracked a rib. "When you're in my house, you live by my rules, you ungrateful bitch!"

He kicked me again, but I managed to somehow scramble to my feet. My wrist where he had grabbed me was dark red and the other wrist that I had landed on hurt like crazy. And my ribs hurt so badly, I felt like I couldn't breathe. But I managed to run out the front door, and I didn't stop running until I got to Freddy's house.

And that was the last time I ever saw my parents. Funny—I don't even miss them.

But I do miss Freddy sometimes.

CHAPTER 17

The weather thankfully holds up, and we're able to go outside as planned.

Getting downstairs is not the easiest task. There's no easy way to get a wheelchair down an entire flight of stairs, so the only way to get down is for Adam to lift her out of the chair and carry her. Fortunately, she's very light, and he's able to do it without even breaking a sweat. He's got another wheelchair down on the first level so he doesn't have to carry her chair down too.

"I'm worried she'll be cold," I say to Adam as I zip up her hoodie sweater. It's nice out, but a bit on the nippy side. I'm wearing a coat, but I feel like it might be hard for her to wear one. A warmer sweater would probably do the trick.

"Go look in the walk-in closet in our bedroom," he says. "She's got tons of clothes in there."

I don't know how I feel about going into Adam's bedroom and sifting through the closet. He notices my hesitation and waves a hand at me. "Come on. I'll show you."

Adam's bedroom, which I suppose used to be Adam and Victoria's bedroom, is much larger than any of the other rooms. It has a large double bed, and the covers are in disarray since Maggie isn't here today. I wonder if Victoria was the sort of woman who liked the beds to all be made every morning—my mother was like that. She drilled it into me so hard that I still make my bed every day, even though I haven't spoken to my mother in eight years.

There's a smaller closet in the bedroom that I suppose belongs to Adam. He keeps the door to that one firmly closed. He swings open the larger door and I can't help but let out a gasp.

"Vicky liked clothing." He shrugs sheepishly. "I don't know what's in here. I haven't touched it since…"

I step inside the massive closet. God, there are a lot of clothes in here. Rows and rows of them. It's practically a department store in itself. And when I check the labels, I realize nothing in here is cheap. Everything is name brand.

There's a certain irony to the fact that a woman with such an amazing wardrobe now dresses primarily in sweatpants, T-shirts, and hoodies. Obviously, Victoria was someone who cared a lot about style. Even in the diary entries I read, it was clear she took a lot of care with her appearance. It must kill her that she's always in her sweats.

And nobody can tell me she isn't aware of it. She knows.

As if reading my mind, Adam says, "I wish she could still wear this stuff. But she spends all her time sitting or in bed. She needs to be in clothes that are comfortable and big enough not to rub against her skin." He fingers a pair of designer skinny blue jeans. "The back pocket on these would cause a pressure sore. And she's so stiff, I don't know how we'd get them on her."

He's got a point, but I still feel bad about the whole thing. So I sort through the closet and pick out one of the nicest sweaters I can find: a blue Ralph Lauren cable knit cashmere sweater that looks like it will compliment her eyes.

"Do you want me to help you put it on her?" Adam asks.

I shake my head. It's just a sweater, for God's sake. "I think I can manage."

When I show Victoria the sweater, I wait for a flash of happiness at the sight of it. *Oh my goodness, Sylvie! It's my favorite sweater!* That was stupid, of course. She doesn't react at all. And when I try to put it on her—well, I sorely regret refusing Adam's offer to help. It is *not* easy to put this sweater on her. Her right arm is stiff like a board and her left arm is fighting me the whole time. I start out by putting her good left arm into the sweater since that is what she's trying to do, but then I feel like I'm about to twist her other arm into an unnatural angle just to get her inside. I can only imagine what Eva would say if she witnessed this display.

Fortunately, Adam must have predicted this was going to happen because he comes down to the living room and rescues me. He gently eases the tangled sweater off her arms, then puts it back on her like he's been doing it his whole life. First her limp right arm, then her good arm, then over her head.

"Don't feel bad," he says when he's got it in place. "It took me a while to master. You'll get the hang of it."

He rests a hand on his wife's shoulder, but she does what she always does—she turns her head away from him.

The weather is perfect for a walk. Sunny but with a nice breeze in the air. I've pulled my hair back into a ponytail, but Victoria's is loose around her face. From the right angle, she looks very pretty when the wind lifts her hair in the air. This is one of those moments when I see a glimpse of how beautiful she used to be... before.

There's a paved path that leads around the house, but Adam wasn't exaggerating when he said it was overgrown. The grass has gone wild and every bush has wayward branches extending into the path. He needs to hire someone to take care of this mess. It would be fine for me to navigate on my own, but wheeling a chair over the path is a challenge. How did Adam ever take Victoria on a walk?

After we've done one lap around the house, I'm already getting tired. I look over at Victoria to see how she's holding up, and her eyes are open wide.

"How are you doing?" I ask her. "Ready to go back in

or do you want to stay outside longer?"

Her brows knit together. She looks like she wants to say something, but she's struggling.

I put my hand gently on her shoulder the way Adam did, but she doesn't look away this time. "What's wrong, Victoria?"

"It's…" She's managing to get the words out, even though they're slurred. "In…"

I shake my head. "What?"

"Glen Head." Her words are slurred but intelligible. "In. Glen Head."

What?

I remember from when I was scouring the map of Long Island that Glen Head is part of the town of Oyster Bay, although it's not anywhere close to here. Why is she interested in some tiny village in Oyster Bay?

"What's in Glen Head?" I ask.

"No." She looks up at me, and a drop of drool escapes from her lips, but she barely seems to notice. "No. Not…" She shakes her head. "No."

Well, this is frustrating.

I've been reading more of Victoria's diary, but I have to admit, I haven't been reading it much. I mean, she loves the guy—I get it. I don't need page after page of how wonderful he is, how good he kisses, blah blah blah. Frankly, given my silly crush on him, it's a bit frustrating.

But maybe I shouldn't have given up so quickly. More and more, I'm getting the feeling there's something

Victoria wants to tell me. And the answer is in that diary.

I'll read more tonight.

She seems unsettled so I go for another lap around the house. It's hard work but the weather won't hold up forever, so we may as well take advantage. Come January, when we're trapped in the house, I'll be glad we got out a little bit.

"Sylvie!"

I freeze, startled by the sound of her saying my name. Every morning, I walk in to see Victoria and say, *Hi! It's Sylvie!* But I never thought it registered with her. Apparently, it has.

"You're right!" I say excitedly. I don't want to make too much of this, but I'm thrilled. She doesn't even say her *own* name. The only name she ever says is Adam. "That's my name. Sylvie!"

"Sylvie!" she says again. And I realize she's pointing with her shaky left hand.

I follow the direction of her extended hand. She's pointing at a tree about twenty feet away from us, near the shed where Adam says they store the gardening supplies. The leaves have all turned red and yellow and fallen on the roof of the shed—it's very beautiful.

"I know," I say. "It's lovely."

And—I swear to God—she rolls her eyes at me. "No." Her voice is filled with impatience. "Sylvie. It's… nub."

There's a part of me that wants to scream. Victoria talks about "nub" all the freaking time. I have no idea what it means. At least once a day, she says "nub" in that urgent voice. At first, I was convinced it had to do with the way I was cutting her fingernails. But now I have no idea. I asked Adam and he didn't know either.

But I've noticed she talks about him in association with nub a lot. *Adam nub. Adam in nub. No nub Adam. Nub Adam.* Any combination you can imagine.

So is "nub" a tree? Is that what she wants? A tree?

"Nub," she says more urgently. Her left hand pointing at the tree is shaking violently.

What does she want, for God's sake? Does she want to climb the tree? Does she want me to climb the tree?

"Do you…" I look back at the tree. "Do you want me to go over there?"

She nods vigorously.

Well, fine. I abandon her chair on the path and pick my way through the wild grass to get to the tree. Or the nub, or whatever it is. I wonder if there are initials carved on the tree—maybe that's what Victoria wants me to see. Or maybe there's a secret message on it that will lead me to a buried treasure.

The tree is… a totally unremarkable tree. I circle it once, just to make sure there are no secret messages written on it—there aren't. It's a very normal tree. The only thing different about it is a small area on the front where the wood is splintered. I reach out and touch the imperfection.

"Nub!" I hear Victoria shout. It's the loudest I've ever

heard her speak.

I have no clue what she's talking about. This is just a splintered area on a tree.

And then I see it. Embedded in the wood.

A bullet.

"Nub," she says, quieter this time but her voice is carried by the wind. "Adam... nub."

I finally know what nub means.

I walk back to where Victoria is sitting. She follows me carefully with her good eye. She's watching my face.

"Gun?" I say.

She nods slowly. "Gun," she repeats.

Chapter 18

Victoria's Diary

December 16, 2016

So I started writing all this stuff down as a way to show my future children how I met their father because I just felt so convinced that this was it. Well, today I was proven right.

Adam finished a draft of his book yesterday. I begged him to read it, but he wouldn't let me. He said he cares about my opinion too much, and it would make him nervous. So he sent it off to the editor, and he is awaiting their opinion. Of course, I'm absolutely *dying* to read it, but I respect his wishes. If he doesn't want me to read it yet, I'll wait. He won't even tell me what it's about or even what it's called.

Anyway, to celebrate, we had this grand plan to go out to dinner after my shift ended today. He was asking me if I could get somebody to cover the shift, but that would be impossible on such short notice. I would only ask for help like that if I were seriously ill. Adam was grumbling about it, but he doesn't get it. When you're in the medical field, you can't skip out on work to have a night out with your boyfriend. You just *can't*.

So I found myself in a packed ER this evening. What's more, right in the middle of my shift, a multi-trauma motor vehicle accident arrived. It was a three-car collision where one person died and we had to send one person straight into surgery because their blood pressure kept dropping and it looked like they had a hemorrhaging spleen. And then there were two patients in a row with chest pain that ruled in for heart attacks and we had to send them straight up to the Cath Lab. Then a third patient with chest pain went into cardiac arrest just as we got him into an examination room.

He didn't make it.

Needless to say, we were shaken after that one. After somebody dies in the ER, there's a somber atmosphere that overtakes the entire place, and it didn't help that we were way behind. Anybody who was not actively dying was not going to get seen in the near future. It meant that when we did finally get in to see one of the non-urgent patients, they were not pleased with us.

I was walking past one of the examining rooms when a man came out and stepped in front of me, blocking my path. He wasn't a big guy, but he was significantly bigger than my five foot four frame. And I didn't appreciate the way he folded his hairy arms across his chest and glared at me.

"My wife has been waiting in that room for *six hours*," he announced. "This is an absolute disgrace. Is anybody ever going to see her?"

I wanted to yell at him that somebody had just died here less than an hour ago, and he was just lucky his family member was still alive. Because delivering that news? It was horrible. But instead, I took a deep breath and gave him my best patient smile. "I'm afraid we've had several urgent issues we had to address. But I promise we'll get to your wife as soon as we can."

I was praying the man would accept my placating words and move on. But he didn't. "That's bullshit. We're going to be waiting here for another six hours, aren't we?"

Another deep breath. "This is an emergency room," I explained. "We have to see the most emergent issues first." I looked over at his wife's room and plucked the clipboard off the door. Fever for two days. Max temp of 101.6, but now 99.8. Not impressive enough. "I'm sorry. We're doing what we can."

"No. I want you to go see her right now." The man stuck his finger in my face, about six inches from my nose. "I'm tired of waiting. My wife *deserves* to be seen. *Now*."

I opened my mouth to respond to him, but before I could get any words out, I heard a voice from behind me: "Is there a problem here?"

I jerked my head around and let out a breath of relief.

I had never been so happy to see Mack standing behind me in his navy blue paramedic uniform. I always respected the fact that Mack was a big guy who could wrangle heavy or drunk patients, but in this moment, I appreciated how intimidating he could look when he wanted to. He had his meaty arms crossed in front of him, and he towered over the man next to me. When he lifted one black eyebrow, the man flinched and took a step back.

"No. No problem." The man ducked his head down. "Sorry."

And then he retreated back into his wife's room without another word.

I couldn't help myself—I burst out laughing. "You totally scared the bejesus out of that guy."

Mack grinned, partially out of pride and (I suspect) partially because of my use of the word bejesus. "I sure did."

"You can be terrifying. You know that?"

He nodded. "When I played football in high school, they used to call me Mack Truck."

"I believe it."

By the end of my shift, I was completely exhausted and in no shape to go out with Adam for a night on the town. I texted him to let him know that I was going to want to crash as soon as I got home. I felt bad about it, but I could barely keep my eyes open.

No problem. Just get home as soon as you can, he wrote.

Adam's apartment was further away from the hospital than my old place. For that reason, he insisted I take an Uber home when my shift ended very late. I argued with him a bit, but ultimately, I knew he was right. Braving the subway at midnight on a Tuesday night was just asking for trouble.

Mack said the same thing. Months ago, before I moved, he saw me leaving close to midnight one night and insisted on going all the way home with me. That's why I can't be too mad at him for getting so judgmental about me and Adam. I know he's looking out for my best interest.

When I finally burst into our apartment at a quarter past midnight, the living room was dark. I assumed Adam had decided against waiting up for me. But after a moment, I realized I was wrong. He was very much awake. And the apartment wasn't actually dark.

It was lit by candles.

Future Children, I want to hold every moment of this experience in my memory. I want to capture every detail because this is a moment I'm going to want to relive for the rest of my life. The dozen candles arranged carefully around the room to set the mood. The trail of roses leading into the living room, for goodness sake. And then Adam. Down on one knee. His green eyes gazing up into mine. Your father looked so handsome at that moment. You can't even imagine.

"Victoria," he said.

I was already crying. I'm not a crier, but I couldn't help myself.

"Victoria." He opened the blue velvet box in his hand. And oh my. You would not believe this ring. Well, I'm guessing you've seen this ring, but I probably keep it in a safe or something because the diamond is gigantic. If I wore this ring on the subway, I would almost definitely be murdered or at the very least have my ring finger sliced off. "I love you so much, Victoria."

"I love you too," I whispered through my tears.

"All I want is to spend the rest of my life with you." He took my hand in his. "Will you marry me?"

Of course, I said yes!

So that is the story of how I got engaged to the man of my dreams and lived happily ever after and gave birth to you… eventually. That part hasn't happened yet obviously, but I'm going to keep recording every detail of our lives together. Short of something very unexpected, I think Adam and I are going to have a great life together.

"This ring…" I stared down at it, unable to get over how… *big* it was. I still can't, honestly. "You must have spent a fortune."

"Well, you're worth it."

I was afraid to ask how much it cost. I didn't want to know if I was wearing a ring that cost more than my college education. But suffice to say, if you ever have any financial problems, you can sell my ring and you'll be out of trouble.

I was shaking so badly from the entire experience that I had to get off my feet before I collapsed. Adam thought it was cute. "I would have proposed to you ages ago if I knew you would react this way," he said.

I laughed. Through the candlelight, I blindly reached out for my Papasan chair in the corner of the room but grasped only air. I blinked, still trying to adjust to the dim light from the candles.

"Where is my chair?" I said.

Adam frowned. "What?"

"My Papasan." A jab of panic took me down from the cloud I had been floating on. "Where is it?"

"You mean that piece of junk chair from your old apartment?" He shook his head. "I tossed it. I put it out on the curb this morning and it's gone now."

My mouth fell open. In spite of his incredibly romantic proposal and ridiculous ring, I was suddenly furious with him. That was *my* chair! It was the only thing from my old apartment that he allowed me to keep, and now he threw it away... without my permission? That chair was your birthright!

"I told you I wanted to keep that chair," I said through my teeth.

"It was a piece of shit, Vicky." His brows bunched together. "It made the whole apartment look cheap. I'd be embarrassed to have people over with that chair here."

"What people? You don't have any friends."

Now it was Adam's turn to look shocked. Honestly, I

was shocked at myself. Why did I say something like that? It wasn't like me to be so mean.

But it's true. Adam doesn't have any friends. He has his agent. And his editor. But other than that, there is nobody else in his life. He doesn't even speak to his parents. There's nobody aside from me.

But that's not the point. I shouldn't have said it.

"I'm sorry." I rubbed at my eyes with the balls of my hands. "I'm just... I'm tired. And this guy died in the ER today and..."

His eyes were filled with hurt. For a moment, I was scared he might take back his proposal. But he didn't. He put his arms around me and kissed me.

"I don't need friends," he said. "I've got you." He squeezed me tighter. "I'm sorry about the chair. We'll get you a new one. Any chair you want."

And that, ladies and gentlemen, was just about the sweetest thing a man has ever said to me. And not just any man.

My future husband. Your father.

CHAPTER 19

I lie in bed, my eyes drifting shut as I finish Victoria's latest diary entry. Just as I suspected, she got the ultimate romantic proposal.

And then Adam threw away her beloved chair. The Papasan chair that she imagined giving to her children.

It was a jerk move. I'm having trouble justifying in my head that he would do such a thing to her, especially since he seems like such a nice guy. And he obviously loves her so much. But then again, I wasn't there. I'm willing to believe this chair was extremely disgusting. I remember when I was living with Freddy, he got a bookcase off the curb, and even though we were dirt poor, I just couldn't allow this bookcase to remain in my home. The wood was all splintered and it smelled like urine.

That Papasan chair might have been as bad as that bookcase.

Anyway, aside from that, Adam was the perfect boyfriend, based on all the things Victoria wrote about him in her diary. She had, in many ways, a charmed life. If I didn't know how things ended up for her, I would probably hate Victoria for how wonderful her life was back then. She had a job she loved, a perfect boyfriend, and she was about to get married to her soulmate.

I can't stop thinking about the bullet hole in the tree.

When Victoria said nub, she meant gun. So is she saying Adam has a gun? And if so, well... so what? So he shot a gun at a tree in their yard. Is that a crime?

Well, at least now I can stop looking for that Papasan chair.

CHAPTER 20

Tonight is our first big storm.

We've been lucky so far with the weather, but the forecast tonight is calling for heavy rain and powerful winds. Gusts up to fifty miles per hour. I don't know what the big deal is though. I mean, I can handle a little rain. It's not a big deal.

"The big deal," Maggie explains to me as I'm preparing Victoria's breakfast, "is you guys might lose power."

That doesn't faze me. In my old apartment, I used to lose power all the time. Of course, that was because I didn't pay the electricity bill.

"Listen," Maggie says, "if there's a big storm, you're always welcome to come stay with me and Steve. We live in an apartment complex, so we usually keep our power. And if there's snow, it gets plowed pretty quickly, so you won't get stranded."

"Thanks." I pull the bowl of instant oatmeal out of the

microwave. "I think I'll be okay here though." I stir the oatmeal. It's thick and gloopy—the characteristics of any delicious breakfast. So no, it definitely doesn't look appetizing, but considering Victoria likely won't attempt even a bite of it, I'm not going to worry too much about it. "By the way, can I ask you a question?"

Maggie tucks a strand of red hair behind her ear. She doesn't seem eager to get to her cleaning chores. She's always looking for excuses to goof off, and talking to me is a popular one. "Sure."

"Do you know anything about Glen Head?"

Maggie is quiet for a moment. "Glen Head?"

"Yeah. It's in Oyster Bay, right?"

The flicker of recognition in her eyes is unmistakable. But she's still silent. There's something about the town that's significant. Otherwise, why would Victoria say it? It's so hard for her to get words out, everything she says has some significance. Like nub.

"The cook and gardener, Irina, used to live there," Maggie finally says. "She moved closer after she started working here. But that's where she had been living before." She hesitates. "I think so, at least."

Adam always gets this strange look on his face whenever the sorry state of the front lawn comes up. He mentioned Irina once by name but then quickly changed the subject. Why is Victoria talking about her? And where is she now? Did she quit?

"So I've got a question for you," Maggie says.

"Sure."

"Who is Freddy?"

My heart drops into my stomach. I'm about to ask her what she's talking about when I see I left my phone on the counter and she's looking right down the screen. Damn.

I snatch the phone right from under her nose. Why won't Freddy leave me alone already? Why can't he move on? I sure have.

Please let me talk to you. I can't stop thinking about you. It's Freddy.

"He's nobody," I mumble.

Maggie raises her eyebrows. "He's nobody who can't stop thinking about you?"

"It's not what you think."

I made a terrible mistake. Please forgive me.

I type the words "please leave me alone" onto the screen, then block the number. Of course, blocking Freddy never helps. He always gets a new number. I had hoped leaving town might deter him, but clearly, he's still determined to be part of my life.

"What do I think?" Maggie looks intrigued.

The last thing I wanted was to make myself interesting. I had hoped that I could get through this entire experience without anybody asking me any questions about my personal life. I don't want to talk about my past. It's just painful.

But then I look up at Maggie's earnest freckled face. It's very hard to spend time with this woman and not want to confide in her. And I've been dying to get the story off my chest. Like Adam, I don't have many friends.

"He was my boyfriend," I say. "A long time ago."

"Is he cute?"

I can't help but smile. "Yes. Very. That wasn't the problem."

"So what happened?"

"I got pregnant." It still hurts to say those words. I wonder if it will ever stop hurting. "But then I got in an accident. I lost the baby and I had other injuries. And at the same time, I lost my health insurance."

I still feel shaken when I remember discovering that my father had taken me off his health insurance policy. At the worst possible time. After all, I needed insurance to pay for the things he did to me. My broken wrist. The bleeding from the miscarriage that persisted for months and required an emergency room visit, a transfusion, and a procedure to get it to stop.

"Freddy and I couldn't pay the hospital bills, we couldn't pay our rent, we were just scrambling to keep our heads above water." I wince at the memory. "I wanted to declare bankruptcy or ask Freddy's parents for help, but he wouldn't let me. It got to the point where all we did was fight. We were really unhappy. So then I finally told him to leave, and... he did. He couldn't leave fast enough."

"And now he wants to get back together," Maggie says.

I nod. "He keeps saying he made a terrible mistake

and he should never have left. But he did. And now I'm done with him. I just want to move on and put the past behind me."

I spent the last year trying to rebuild my life. And now Freddy wants me back? No way.

"Wow," Maggie breathes. "I don't blame you for not taking him back. I think I'd have trouble getting over all that too. Sometimes it's better to have a fresh start."

"Yeah," I mumble.

Maggie taps her finger against her chin. "I'll have to ask Steve if he knows any guys we can set you up with."

"That's okay. I don't feel like getting into any relationships right now.

She clucks her tongue. "Okay, but you have to get back on the horse sooner or later. Right?"

I close my eyes for a moment, remembering that awful night. Freddy didn't come home until two in the morning. It wasn't his fault—he was doing janitorial work at a large office building in the city and it was a night shift job. His last job, working as a security guard, had been better but some stuff at the company went missing and they fired him, even though he swore up and down he would never have stolen anything. I told him to his face that I believed him, but I wasn't entirely sure. Given our financial situation, I wouldn't have blamed him for breaking the law. It's not like I was never tempted.

So it wasn't like he was out with his friends, drinking at a bar. He was working. But the fact of the matter was that I was trying to sleep and had to be up at six in the morning to walk a couple of kids to school for minimum wage. And I didn't appreciate the amount of noise he was making as he took off his shirt and pants and then flipped around about five times on our creaky mattress to get comfortable. The last straw was when he put his arm around my body.

I flipped over in bed and glared at him in the darkness. "Are you serious? Are you trying to make it *impossible* for me to sleep?"

The room was dark but my eyes had time to adjust, so I could see the surprise on his face. "No. I just wanted to put my arm around you."

"Well, you're keeping me awake. I've got to get up early in the morning, you know."

"Sorry. I just got home."

"I mean, I'm *exhausted*. I need to get a good night's sleep. Why is that so hard for you to wrap your head around?"

He propped himself up on his elbows. "You think I'm not tired, Sylvia? I've been cleaning up fucking garbage for the last eight hours. All you have to do is walk a couple of kids to school."

"So find a better job."

"Right. Because it's that easy." He flopped back down against the pillow. "Obviously, this is my *dream* job. Mopping floors and hauling around trash—it's fantastic. I would never want to find anything else."

"Don't be an asshole."

He punched the bed with his fist. "I don't know what you want from me. This is the best I can do right now."

I realized he was right. This *was* the best he could do. I had fallen in love with Freddy in high school, and everything about him seemed so glamorous then. There was nothing glamorous about our lives right now. We were stuck in a hole we would never get out of. We were still trying to pay off my medical bills. Freddy couldn't seem to get a decent job and neither could I.

I wasn't happy. And neither was he. Worst of all, we were dragging each other down.

"You should go," I said to him.

He groaned. "Look, I'm sorry. Let's talk about this in the morning

"There's nothing to talk about. This is… it's over."

"*What?*" He tried to reach for me but I pulled away. "Sylvie… come on… you know I love you."

"The only reason you're still with me is that you feel responsible for my parents kicking me out and losing our baby." I swallowed a lump in my throat. "Well, you're not responsible. Both those things weren't your fault. So you can leave—guilt-free."

"Sylvie…"

"I told you to *leave.*"

I watched him in the dark room. I wanted him to disagree with me. I wanted him to tell me that he loved me too much and that he couldn't possibly leave. But instead, he got out of bed at two in the morning and started getting dressed. He shoved a bunch of his belongings into a suitcase and went out the door without saying goodbye. I could hear the front door slam on his way out.

I went to the window and saw his Ford Fiesta parked on the street. He bought it used a few months ago when he got mugged and beaten up on the subway by a bunch of thugs on his way home from work at one in the morning. He got it cheap but it had already cost us over a thousand dollars in repairs. Deeper into the hole.

I watched him throw his duffel bag into the car, get into the driver's seat, and speed away.

I had thought I would feel relief when he left, but I didn't. I felt sad that the only man I had ever loved had left. And angry that it was so easy for him to go. He was just waiting for me to give him permission. I thought maybe he would come back the next day, after he had a chance to cool off. But he didn't.

I can't let go of my anger—he abandoned me the second I gave him permission to do so. And I still have the nagging feeling that I was right when I told him to go. Freddy and I were good together once upon a time, but not as adults. We were better off on our own.

Then after a year had gone by, he came back. He claimed he still loved me and he wanted to give it another try. But it was too late by then. I had decided that I was better off without Freddy Ruggiero.

CHAPTER 21

By the time I feed Victoria her dinner, the rain is already coming down hard. The trees outside are shaking and the branches are whipping back and forth. Maggie headed out a couple of hours ago, renewing her invitation to come stay with her and Steve, but I turned her down. I didn't want to leave Victoria, especially if the power went out. This is my job, after all.

While I help Victoria guide a shaky spoon filled with sweet potato to her mouth, she has one eye on the food and the other is pointed in the direction of the window, where the droplets of rain are slamming against the windowpane with some ferocity. I can hear a branch scraping against the side of the house as it shakes in the wind. It's hard to know how much she understands about the situation. I explained to her about the rain and she just stared at me like she often does when I'm telling her something. She didn't react, which is nothing unusual— I've yet to see her even smile.

But she knows my name. She understood that much. And she remembers when someone fired a gun at the tree outside her house.

Adam comes into the room with the syringe filled with her medications. Victoria stiffens at the sight of him, and I know any chance of getting her to eat is out the window.

"I want to get her into bed early tonight," he says. "In case the power goes out."

I step aside for him to get at her feeding tube. I clipped Victoria's nails down to the quick, so when she scratches at his hand, she can't break the skin. When that doesn't work, she attempts to grab at his wrist, but she's too weak. He's easily able to overpower her and inject the medications.

"She hates it when you do that," I observe.

"She doesn't like stuff going down the tube. It must be uncomfortable."

"Yes, but…" I lower my voice a notch, as if it would matter—Victoria can hear every word. "She hates the medication. More than the tube feeds." I chew on my lip. "Does she really need them? They seem to make her very tired."

Lately, I've been wondering if the reason Victoria is so lethargic in the morning is because of whatever medications she's getting at night. She barely seems able to keep her eyes open within an hour of getting her meds.

He raises an eyebrow. "*Yes*, she needs them. The

medications keep her from having seizures."

"Right. Sorry. I didn't mean to question you."

His shoulders sag. "No, it's okay. They're strong medications and I don't want to knock her out. But she was having seizures at the hospital and it was really scary. So there isn't anything I can do."

Even though she only just received the medications and they couldn't possibly have hit her bloodstream yet, the fight seems to have gone out of Victoria. Her shoulders sag and her head tilts to the side. There's no chance of getting her to eat now.

"Why don't you finish up with her and come get me?" Adam looks down at his watch. "I'll get her into bed and then we could have dinner."

"Sounds good."

Adam and I have been eating dinner together a few nights a week. He cooks something simple or I cook something simple, and we eat in front of the television. It's nice to have the company. And the last thing I want is to be alone in this huge house if the power is out. I'd imagine he feels the same way.

I feel guilty about it though. I'm sure Victoria wouldn't want another woman having dinner with her husband every night. Once I suggested to Adam that we bring her down to join us for the meal, but he pointed out that it would be a lot of hassle to get her down the stairs. I didn't want to push him too hard, but then I felt guilty. It doesn't seem fair to Victoria that she should have to eat every meal isolated upstairs in her room.

With Adam gone, I scoop up more sweet potato and hold it to Victoria's lips. Her eyelids are sagging and she barely seems aware of my presence anymore.

"Sorry, Victoria," I say.

She blinks a few times and her eyes fill with tears. "Sylvie," she slurs.

There's a box of tissues by her bed. I reach for one of them and hold it out to her, but she doesn't take it. "What's wrong, Victoria?"

"Glen Head," she whispers. "In... Glen Head."

I frown at her. After she talked to me about Glen Head the first time, I looked up the town. It's not even a town, but something called a "hamlet," which is like a small village within the town of Oyster Bay. (Trivia: Oyster Bay is the birthplace of former President Theodore Roosevelt and the arguably more famous Billy Joel.) It's a good two-hour drive from here, so I'm not going to pop over there and check it out just out of curiosity.

"Mmmmmm," she slurs as her head starts to loll to the side.

"What's in Glen Head?" I press her.

She shakes her head. "No. He's..."

She says something else that's so slurred, I can't make it out. And then her eyes drift shut.

CHAPTER 22

When I finish up with Victoria and come downstairs, Adam is cooking spaghetti in the kitchen and talking on his cell phone. He's swirling the spaghetti around in a pot of boiling water as he laughs at something the person on the other line says to him.

"Don't worry," he says. "We'll be fine." He pauses to listen. "Yeah, just stay away from the electrical outlets. If the power goes out, it'll probably come back by the morning."

After a few more exchanges, he hangs up the phone and flashes me an apologetic smile. "That was my mom," he says. "She lives on the island too, and she's freaking out about the storm. I always call to check on her when a big one is coming."

"That's so sweet."

He grins. "Well, I'm a sweet guy."

I can't argue with that assessment. Given how attentive Adam is to a wife who can't give him anything in return anymore, I'd expect he'd be equally attentive to his elderly parents. It worries me though that he spends so much time and effort taking care of other people. Adam seems like he's on a fast track to burn out.

I tend to the spaghetti while Adam goes upstairs to get Victoria into bed. By the time he comes back down the stairs, I've got two heaping plates of spaghetti and tomato sauce on the counter with two glasses of water. Just as he reaches for one of the plates, the lights flicker above.

And then they go out completely.

"Whoa," I say. The room lights briefly from a flash of lightning, and thunder crashes a moment later. With the lights out, I can barely see the plate of food. "It's dark in here."

"I put candles all around the room. I just need to find a lighter." Adam goes to the kitchen counter and fumbles around in a drawer. A moment later, I see a flash of fire. "I'll go light them."

He lights the candles one by one until the room is bright enough for me to at least see my spaghetti and make out the curves of Adam's handsome face. We bring our food over to the sofa like we always do, but we won't be able to watch television this time like usual. We'll have no choice but to… talk.

"Wine?" he asks me as he heads back to the kitchen.

A voice in the back of my head is telling me it's not a brilliant idea to have a glass of wine with my incredibly sexy boss when we're trapped together in his house and the lights are out. But I haven't had a drink since my first night here, and this storm is making me anxious. "Sure," I say.

He returns with two glasses of white wine. He places them both on the coffee table with our food, then he picks up his plate. "Glad I went for a run this morning," he says. "The ground will be a mess tomorrow."

"There will probably be leaf-paste everywhere," I comment.

"Leaf paste?"

"You know, that mix of dirty leaves and water that becomes kind of like a paste?"

He laughs. "Oh right. Exactly."

I take a sip of the white wine. I'm sure it's more expensive than the usual stuff I get for ten bucks a bottle, but it tastes the same to me. "I admire your discipline though. How long have you been running?"

"Honestly? Only since Victoria came home."

"Really?" Most men wouldn't see their wives getting injured as a motivation to get in better shape. "Why?"

"Well…" He runs the tip of his finger along the rim of the glass. "The thing is, lately I've had a lot of… pent up energy… if you know what I mean…"

I suck in a breath. Adam has lowered his eyes, and I have a feeling if the lights were on, his cheeks would be pink. "Oh…"

"That sounds bad." He glances at the stairwell. "I don't mean it like that. What happened to Victoria was horrible, and I want to take care of her for the rest of her life. I made a vow to do that, and I'm going to keep it. But… sometimes it's…"

"No, I understand."

He drops his head back against the sofa. "I want to go the distance. For Victoria. But… it's going to involve a lot of long runs and cold showers." He takes a deep breath. "And who knows? Maybe she'll get better…"

Except he told me on the first day here that all the doctors told him she wouldn't. Victoria will never get better. She will be like this for the rest of her life.

The thunder crashes again and I shiver. Adam frowns at me. "Are you cold, Sylvia?"

"I… a little." I hadn't realized it before, but it's suddenly freezing in here. "Is the heat on?"

He shakes his head. "I think it went out. Listen, I'll get the fireplace going, but you might want to get another sweater."

I tug at the hoodie I'm wearing over my T-shirt. "I don't know if I have anything… warm enough…"

He hesitates. "Why don't you check Victoria's closet? Might as well. There's so much clothing in there and it shouldn't go to waste. I think you're about the same size as she is."

There's something about scavenging around in Victoria's closet for something to wear while hanging around with her husband that feels wrong. "That's okay."

"Are you sure? It's going to get pretty cold in here soon, even with the fire."

I shiver again. It's uncomfortably cold right now. I'm sure the fire will help, but I can't even focus on eating my food. Maybe I should get over myself and borrow a sweater from Victoria. It's not like she'd even know about it.

Finally, I decide to just do it. While Adam fiddles with the fireplace, I grab a flashlight from the kitchen and mount the stairs. In the dark, they seem even more steep and scary. I cling to the banister, taking them slowly. I don't want to fall like Victoria did.

Victoria's giant, walk-in closet seems even more gigantic by flashlight. How does one woman have so much clothing? She's so lucky. Or at least, she was.

I sift through expensive cashmere sweaters but reject each one. Finally, I pick out a gray woolen sweater that's mildly ugly but looks warm. It looks like something she's had for a long time, before she had a rich husband to fund her wardrobe. I'm not trying to look sexy today—this is perfect.

Small orange flames are coming out of the fireplace when I get back downstairs, but the room is just as cold. In addition to getting the fire going, Adam has brought a couple of quilts out to the couch, so I waste no time in wrapping one of them around me. He smirks when he sees me bundling myself up.

"Better?" he says. He sits down next to me and drapes the other quilt over his legs.

"A little." I take another sip of wine. The alcohol might warm me up. "Still kind of cold though."

"Do you want another blanket?" He pulls the one he's got on his legs off him and holds it out to me. It reminds me of how he offered me his scarf that first day at the train station.

I shake my head. "No. My body is warm enough but my face is cold."

"Your *face* is cold?"

"Yeah. Like my nose and my cheeks. And my eyeballs."

He laughs. "Your *eyeballs*?"

"Don't laugh. My eyes are really cold."

"I just… I'm not sure how to help you with that."

I let out a breath. If it weren't so dark in here, I suspect I'd be able to see the puff of air. "You don't have to help me. You don't always have to be the hero, you know."

He lifts an eyebrow. "The hero?"

"Well…" I pick at a loose thread on the quilt. "You just… you do a lot. For Victoria. For your parents. It's nice of you, but… it's just a lot for any one person."

"Yeah…" Adam's features flicker in the dim light of the room. "I'm not going to lie. It's been… hard."

Without entirely meaning to, I reach out and touch his arm. "I know it has."

He furrows his brow. "I just wish…"

The thunder cracks again and I pull the blankets tighter around me. Our food is completely forgotten on the coffee table—it's probably ice cold by now anyway. I can't help but notice Adam and I are sitting very close together on the couch. I know I should move, but I don't want to pull away from his body heat. Isn't that what you're supposed to do when it's cold out? Cuddle together for body heat?

Except we might be a little too close.

"Sylvia," he whispers.

I shut my eyes. If I can't see how attractive he is, I won't be as tempted. But this situation is impossible—between the dim lighting, the cracks of lightning and thunder, and the allure of his body heat, it's like someone set it up to guarantee we'd do something we shouldn't. I know all those months of loneliness are wearing on him.

I should pull away. I know I should. But I haven't kissed a guy since Freddy. And that was a very long time ago. Both of us have been alone for so long.

Pull away, Sylvie!

Neither of us is saying anything. We're just sitting on a sofa, looking at each other, cuddling under the blanket for warmth. My heart won't stop pounding in my chest. My lips are a foot away from his. It would be so easy.

Crash!

Both of our heads simultaneously swivel in the direction of the staircase. The noise came from upstairs. In the direction of Victoria's room. Except she can't be making noise. She's in bed, sound asleep. But then again, she's the only other person in this house.

Adam leaps off the couch like it was on fire. "I'll go see what that was."

I jump up too, allowing the blankets to fall off my body. "You can finish eating. I'll go."

"It's fine. I don't mind."

"I don't mind either." When he looks doubtful, I add, "It's my job, right?"

He scratches at the stubble on his face. "Okay. Give me a yell if you need any help."

As soon as I'm heading up the creaky stairs again to the second floor, I regret my generous offer. Especially when I realize at the top of the steps that I forgot the flashlight downstairs. The first floor was well lit with all the candles and the fireplace, but the second floor is black as night. I blink a few times, trying to adjust my eyes, but it helps only minimally.

I debate going back downstairs to get the flashlight, but I'm scared to descend the stairs without a flashlight in hand. I know there's one in the top drawer of the dresser inside Victoria's room. So if I can find the room, I can use that flashlight. But finding a room is a challenging task. I keep my hand along the wall, feeling the bumps and cracks in the plaster. Victoria's room is the last one on the right. I feel the first door, second, then the third—Victoria's room. My fingers fumble for a doorknob, and I throw the door open.

It's pitch black inside Victoria's room. The only sound is the rain pounding against her window. "Victoria?" I whisper.

No answer. She must be asleep.

Except what was that noise?

I feel around until I locate the dresser. I slide the first drawer open and fumble around with papers and identifiable objects. I finally feel a flash of relief when my fingers close around a cylindrical object. I locate the switch with my thumb and flick it on.

The room fills with the beam from the flashlight. I have to blink again, adjusting my eyes to the light. I turn the light across the room, shining it in the direction of Victoria's bed, so I can make sure she's all right and sound asleep.

But when I shine the light on Victoria, I realize she's not asleep at all. Her eyes are open, and she's staring at me with her one good eye.

It's the last thing I expected to see. My heart leaps into my chest. She was passed out only a couple of hours ago. Now she's wide awake.

"Victoria," I say. "You… you startled me. I thought you were asleep."

She just blinks.

"Is everything okay?" I ask her. "I heard a crash."

I look down at the floor, to see what might have made the noise. I see now that the glass of water that had been on Victoria's night table when I went downstairs is now on the ground. Water has spilled all over the floor by her bed. Clearly, that's what made the noise. And it must have awakened Victoria from her sleep.

Of course, if Victoria was asleep when the glass fell,

what made it fall? Glasses don't suddenly roll off the table. Did she wake up and reach for it? I've never seen her do anything like that.

"I'll get that cleaned up," I tell her.

Armed with my flashlight, I make my way over to the bathroom to grab some tissues to get it all cleaned up. It's not much water, and it won't take long. When I come back, Victoria still has her eyes open and she's watching me. I feel her eyes on my back as I wipe down the floor. Thankfully, the glass was made of plastic and didn't break.

"Mmmmm," Victoria says.

I lift my eyes from the ground, where I'm wiping up the last of the water. "What?"

Victoria's lips work like she's trying to say something. I think M words are harder for her. She tries again, concentrating all her effort: "Mmmmmine."

Mine?

I look down at where her gaze is directed. My sweater. Or, I should say, *her* sweater. I'm wearing her sweater. And she noticed.

"I'm so sorry," I say quickly. "I should have asked, but Adam said it was okay. The heat is out and I was so cold." I pull it off, even though it's almost unbearably cold without the sweater. "I won't wear it anymore. I'm sorry."

Victoria's expression does not change. "Mine," she says again. The word is much clearer this time.

I stuff the sweater into her drawer. You couldn't pay me a million bucks to wear the sweater at this point. I'll just wrap myself in blankets and I'll be fine. I look back at Victoria, hoping to see that strange, intense look has disappeared from her face. It hasn't.

"Mine," she says.

My heart is pounding. She's stuck on this. But what can I do? I returned the stupid sweater. What more does she want from me?

"If you're all right, I'm going to go now," I back away, towards her door. "I'll be back to check on you in the morning."

It's only after I leave the room that I realize the thing Victoria was telling me was hers might not have been the sweater. So instead of going back downstairs to tempt fate with Adam, I go to my bedroom and read by flashlight until I pass out.

CHAPTER 23

Victoria's Diary

January 5, 2017

I don't even know where to begin with the crazy evening I had tonight.

The night started perfectly. We were at dinner and talking about what sort of wedding we wanted to have. Wedding planning is so fun! I feel like such a girly girl saying something like that, but it is! Adam wants to get married sooner rather than later. He's really excited about the whole thing. It's sweet. Carol always talks about how her boyfriend Jeff is terrified of commitment, but Adam is all in.

We agreed we wanted something small. I was nervous that Adam was going to want a huge, extravagant wedding, given the way he likes to throw around money, but he is on the same page as me about keeping it small and simple.

He reached across the candlelit table to take my hand. "I'd be okay with it just being the two of us. Maybe at a courthouse. Or Vegas, if you'd like that better."

"There's no family you want to invite?"

Adam winced and let go of my hand. On our third date, he admitted he wasn't on speaking terms with his parents. That did strike me as a bit odd. My mother died from cancer when I was in middle school, and my father had a heart attack while I was in college. I was an only child, and neither of them had siblings, so that left me without much in the way of family.

I know it sounds stupid, but I always fantasized about marrying a man who had a huge family, so I could finally have that family experience. A mother and father-in-law to replace the mother and father I lost. A brother-in-law or sister-in-law to make up for the siblings I never had. But Adam can't give me that. He told me he hasn't spoken to his parents in nearly ten years. He also has a brother that he hates.

"I know you're angry at them," I said. "But it's been a long time. Don't you think... now that we're starting a new life, it would be nice to try to make amends?"

Adam picked up his wine glass and swished around the dark red liquid. "No. I don't."

"Well, why not?"

"You just don't get it."

"Maybe you can explain it to me." And then I could explain to *him* why he was being stubborn.

He wouldn't look up from the wine glass. "They never supported me when I said I wanted to become a writer. They told me it was a waste of time. A waste of my life."

I can understand that. Deciding to become a writer is a gutsy move, and to do it without the support of your family is even harder. "But they must see now how wrong they were!"

He lifted the wineglass and brought it to his lips. He tilted it back until he drained the whole thing. "You would think. But no. Also, they didn't like my first book."

"*All in the Family*?" I had read his first novel years ago, well before he was a part of my life. I tried to recall the plot. All I remembered was loving it—it was an unputdownable thriller. I remember thinking it was deliciously evil. But I was having trouble remembering exactly what happened. "What didn't they like about it?"

"They thought some of the characters were based on them." He shrugged. "They felt I had portrayed them unfairly."

"Were the characters based on them?"

He shrugged again. "When you're a writer, it's hard not to draw on your own experiences. So... I suppose I did. To some extent."

I made a mental note to get a copy of *All in the Family* and re-read it. Adam had a whole shelf of them in his bookcase in the living room. I could just borrow it. It certainly wouldn't be a chore to reread. As you know, your father is a brilliant writer.

"Look, Vicky, I know you have this romantic idea about a big family, but my parents are terrible people." Adam leaned back in his seat. "I'd prefer just to forget all about them. Anyway, we can make our own family. Right?"

My heart leaped in my chest. That was something I had never heard him say before. "What do you mean?" I asked carefully.

"I mean…" He grinned at me. "I was thinking we should start making some babies as soon as possible. What do you think?"

I couldn't stop grinning like an idiot. Before I met Adam, I never thought about having children. It just seemed so far off the radar. But the second I met him, my first thought was that I wanted this man to be the father of my kids. After all, that's why I'm writing this.

"I think I could be convinced," I said coyly. He had definitely gotten me to forget all about his parents.

He winked at me as he filled his glass with more wine. "How many kids do you want?

I got a warm fuzzy feeling in my belly. All of a sudden, I couldn't wait to get knocked up. "Three?"

His eyes lit up. "You read my mind. Two boys and a girl."

I laughed. "I don't know if we have too much control over the boy and girl part."

"Fine. I won't be mad if we have three boys."

And we spent the rest of the meal fantasizing about our future children. It was so dorky yet really fun. We didn't get too far with the wedding planning, but there's no pressure there. We're not going to get married for a little while. And it will be a small wedding, so we can plan it quickly.

Everything was great until we got home.

We couldn't keep our hands off each other in the elevator. I thought for sure we were going to go straight to the bedroom to, um, go to bed for... sleep. But then Adam made a pitstop in the bathroom and that's when everything went wrong.

Adam came out of the bathroom, clutching a tube of toothpaste. Correction: *his* tube of toothpaste. Even though I've been living with him for several months now, he has not abandoned his determination that our belongings need to be kept separate. The stuff on the bottom shelf of the refrigerator is still mine and the top shelf is his, and everything in the middle shelf needs to be labeled. He became furious at me last week when I used some of his milk to make cereal. But seriously, why do we need *separate milk*?

And yes, we also have separate toothpaste. I don't know why we can't share the same goddamn tube of toothpaste, but he was adamant about it, and it seems silly to fight over something so trivial. Adam is a little OCD— it's just something I need to get used to. It's almost endearing.

But now he was gripping his toothpaste, labeled in that black marker I've come to hate. His face was bright red.

"Did you use my toothpaste?" he asked.

"I…" Okay. There was a chance I might have used his toothpaste this morning. I was feeling groggy and just grabbed the first tube I saw. I didn't think it was that big a deal. "I don't think so…"

"So who used it then?" He got closer to me and shook the tube of toothpaste in my face. "Did a burglar come in and use the toothpaste? Because *somebody* squeezed this tube right in the middle."

Right. That's the reason I can't use his toothpaste. Because I squeeze from the middle instead of from the end. Which is morally wrong.

When I used his milk, I apologized right away. But this was getting ridiculous. After all, we're going to have children together. And children sometimes squeeze from the middle of the toothpaste tube. Adam had to learn to mellow out. Just a little.

"I think it's silly that we can't share a tube of toothpaste," I said. "It's just toothpaste, Adam."

His eyes darkened. "So in a nutshell, you're not capable of respecting my things. Even though I'm letting you live in *my* apartment rent-free."

"Rent-free? We're *engaged*."

"Well, you're not paying the rent. So I would say you're living here rent-free." The toothpaste trembled in his hand. "You couldn't afford to live here on your own."

My cheeks burned because he was right. "Fine. I couldn't afford to live here. But that doesn't mean we can't share toothpaste."

Adam looked down at the tube of toothpaste. He threw it into the trash bin so hard, the sound made me jump. "I'm going to go buy a new tube of toothpaste," he said.

And then he grabbed his coat and stormed out. He slammed the door so hard when he left that the entire apartment shook.

That was two hours ago. I've called him multiple times, and he's not picking up the phone. I don't know what the hell is going on. He's really mad at me. Over toothpaste. We just had a gigantic, blowout fight over *toothpaste*.

But they say that's what it's like having long-term relationships. You fight over silly things. Like changing the toilet paper roll. Or leaving the toilet seat up. Obviously, bathroom-related grievances are common.

I'm crazy about Adam. And yes, the man has his eccentricities. If I want to marry him, I have to accept it. I wish I hadn't said anything. I should've just apologized.

After all, nobody is perfect. Even Mr. Perfect.

CHAPTER 24

I oversleep the next morning. The power came back on
sometime in the early hours of the morning, and the
flashing light on my alarm clock says it's three in the
morning, but the sun shining through the window says
otherwise. In any case, my alarm never went off.

My watch reveals that it's after eight, so I stumble out
of bed in the direction of Victoria's room. I peek in on her
and she's out of bed, which means Adam must've gotten
her up. The television is on, but her eyes are shut and her
head is sagging to the side in her headrest. She's sound
asleep.

I go downstairs to make her breakfast, even though I
know she won't eat it, but I find Adam already down there,
washing dishes. He smiles cheerfully at me, with no
suggestion to the fact that something really wrong almost
happened between us last night.

Reading Victoria's diary entry last night about him
throwing a fit over the toothpaste revealed another side to

Adam I had never seen before. He doesn't seem like the sort of person who would do something like that. But in a way, it makes me like him more. Like Victoria's friend Carol used to say, he seems like Mr. Perfect. It's good to know that he has flaws like everyone else. Nobody likes a person who's too perfect.

It's also good to see he made up with his parents. Whatever animosity he had towards them seems to be long gone. Maybe Victoria's accident had something to do with that.

"Eva couldn't make it in this morning so I took care of Victoria," he says. He puts a plate on the drying rack. "Everything is taken care of."

I go for the cabinet with the oatmeal and reach for the box. "I'll fix her some breakfast."

"It's okay. I told you I took care of it."

I pause in the middle of opening a packet of oatmeal. "You fed her?"

He lifts a shoulder. "I gave her some tube feeds. She was too asleep to eat anyway. She never eats in the morning, does she?"

I feel a little guilty about that. I always at least *try* to give her a chance to eat, but he's right that she seldom does in the morning. I'm usually lucky if she takes one bite.

"If you don't need anything else," Adam says, "I'm going to head upstairs to do some writing. I need to get some work done today."

"Are you working on a new book?"

A smile touches his lips. "Yes. But I'm at the stage where I feel like everything I'm writing is crap. Yesterday I tore up five pages and tossed them in the trash."

I roll my eyes. "I'm sure it's not crap. All these reviews online say you're this amazingly brilliant writer. And you're a number one bestseller."

He waves a hand. "No. I'm just lucky."

"Bullshit."

"It's true." He shrugs. "There are a ton of talented writers out there. I was lucky enough to land a good agent, who landed me a good publishing deal, and that opened a lot of doors for me. But it could've gone another way."

I lean against the kitchen counter. "Did you always know you wanted to be a writer?"

"Pretty much." His eyes become distant. "In life, things never go quite the way you want them to. But when you're creating your own fictional world, you can make everything happen exactly how you want it to. That's what I love about writing."

"I know what you mean. I would definitely like to rewrite parts of my life story."

"How about you?" He raises his eyebrows. "What are your career aspirations?"

They always asked me this in school. *What do you want to be when you grow up, Sylvia?* I never had a good answer. My parents were sensible, middle-class folks who thought that I should be a teacher. After all, I sucked at school—and don't they say that those who can't do teach?

But I never had a passion for teaching. I felt like I was just drifting aimlessly through life until I met Freddy. I thought he was my lifeboat until he abandoned me like I was nothing.

"I don't know." I drop my eyes. "That sounds pathetic, doesn't it? I mean, I'm old enough to know what I want to be when I grow up. Since, you know, I *am* grown-up."

Adam laughs. "That's okay. You have a lot of time to decide. And in the meantime, we can use you here as long as you want to stay. It's nice having you here."

I squeeze my fists together. He seems unwilling to address the elephant in the room. Does he not realize how close we came to kissing last night? Maybe he has the right idea though. Maybe it's better to just pretend it never happened.

After all, it's never going to happen again.

CHAPTER 25

Victoria is especially lethargic today. I wasn't able to feed her any of her lunch, and dinner is going just as badly. She seems listless as I offer her spoonfuls of puréed carrots. On the plus side, she hasn't given me any dirty looks for what happened last night.

I still can't quite understand how that water glass tipped over.

Maybe I don't want to know.

I've been feeding her unsuccessfully for close to an hour when Adam peeks his head in. "Is this a good time to give her some medications?"

Victoria's eyes widen at his statement. This is the most awake she has seemed all day.

"Give me another twenty minutes," I say.

He nods. "Okay. I'll be back."

Victoria had a mouthful of carrots and some of them drip out of the right side of her mouth. I try to clean it away with a napkin, but she pushes me away. "Sylvie," she says.

I've noticed that whenever she says my name, she wants to tell me something important. "Yes?"

"Nub." Her blue eyes are like saucers. "Adam nub."

I know now that she's talking about a gun. But I don't know what she's talking about. I have not seen a gun in this house. I'd think she was making it up if I didn't see that bullet hole.

"You…" She points at the wall. "Nub. In the…"

I watch her face. She's struggling to come up with a word. It looks so frustrating. She knows exactly what she wants to say, but she can't say it. I can almost see the wheels turning in her brain, but she's not going anywhere.

"Coppit," she finally says triumphantly.

Well, great. I still have no idea what she's talking about. "Carpet?"

"No. *No.*" She squeezes her eyes shut for a moment then opens them. "Coppit. Coppit. The… coppit."

No matter how many times she says it, it's still a nonsense word. But then I look at where she's pointing. She's not pointing at the wall. She's pointing at her closet.

"Closet?" I ask.

She nods vigorously. "Yes. Adam coppit."

Is she trying to tell me there's a gun in her husband's closet?

Well, maybe there is. And if so, is it that big a deal? I can imagine wanting to have a gun out here for protection. If he has a gun in his closet, that's his business. It's not like he's keeping it on a holster and swinging it around.

But there's a pleading look in Victoria's eyes. She wants me to get the gun. But I can't do that. He would fire me.

Anyway, I trust Adam to have a gun. It's not that big a deal.

"It's okay," I tell Victoria. "I'll take care of it."

But I already know I'm going to do nothing.

CHAPTER 26

Adam makes TV dinners for dinner tonight.

Swedish meatballs. Which is one of my favorite TV dinners. I'm sure Adam thinks TV dinners are low brow food, but it's sort of a treat for me. When I was struggling to make the rent, I couldn't afford to plop down five dollars for a plastic container of meatballs, noodles, and sauce. My weekly food budget was about ten bucks. I ate a lot of Ramen noodles.

I'm just glad it isn't raining anymore. The sky has been mostly sunny today, although it's gotten very cold all of a sudden. I have a feeling I'm not going to be able to take Victoria out for walks much longer. I wanted to take her today, but I was worried the ground was too slippery with leaves and water from the storm last night.

"I think I'll take my food upstairs and eat in my room," I say as the microwave chimes to signify food is ready.

Adam frowns. "Oh. Okay."

He doesn't look happy about it, but he doesn't protest. He gets it.

I put the food on a plate and I'm about to head upstairs when the doorbell rings. I glance over at Adam, who looks as surprised as I am. "Are you expecting any visitors?" I ask.

He shakes his head no. "We don't get many solicitors out here."

He abandons the microwave and goes over to open the door. As he's looking through the peephole, I glance out the window. There's a car in our driveway that looks painfully familiar. A green Ford Fiesta with scratched paint. I clasp a hand over my mouth.

"Adam!" I say. "Don't—"

But it's too late. Adam has already opened the door and now Freddy is standing in the doorway. He's holding a bouquet of flowers. Not roses, like what Adam used to buy for Victoria, but carnations. Something cheap. Not that I should be surprised.

"Sylvie!" Freddy pushes past Adam and now he's in the foyer. He's in the house, just like that. "Sylvie, I've got to talk to you."

I take a step back. My mouth opens to form words, but nothing comes out. I finally understand how Victoria feels.

"Can I help you?" Adam asks.

"Yeah." Freddy glances at him, then looks back at me. "Sylvie and I... we..."

He is struggling to explain our relationship. He can't. We never got married. Since he left, I would say we're nothing.

Freddy pushes past Adam to talk to me. I can't help but notice that in spite of everything, Freddy looks good. He always kept his dark hair shaggy, but now he's clipped it short and professional. He's wearing a white dress shirt and nice pants. He looks like a white-collar worker. It looks like he cleaned up his act. I wonder if he went back to school like I always told him he should.

"Sylvie, can we please talk?"

"How did you find me here?" I say.

"Your old landlord told me."

My hand squeezes into a fist. "He told you?"

"I slipped him a twenty." He grins crookedly, like he's proud of himself for bribing my landlord. "Anyway, it wasn't like it was a big secret. You coulda told me where you were going."

"Maybe you should take the hint that I don't want you to know." I take another step back and hit the kitchen counter. "It's over, Freddy. That chapter in our lives is done."

"I should never have left even when you told me to." He frowns. "But you don't get it. I was hurting too. It was just so… frustrating. All we did was fight. But that didn't mean I didn't love you. I *do* love you. I just kept beating myself up because the whole thing was my fault…"

That was the worst part. Freddy kept blaming himself.

If only he'd insisted on coming inside with me when I talked to my father. Our whole life could have been different. He could've protected me.

But he didn't.

"I'm sorry." My voice breaks. "I just don't want to see you anymore."

"Sylvie, come on…"

He takes another step towards me. I try to back up, but I've got nowhere to go. I hit the counter behind me. I had almost forgotten Adam was in the room until he clears his throat and taps Freddy firmly on the shoulder.

"Hey," Adam says. "I'm going to have to ask you to leave.

"Sorry, buddy." Freddy barely glances over his shoulder. "This doesn't concern you."

"It concerns me if it's happening in my house." Adam's voice is cold, and a bit scary if I'm being honest. "I want you out of here. Right *now*."

Freddy pauses. He turns to look at Adam and sizes him up, probably trying to figure out if he can take him. Freddy used to be pretty decent at fighting. He got into scuffles from time to time, and he always held his own. I'm not sure who would come out on top in a fight between Adam and Freddy.

It makes me think of that gun. The one that Victoria claims is in Adam's closet.

But it doesn't come to that. Adam whips out his cell phone. "I'm dialing 911. The cops can be here in two minutes."

I see Freddy hesitating. It looks like he's got his life back on track, and I'm sure the last thing he wants is to be thrown in jail.

"Sylvie," he says in a low voice. "Will you come outside with me to talk?"

Before I can answer, Adam speaks up: "She said she wants you to leave. Leave. Now."

Freddy's shoulders drop. There's a part of me that wonders if he's going to risk it and stay. There's a part of me that wants him to stay. After all, I used to love this man. I thought we were going to start a family together. But then he shuffles in the direction of the door. I finally relax when I see him get back in his car and drive away.

I can't even look Adam in the eyes. "I'm sorry about that."

"Don't worry about it. That's what I'm here for."

I look up at Adam. He's been through the same thing I have. The loss of a child before it could be born. Having the person who he thought was the love of his life taken away from him. He gets it. He knows what I've been through because he's been through it himself.

And then I completely lose it. I start sobbing like a baby and Adam takes me into his arms and holds me. I haven't been held like that in such a long time. It feels so nice. He strokes my hair as I rest my head against his shoulder. And when I lift my face, he kisses me so gently on the lips that I can't help but kiss him back.

What happens next is so very wrong. But I don't even care anymore.

CHAPTER 27

I wake up the next morning in Adam's bed.

The master bedroom has its own bathroom, and I can hear him showering. He's singing. I try to identify the song. I think it's something by Bruno Mars. He sounds very happy. At least, I've never heard him singing before, so I would think it means he's happy.

He comes out of the bathroom with a towel wrapped around his waist and a big grin on his face. Yes, he's definitely happy. I guess it's been a long time for him since he's gotten lucky. Maybe he was starting to think it might never happen again.

"Hey." He leans over the bed and kisses me gently in the mouth, bringing back very nice memories of last night. I allow him to do it for a moment, then I pull away. "You're finally up. You really know how to sleep, Sylvia."

I avert my eyes as he lets the towel drop, and I don't look up again until he throws on some clothes. I shouldn't have done what I did last night. I should have pushed him away. But after the way he intervened when Freddy showed up, I wasn't thinking straight.

"Adam," I murmur. "Listen…"

His T-shirt sticks slightly to his damp chest. "Oh. Shit."

"What?"

The smile drops off his face. "You're about to tell me that last night was a terrible mistake and we can't ever do it again."

"Well…" That's exactly it. "It's just that… Victoria…"

His brows bunch together. He sits on the edge of the bed next to me. "Sylvia, I love Victoria. You know that. I'll always love her. But…"

"But?"

He rakes a hand through his wet hair. "Are you seriously going to make me complete that sentence? Victoria has major brain damage. We don't have a marriage anymore. Am I telling you anything you don't know?"

I drop my eyes. "No… but she's still in there. Part of her, at least."

He shakes his head. "Maybe a small part. I don't know. But, Sylvia, I'm thirty-five years old. I want to take care of Victoria, and I'll do that, but that can't be it for me. It *can't*. I mean, if this were it for my entire life, I…" He takes a deep breath. "I'd blow my brains out."

Even though what he's saying sounds awful, I can't entirely blame him. He has been an amazing husband to

Victoria up to this point. He has stood by her when a lot of spouses might not, especially somebody as young and handsome as he is.

But the part that really bothers me is I think there's a bigger part of Victoria still in there than he is willing to admit. It would be one thing if she were a vegetable who never opened her eyes, but she's not. She talks, albeit rarely. She knows what's going on. She remembered when a bullet hit the tree outside the house. She knew when I was wearing her sweater. She claims there's a gun hidden in Adam's closet. And for some reason, that scares her.

But I get that he feels lonely. After all, Victoria isn't capable of even a simple conversation anymore. And I can see why he feels having sex with her would be an ethical gray area. He admitted that ever since she's been home, he's had to take cold showers.

But this morning, he took a nice hot shower.

Adam leans forward and kisses me again. And God help me, I let him do it.

CHAPTER 28

Adam and I have been hooking up for two weeks.

Every night after he gets Victoria into bed, we have dinner together and then retire to his bedroom. And then we make love for hours. I was so infatuated with Freddy when I was younger, but this is something entirely different. The truth is, I think about him all the time. He's my last thought when I go to bed at night and my first thought when I wake up in the morning. I dream about him.

But I haven't spent another entire night in his bed. First of all, I still think of it as Adam and Victoria's bed. It's not my bed to be spending the night in. And second of all, I don't want Eva or Maggie to catch me coming out of there in the morning. Maggie would just laugh and tease me, but I'm scared of what Eva would do. At best, she would give me the glowering of a lifetime.

I feel guilty about Victoria too. She doesn't know what's going on between the two of us, but she's got to suspect. And even though she does have a serious brain injury, she's with it enough that she would understand I'm sleeping with her husband. I still remember the way she looked at me that night in her room when the power was out.

Mine.

The truth is, I'm still reading Victoria's diary, but for a different reason. She's writing about her engagement with Adam. He's so sweet and romantic to her in ways he can't be with me given our arrangement. And sometimes I read her entries and just savor them, imagining that I'm the one going on a horse-drawn carriage ride around Central Park or that we are the ones going to see a Broadway show with orchestra seats.

That is not to say there's no romance. This morning when I open my bedroom door, a dozen roses are lying on the ground. Nobody has ever given me roses in my entire life—Freddy could never afford them. I almost burst into tears. I feel a surge of happiness until I look up and find Eva staring daggers at me.

"Hi, Eva," I manage.

She narrows her eyes at me. "I know what you are doing."

I snatch the roses off the floor. "I… I don't know what you mean."

She snorts. "Do not tell lies. I knew the second I saw you this would happen. It always happens this way. Do you think you are the first? You are not."

A sweat breaks out on the back of my neck. "I'm sorry..."

"No," Eva says. "*You* are the one who will be sorry. You will be punished for the despicable thing you are doing. I promise you."

And with those words, she walks past me and stomps down the stairs. I hear the door to the house slam behind her and I let out a breath.

The house is completely silent now. Presumably, Victoria is in her bedroom. I put the roses down on my dresser and creep down the hallway to her bedroom. When I open the door, she's in her usual spot. Sitting by the window, her eyes closed.

Ordinarily, I would go downstairs to make her breakfast, but I feel so shaken by my confrontation with Eva, I feel like I should say something to Victoria. So I walk over to her and plaster a giant smile on my face.

"Hi, Victoria!" I say in a voice that I hope is loud enough to jar her awake.

It works. She opens her blue eyes just a crack.

"How about some breakfast?" My voice sounds strangely chipper to my own ears. That's what two weeks of good sex will do.

Victoria's eyes open slightly wider, but she doesn't say anything.

I hear a knock on the door to the bedroom, which is superfluous considering the door is already open. Adam is standing in the doorway, in his jogging shorts and a damp

T-shirt.

"Hey, Sylvia." He winks at me. "I'm going to make some eggs for breakfast. Should I throw a couple on for you?"

I glance over at Victoria, whose eyes are now completely open. I get a sinking feeling in my chest. She knows. She knows what's going on between us. It's all over her face.

"No, thanks," I mumble.

"You sure?" He wags his eyebrows at me. Oh God, could he make it any more obvious we're sleeping together? "It's no trouble."

"Nope." My smile is starting to hurt my cheeks. "I'm good."

Adam wanders away, but Victoria is still staring at me. If I had any doubt that she knows what's going on, it's gone. Whatever little she can comprehend, she comprehends that I'm sleeping with her husband.

"I'm so sorry," I murmur. "I just…"

I don't know how to complete that sentence.

Victoria looks like she's contemplating her next words. She looks like she's got something to say. And I'm going to bet none of it is very nice. For the first time, I'm grateful for her inability to speak.

"Sylvie," she finally says.

"Yes?" My heart is pounding in my chest. I'm bracing myself for whatever horrible thing she's going to say to me, which I will absolutely deserve.

"You…"

I bite my lip. "I know. I'm so sorry, Victoria."

"He'll kill you."

I've never seen or heard her say so many words at one time. And the slur she usually has in her speech is nearly gone. My mouth falls open. "What do you mean? What are you talking about?"

"Gun." Victoria's good eye bores into me while the other stares out the window. She got out the word correctly this time. "Get… gun."

And those are the last words she says to me all day.

CHAPTER 29

Victoria's Diary

March 22, 2017

This night. I don't even know what to say.

I haven't stopped crying for the last hour.

Tonight Carol threw an engagement party for me and Adam. Well, it wasn't so much a party as it was a bunch of us getting together at a bar and grill a few blocks away from the hospital and taking up five tables to have dinner, and drinking way too much.

A lot of the people invited were from the hospital, so there were a fair number of us wearing scrubs. I, on the other hand, wore my blue skirt paired with a white blouse and black pumps. It was the second thing I put on. Originally, I came out of the bedroom wearing my new little black dress, but I could tell immediately from the look on Adam's face that I needed to change.

Adam has his good and bad points. Carol still jokes around that he's Mr. Perfect, but like I said, nobody is perfect. He's extremely particular about how he wants the house and also about how he wants... well, *me*. When we go out for meals, he insists on approving my outfit. It's important to him. And if he doesn't like what I'm wearing, I have to go back in the bedroom and put on something different.

When I write it down, it sounds... weird. I know it. Everyone has their own personality quirks. It's not like I'm perfect either. Like, as Adam points out, I'm a bit of a slob. More than a bit, even. And of course, he has a ton of good points: he's sweet, affectionate, generous, and a brilliant writer. His editor loved his new manuscript and says it's going to be the biggest one yet.

And now I'll probably never read it. Because he and I are done.

Adam and I were sitting in the middle of the overcrowded table, and Carol and her boyfriend were across from us. And next to Carol was Mack, who came alone. I've never thought of Mack as being a particularly quiet guy—I'm used to the sound of his hearty laugh—but he had barely said two words the whole night. He just kept playing with his napkin and looking in my direction.

We had a mountain of food in front of us. And it was the kind of food that Adam and I *never* get when we're out together: french fries, hot wings, onion rings, sliders. Everything on the table was coated in a layer of breadcrumbs or a layer of grease or both. And instead of wine, I was drinking a Corona. My belly was stuffed with fried food and cheap alcohol. But I felt good!

"So when are you two tying the knot?" Carol asked. As she leaned forward, I could smell the beer on her breath.

Adam reached out to grasp my hand under the table. "We've got tickets for Vegas in three weeks."

"It's just the two of you?" Mack asked.

I popped an onion ring in my mouth. "Just the two of us."

Adam squeezed my hand. "Nobody else matters."

"That is *so* sweet!" Carol cried. She smacked her boyfriend in the arm. "Why can't you be sweet like that?"

Of course, Carol's boyfriend, Jeff, is a nice guy. I've known him for even longer than I've known Adam, and he's very easy-going and can be romantic when he needs to be. And I'm sure he doesn't make Carol use a separate toothpaste. Or freak out when she accidentally uses his.

I stuffed a few more french fries in my mouth. Somehow I'd forgotten how much I liked french fries. Adam likes all these upscale things, but that's not how I was raised. Maybe I'm just a lowbrow type of girl.

"Slow down there, Vicky," Adam said. "You're not going to be able to fit on the plane seat if you have too many more of those french fries."

Carol, who had way too many beers to drink, giggled at Adam's joke. I laughed too, but I felt my face grow hot. I couldn't even look at Mack. I could only imagine the expression on his face.

Our waitress came over to the table to offer us another round of drinks. Even though I knew I shouldn't, I got another beer. Carol got another too, but Mack shook his head.

The waitress put her hand on Adam's shoulder. "And how about you, sugar?"

The waitress had been hitting on Adam since he arrived. That's not entirely unusual. Adam is a very good looking guy and women hit on him. A lot. Even in front of me sometimes, which I really don't get. Do they think I'm his *sister*? Do they *want* the sort of guy who would dump the woman he's having dinner with for a more attractive option? Regardless, it happens. And it's irritating.

He smiled up at her. "I can't decide."

"Well," she said. "I always say, if you're not sure, you should have another!"

She giggled at her own joke. I couldn't help but notice the waitress had spectacular breasts packed into a tight little white shirt. Adam seemed to be noticing as well.

"Any beer you recommend?" he asked.

She tapped her finger against her chin. "Well, I think you would like our switchback ale. It's very rich and smooth."

His smile widened. "Like me."

She sidled a little closer to him. "Exactly what I was thinking."

I couldn't believe this. Yes, Adam did flirt back with waitresses sometimes, but the fact that he was flirting so aggressively in front of all my friends was a real slap in the face.

And it was even more of a slap in the face when she returned with his drink, as well as a cocktail napkin with her phone number scrolled on the back that she lay down in front of him accompanied by a suggestive wink.

"Oh my God!" Carol squealed. "Adam, that waitress just gave you her number!"

"Wow," Mack said.

"It's not that surprising," Carol said. "Adam is really hot." She giggled and nudged Jeff, who rolled his eyes.

Adam laughed. "I guess she didn't realize I'm already taken."

And here's the worst part: he didn't rip up the napkin or crumble it up. He folded it in half and put it in his pocket.

All that beer was sloshing around uncomfortably in my belly. I pushed my chair back so quickly, it nearly fell over. I rose unsteadily to my feet. "Excuse me," I managed.

I stumbled in the direction of the ladies' room. I didn't have to pee exactly, but I had enough to drink that I did *sort of* have to pee. But mostly I just wanted to get away from the table. My fiancé was hitting on another woman at our engagement party. I couldn't sit there another minute.

Before I could wrench open the door to the ladies' room, I felt a hand on my shoulder. I whirled around and saw Mack standing behind me. There was a deep crease between his black eyebrows.

"Vicky," he said.

"I need the bathroom," I mumbled.

"I need to talk to you."

I averted my eyes. "Not now."

"Yes, *now.*" He shook his head. "I know I promised I was going to keep my mouth shut about Adam, but I'm sorry. I can't."

"Mack…"

"He's a jerk to you." His right hand squeezed into a fist. "He's been putting you down all night and making jokes at your expense. And then hitting on that waitress right in front of you… I mean, Jesus Christ…"

"It was just harmless flirting…"

"It wasn't harmless flirting!" He raised his voice several notches. "He wasn't respecting you. I know it's none of my business, but—"

"Right." I swallowed down some bile in my throat. "It's none of your business. You wouldn't even tell me why you broke up with Kaitlyn, so don't act like we have that kind of relationship."

He sucked in a breath. "Vicky…"

"Don't say it's not true." I snorted. "When it comes to *your* personal life, it's all a big secret. But when it's *my* personal life, you can weigh in all you want. Why don't you tell me why *you* broke up with Kaitlyn? Tell me what egregious thing the wonderful Kaitlyn did that was *so* unacceptable?"

Mack's shoulders sagged. "You really wanna know?"

I meant it when I said it—I did want to know. But the way he said it, now I wasn't so sure.

"The reason I broke up with Kaitlyn," he said, "was because…" He took a deep breath. "Because I was in love with you."

What?

My head was swimming. I'm still not sure I even heard him right. Mack was *in love* with me? What the heck was he talking about? How was that possible? I was engaged to another man. And Kaitlyn was… Well, she was *gorgeous*. And why was he telling me this now, when I was three weeks away from marrying Adam?

He raked a hand through his black hair. "I know the timing sucks. I wasn't going to say anything. But… I can't stand by and let you make such a big mistake. Especially when…"

I shook my head. "Mack…"

"Look." He crinkled his nose in that way I used to find so cute. I guess I still do. "I don't expect you to love me back. I get it. I missed my shot. But… this isn't about me. This is about you, Vicky. Please don't marry this guy. Please."

"I…" I looked up at Mack's face. At his soft brown eyes and messy black hair. Why couldn't he have said all this to me the day before Adam walked into the emergency room? Not now, when it's too late. "I… I think I'm going to be sick."

And then I ran into the bathroom and vomited quite impressively into the toilet bowl. Mack was smart enough not to follow me into the ladies' room, which would have been mortifying. But I could hear the door crack open and his voice enters the room: "Vicky? You okay?"

"Please get Carol," I croaked.

The next voice I heard in the ladies' room was Carol's, thank heavens. She came into the stall with me and rubbed my back, and kept my hair out of the toilet bowl. (I had it down—the way Adam liked it.) I wasn't even that drunk. I think it was all the fried food. And possibly a little bit Mack telling me he was in love with me.

When I finally managed to make it back to the table, Adam leaped to his feet and went to get us an Uber to get home. All that nonsense with the waitress seemed forgotten. I was relieved. I had been so angry about it at the time, but now I just wanted to forget the whole thing.

My head was throbbing the entire ride home. Adam helped me out of the car, and I was walking like a little old lady up to our apartment. All I wanted to do was sleep for a week. Fortunately, Carol had timed the party so that I didn't have a shift the next day. I planned to spend the entire next day sleeping, if not the whole week.

Except the second we got inside the apartment, Adam slammed the door shut behind me. It was loud enough to make my head throb. For a moment, I hoped it was an accident and not another temper tantrum. But then I saw the look on his face and I knew I was in for it.

"You're unbelievable, Victoria," he said.

I rubbed my temples. My eyes felt bloodshot. I would have shelled out a hundred bucks to end this conversation right now. "What? What are you talking about?"

His lips curled into a sneer. "You think I didn't see you sneaking off with that big, fat paramedic guy?"

My stomach sunk as the reality set it. Adam was pissed off. There was no chance I was getting to go to bed right now or any time in the near future. "I wasn't sneaking off with Mack. I talked to him for two minutes on my way to the restroom."

"You expect me to believe that?"

My knees trembled beneath me. "Adam, it was nothing. Nothing happened."

"You think I don't see the way he looks at you. And you were flirting with him all night…"

"I was flirting?" In spite of the throbbing in my temple, I felt a spark of fury. "*You* were the one who got the waitress's phone number! Don't you think that was inappropriate?"

"She gave it to me! It's not like I asked her for it."

"You could have given it back. Or torn it up."

He stared at me, his green eyes darkening. "You know what? I'm glad I didn't. Maybe I'll give her a call."

I stared at him. I already knew Adam had some issues with jealousy. That was not a big surprise. But we've never fought this badly over his jealousy.

"It's obvious I can't trust you," he said. "Every time I turn my back, you're flirting with another man." He narrowed his eyes. "Are you sleeping with him, Victoria?"

"No!"

"I don't believe you." He looked over to the kitchen table, where I had dropped my purse. Before I knew what was happening, he made a beeline for my purse and fished out my iPhone. "I bet if I looked in here, I'd find a million text messages from that guy."

Well, there would be *some*. But not a million. Like, two-hundred—max. And they were all very innocent. "That's not true."

He jabbed at the screen of my phone. "What's your password, Victoria?"

The throbbing pain in my temple intensified. "I'm not going to tell you that."

"Why not? Because you've got something to hide?"

I could have given him the password. I could have opened up my text messages with Mack to show him how innocent they were. But somehow, I didn't think that would be enough. He would look over every exchange and imagine things that weren't there. And even if he didn't, I still didn't think I should give him my password. Why should I?

"No," I said firmly. "Because it's *my* phone. You wouldn't tell me the password for your phone."

"Because *I'm* not cheating on you with another woman."

I couldn't even believe what I was hearing. Did he honestly think I was cheating on him? "I'm not cheating on you, Adam."

"Bullshit." He shook my phone at me. "What's your password, Victoria?"

"Adam..."

"Tell me your goddamn password!"

Adam got this look in his eyes that I'd never seen before. It made me take a step back. My head was still throbbing but I wasn't even thinking about that. For a moment, I thought for sure he was going to reach out and strangle me with his bare hands. But instead, he lifted my phone in the air and hurled it at my face.

I thought he was throwing it at my face anyway. I don't know if it was bad aim or what, but the phone missed my head and slammed into the wall behind me hard enough to make a tiny dent. I heard glass shattering as the phone hit the ground. Adam gave me one last look, then he spun on his heels and walked out the door, slamming it hard behind him.

And that was the night of my engagement party.

So my phone is wrecked. The screen is so shattered, I can't see anything. But what's even more wrecked is my engagement. I can't marry Adam. Not after what he did tonight. It turns out Mack was right all along.

I've already locked the deadbolt on the door. In the morning, I'll pack up all my stuff and find a place to stay. Maybe Carol will let me crash at her place. All I know is

I'm done with Adam.

I started this journal so my children could read about how I met their father. But it looks like the father is not going to be Adam Barnett.

I feel so stupid.

March 23, 2017

I'm a little embarrassed to be writing this post.

I took him back.

I know. Last night was awful. I skimmed over what I wrote after our fight, and I remember how angry I was. There was no chance I would ever take him back. Not in a million years.

All night, I was tossing and turning. I kept imagining the conversation I would have with him when I returned his insanely expensive ring. But when I thought about that conversation, I didn't feel good or relieved. I felt *awful* at the idea of losing him. It made my chest ache.

I mean, this was the guy I planned to marry. I planned to have a family with him. How could it be over?

Adam showed up at the door at ten in the morning, looking about as bad as I felt. His hair was disheveled, he had a day's growth of a beard, and his eyes were bloodshot. He told me he had slept on a park bench, which made me feel awful. He looked like he was about to burst into tears.

I still wasn't ready to take him back. But I did let him

in.

"I'm *so* sorry about last night," he said. "I had too much to drink and I just..." He rubbed his eyes. "I can't believe the things I said to you. That's not me. You know that, Vicky."

I did know that. Adam had a bit of a temper and got angry over stupid things like toothpaste, but him throwing my phone was not like him.

"I'm never drinking beer again," he groaned.

"You can't blame this on the beer."

"I know." He winced. "I'm not. I'm sorry. I don't know what got into me. I know you would never cheat on me. And I would never cheat on you. Ever."

It was at moments like this I wish more than ever that my mother was still alive. Carol gives me advice sometimes, but it's not the same—she thinks Adam is Mr. Perfect. And Mack has an ulterior motive, so I can't trust what he has to say. I didn't know what to do.

But I couldn't imagine my future without Adam in it.

"I love you so much, Vicky." He reached for my hand and I let him take it. "You are the best goddamn thing that's ever happened to me. Better than hitting the *New York Times* bestseller list. You're my whole life." He blinked his bloodshot eyes. "Please... let me make this up to you. *Please.*"

Finally, I told him I would think about it. He went to take a shower, and then even though he must've been feeling like crud, he took me out to lunch. And then we got gelatos. And he bought me flowers. And he spent the whole day telling me how much he loved me and how I was the most amazing woman he's ever met.

I'm not made of stone.

Adam is a good guy. I know that. What he did last night was really out of character, and I have to believe it must've been from how much he had to drink. I'm going to give him one more chance, but believe me, I'm going to make him work for it. I'm not going to put up with any more garbage. I won't be his punching bag. I won't.

I started writing this for my future children to tell them the story of how I met their father. But if that doesn't end up happening with Adam, at least this will serve as a reminder to me that even the best relationship can go sour.

CHAPTER 30

Victoria's story about their engagement party must be an exaggeration.

I can't imagine it. As Adam unpacks the Chinese food takeout feast that got delivered a few minutes ago, I try to envision him throwing a phone across the room. I can't do it. He's not like that. He's been nothing but kind and gentle around me.

"You've been really quiet tonight," he comments as he peers into a container of kung pao chicken. "Hey, did we order two of these chicken dishes or just one?"

"Who is Mack?" I blurt out.

Adam lifts his eyes from the container of chicken. "Mack?"

I can't tell him about the diary I've been reading. If I told him about it, he'd think I was violating Victoria's privacy. He wouldn't believe that she gave it to me to read, because he thinks nothing is going on upstairs with her. He doesn't see what I see. "Victoria said the name."

"Oh." He looks in the brown bag of food again and yanks out some chopsticks. "It doesn't sound familiar."

"She used to work with him... I think he was a paramedic."

He shrugs. "I don't know. She had a lot of coworkers at the hospital. It's a busy place."

"So the name doesn't sound familiar to you?"

"Not really." His face is completely blank. If he's lying, he is an incredible liar. "Why do you ask?"

"I just thought..." I wring my hands together. "I feel bad that Victoria never has any visitors. She mentioned him, and I thought maybe..."

Adam steps away from the bag of Chinese food. He frowns at me. "She had a few visitors when she first got home, but they used to upset her. So... I stopped inviting people."

"Oh..."

"It's hard to blame her." He bites his lip. "I'm sure she doesn't want people she used to know to see her like this. She used to be intelligent and charming and beautiful, and now she's... Anyway, it's got to be hard."

"That's true..."

He makes a good point. If Victoria had feelings for this guy or he had feelings for her, I'm sure she wouldn't want him to see her like she is now. But that's silly. She's lonely. She'd probably be happier if she could reconnect with some of her old friends.

Or maybe I just want to do something nice for her

because I feel so damn guilty about Adam.

Adam has gone back to unpacking the food from the bag. We got way too much—enough for at least four people, but it's fine—we'll have leftovers tomorrow night. "Hey," he says. "I've been thinking about Thanksgiving next week. Do you need a few days to go see your family?"

My family. That's something I haven't spoken to him much about, and he's been good enough not to ask. Given he had some sort of falling out with his own parents, maybe he would understand. I was never close to my father. I always felt like I was disappointing him in one way or another. My grades were never what he wanted them to be. He always acted like he expected more from me than what I felt like I could give him. He had given me a roof over my head, food, and a good education—so what did I have to show for it? And my mother always just followed his lead.

Another C? Is that really the best you can do, Sylvia?

But then again, I can't bring myself to tell Adam that the last time I saw my father, he kicked me in the ribs hard enough to break them. That's not a story I want to tell anyone.

"I'm not close with my family," is all I say.

"Well then," Adam says. "I was thinking we could have a little feast. Here."

I feel a smile touch my lips. I haven't had a real Thanksgiving dinner in years. "Okay. What did you have in mind?"

"Well…" He pulls me close to him, his hands on the small of my back. I love the smell of his aftershave—it always gets me. "I just thought I could make a turkey and you could help with a couple of the sides. Nothing big."

"Would you invite your parents?"

He shakes his head. "They're going to my father's brother's house."

I can't hide my relief. The last thing I want is to explain this awkward situation to Adam's parents. They'll surely recognize something is going on between him and me.

"I thought we should just keep it small," he says.

I nod vigorously. "That sounds great."

He leans in to kiss me. "So it will just be you, me, and Victoria."

Wait… what?

Maybe it was unreasonably selfish, but I had thought the meal would just be him and me. Or me and him with Maggie and her boyfriend. I can't even imagine how awkward it will be with the three of us around the table. I used to want to bring Victoria down for meals, but now I see it would be a mistake.

"Um…" I disentangle myself from his embrace. "You want Victoria to join us?"

"You don't?" He raises his eyebrows. "It's Thanksgiving, Sylvia. Victoria is my wife."

"But…" Doesn't he understand how weird it would be? "I know you want to be nice, but I think it will upset her. I think she knows about... you know, *us*..."

He snorts. "She doesn't know."

"She does, Adam."

"You're imagining things." He shakes his head. "She has severe brain damage, Sylvia. The doctor said she's like a two-year-old child. She doesn't know what's going on. She can't even remember things from one day to the next. She barely even knows who you are."

"She remembers my name."

"Does she? Then how come every time you walk into the room, you say, 'It's Sylvie'?"

He's right. I do say that every time I walk into the room.

"We have to include her," Adam says firmly. "She'll enjoy it. You can dress her in one of the nice outfits from her closet and do her hair. And then after dinner, we'll bring her back upstairs and... then we can be alone together."

I don't think Victoria will enjoy this dinner, but on the other hand, it's just one night. And Adam seems to feel strongly about it. I guess it won't be the end of the world.

CHAPTER 31

Victoria's Diary

April 19, 2017

Today I got married.

I'm married!!

I can't even believe it. And honestly, the entire trip has been magical so far. Like a fairytale. Well, a fairytale that happens in Las Vegas. But I love Las Vegas. I want to move here. The hotel we're at is like something out of a storybook. The entire first floor is made out of waterways and this morning Adam and I took a gondola ride. A gondola ride! Honest to goodness!

Adam has been the most romantic and sweet guy in the world for the last three weeks. We should fight more if this is the result. He brought home flowers every night, and he's always telling me how much he loves me and how he's the luckiest guy in the world to have me. He even bought a new toothpaste and he said it was for the two of us. We're finally sharing toothpaste! It's like the fear of losing me turned him into a different person. I'm so glad I didn't do anything crazy and leave him that night.

The chapel where we got married was actually really tasteful. I was scared that it was going to be extremely gaudy because, you know, Vegas. But it was a sweet little white chapel with purple trim, and the inside had lots of seats like a real church. And the person who married us was a man in a suit—not Elvis or anything. Yes, Elvis was an option, but we decided against it (although I was a little tempted).

We couldn't stop grinning at each other when the minister read us our vows. It was so surreal. One year ago, I didn't even have a boyfriend. Now I was pledging my life to this man. And I felt really good about it! I made the right decision.

Then we went back to our hotel and Adam carried me across the threshold. It was so freaking romantic! And then we spent the next two hours in bed.

In bed with my husband.

My husband! Husband husband husband... I can't stop saying that word! This will never get old.

I knew it. I knew from the second I laid eyes on him, this was going to happen. This was fate. Adam was fated to cut his hand and end up in the emergency room, just so we could meet.

After we were spent, we shared a bottle of Bailey's

Irish Cream from the minibar, then ordered room service for dinner. At that point, Adam said he wanted to go play some blackjack at the casino downstairs. He wanted me to come with him—he said I would be his good luck charm. I was tempted but I was too absolutely exhausted from the day.

So, in summary, in case you missed it, I'm now married. (Eeeeek!) And I'm lying in our king size bed, re-reading Adam's first novel, *All in the Family*. I was reading it yesterday during the plane flight over here, and now I'm nearly finished with it. It's just amazing as I remember—no wonder it was so popular.

I'm not surprised the book upset Adam's family. The plot centers around a guy in his twenties with an incredibly toxic family. If this book is based on reality, I don't blame Adam for not wanting anything to do with his parents. It sounds like they were miserable people who rooted for him to fail every step of the way.

In the novel, the parents finally threaten to cut the protagonist out of their will in favor of his sycophantic older brother. The hero subsequently plots the death of his parents and his brother, which is ultimately successful. And he gets away with everything.

So in summary, I can see why his parents weren't fans of the book.

Still, I haven't given up on the idea of a reconciliation between Adam and my new in-laws. Someday Adam and I will have children, and I would love for those children to know their grandparents. But I'm not going to ruin our honeymoon by bringing it up right now. We'll talk about it when the time is right

In the meantime, I'm going to keep reading and wait for my husband to get back to our hotel room.

My husband.

I can't believe I'm married!

April 20, 2017 (very early)

I cannot believe this.

It's four in the goddamn morning and Adam still hasn't come back to our hotel room. At first, I was waiting up for him to be romantic, but around two in the morning, it stopped being romantic. I called him and he didn't pick up. I called him *repeatedly.*

At three in the morning, I went downstairs. I walked around the casino like a crazy person, trying to find my husband. I probably sounded like such a loser.

"He's about five foot eleven, brown hair, early thirties," I said to one waitress who was carrying a full tray of cocktails. "He's really... um, handsome."

She gave me a sympathetic look. "I'm sorry, hon. I hope you find him."

Of course, I didn't. I called him about twenty more times and left increasingly furious messages. I still haven't heard back.

I thought about calling the police. I'm still thinking about it. I mean, something really bad may have happened to him. What if he got mugged and is lying unconscious in the street? But I can just imagine how it would sound if I called the police and explained that my husband went to the casino a few hours ago and now I can't find him. They would laugh at me.

I really hope he's all right.

And if he is, I'm going to kill him.

April 20, 2017

Well, I never would have expected my honeymoon to end up this way.

Adam didn't get back until this morning. The sun was already up when he returned to the hotel. I was engulfed by our giant king-size bed, tossing and turning for most of the night. I probably got an hour of sleep in scattered ten-minute blocks. So when he walked in the door wearing the same clothes from last night, not looking like he'd been beaten to a bloody pulp, and whistling a little tune under his breath, I wasn't sure if I wanted to hug him or throw something at him.

"Where were you all night?" I screamed at him. I'm not even going to pretend I wasn't screaming. I was definitely screaming. The fight we were going to have was going to be a screaming fight.

"At the casino," he said.

Of course, I knew that was a lie. I had looked for him at the casino. If he had been at that casino, I would've found him.

So then his story became that he went to *another* casino on the strip, because he heard those casinos were better. I asked him where he heard that, and he mumbled something about how a waitress had told him. And that's when we got to the crux of the story.

"Did you go to the other casino with that waitress?" I asked.

He just shrugged and looked away. "What's the difference?"

Right. Because why should I care if my husband went on a date with another woman on *our wedding night*? Why should that bother me?

The truth is, I'm starting to realize that all the things that first attracted me to Adam are the things I hate about him now. I mean, I'm glad my husband is handsome, but why does he have to be *so* unbelievably handsome? Why does he have to have so much money to throw around? Why does he have to give girls Jell-O legs when he smiles? Why does every woman who meets him have to fall half in love with him?

And why does he have to flirt back?

Of course, it's the last part that bothers me. If he didn't flirt back, it could be something we would joke about. *Ha ha, the naïve waitress thinks she's got a chance with me.*

"Stop acting so jealous, Victoria," he said. "Is that what you want to be? A jealous, nagging wife?"

"No, I want to be a wife whose husband doesn't abandon her on her wedding night!"

It only got worse from there. I'm not going to re-create it here. But believe me, it was brutal. If you want to imagine the worst conversation you would ever want to have with the man you married yesterday, that was our fight.

But even so, I thought we would work it out. I mean, we just got married! But when the fight entered its second hour, I could see the red in Adam's cheeks, and I knew he was never going to admit what he did was wrong. Because he didn't *believe* it was wrong. The only way this fight was ever going to end would be if I apologized for yelling at him and admitted I was a jealous, nagging wife. And heck no, I was not going to do that.

Still, I was surprised when he started packing his things.

"What are you doing?" I said as I watched him throw his jeans and shirts into our big brown luggage.

"What do you think?" He took a moment to fold one of his shirts. "I'm not going to share a room with somebody who thinks I'm a cheater. I'm leaving."

"You're getting another room?"

"No, I'm going back to New York."

I opened my mouth to ask him if he was serious, but I

didn't have to. I could see in his eyes that he meant it.

So that's that. My husband has packed his things and abandoned me one day into our honeymoon. I don't even have a bag to pack my clothes, because he took it with him. And our return plane ticket isn't for another week and it's in Adam's name, which means if I want to go home, I'll have to buy a new ticket myself.

How did this become my life?

April 24, 2017

At some point, you realize you have two choices:

1. You admit that your two-day-old marriage was a huge mistake. And when you come back to work from your honeymoon, and everyone asks you how it was, you get to tell them you got divorced during the honeymoon. Making it the worst honeymoon ever in the history of the world.

2. You suck it up and try to make it work

If I told Victoria of one year ago what Adam had done to me and that I took him back, she would have laughed. She would have insisted I had more pride than that. But when I got home and Adam immediately threw his arms around me, my resolve faded.

This man is my husband now. I made a commitment to him. I do *not* want to get a divorce three days into my marriage. I don't want to throw everything away over one bad fight. I mean, every marriage has growing pains.

Right???

Chapter 32

What sort of man cheats on his wife with another woman on their wedding night?

I contemplate that question in my head as I watch Adam sleep beside me. As handsome as he is, he's even more attractive when he's asleep. He has this sexy stubble on his chin and his lips blow air softly in and out. After reading Victoria's story about what happened on their wedding night, I didn't want to come to his room. But he was so nice and charming, it was hard to say no. He said all the right things, just like he said all the right things to Victoria to get her to forgive him. And here I am.

I need to stop. I need to tell him I can't do this anymore. I can't do it to Victoria. No matter what he says, I know she knows.

But it's harder than I thought. After all, look at what he did to her—and she stayed with him. My situation is much worse. At least she had a good job. If I left, I'd have nothing. Not even a place to live. Of course, Freddy would let me stay with him, but no, I can't.

I don't know what to do.

While Adam is still asleep, I slip out of the bed and quietly leave the room. I had hoped to get back to my room without anybody noticing, but I nearly collide with Maggie, who is vacuuming the hallway. When she sees me sneaking out of Adam's bedroom, her eyes go wide.

"Oh," she gasps.

"Maggie." I feel the heat in my cheeks. I did not want to run into Maggie, but it's better than running into Eva. "This isn't how it looks…"

She cocks her head to the side. "Really?"

I let out a breath. I'm not going to stand here and insult Maggie's intelligence. "Fine. It is how it looks." I glance at the closed door to Adam's bedroom. "I didn't mean for it to happen though. It's just… I mean, I've been living here and… the house is so empty… and cold…"

Suddenly, I feel like I'm about to burst into tears.

"It's okay," Maggie says quickly. "I mean, *I* sure don't mind. I sort of suspected, to tell you the truth. I didn't want to say anything though." She smiles wryly. "And it's not like I can blame you. He *is* pretty hot."

"Please don't tell Eva."

She throws back her head and laughs. "Yeah, that would involve me having a conversation with Eva. No way. Don't worry, Sylvie. Your secret is safe with me. I swear." She hesitates and looks down the hall at Victoria's bedroom. "Just make sure Victoria doesn't find out."

I frown. "What do you mean?"

Maggie lowers her voice a notch. "Adam thinks Victoria has no clue what's going on, but he's wrong. Her speech is messed up, but she knows exactly what's going on around her." She squints at me. "You know it too, don't you?"

I nod slowly.

"I've been working here since Victoria and Adam first moved in," Maggie says, "and let me tell you, Victoria is a very jealous woman."

I get this sick feeling at the pit of my stomach. "She is?"

"Yes, *very*." Maggie hesitates. "This is just between you and me, right?"

"Of course."

She leans in very close to me so that she's nearly talking into my ear. "So we used to have this woman here who did gardening and cooking. Irina. But Victoria was insanely jealous of her. Almost obsessed. She thought Irina and Adam were sleeping together."

Irina. The one who used to live in Glen Head. The place Victoria mentions every few days, with what seems like increasing urgency. This can't be a coincidence, can it?

"Were they sleeping together?" I ask in a voice that's barely a whisper.

Maggie doesn't answer right away. She glances around the hallway. "I don't know for sure, but I don't think they were. But on the other hand, it wouldn't have surprised me. Adam and Victoria… They did not have a good marriage."

This isn't entirely a revelation based on what I've been reading in Victoria's diary. But hearing it from an outsider just confirms what I suspected to be true.

"Anyway." Maggie straightens up and brushes off her jeans. "I shouldn't be gossiping. Every marriage has its problems, right?"

Right. It's not like I can talk. The closest thing I ever had to a husband was Freddy, and that was a disaster.

"Thanks for telling me," I say.

Maggie winks at me and gets the vacuum started again. "No problem. Just… you know, be careful."

I'd feel a whole lot better if people would stop warning me to be careful.

CHAPTER 33

Victoria's Diary

August 28, 2017

When I got home from work today, I felt like I could barely stand up. It was an exhausting shift in the ER. The last patient I saw was a man whose family brought him in with concern for a stroke, but he kept insisting he didn't have slurred speech. "I'm just from the south—that's how we talk," he kept saying. (It turned out to be a stroke.)

My head was pounding when I finally stumbled into our apartment. Adam was watching television on the couch, and when he saw me come in, he patted the seat next to him. That's the best thing about being married— when you get home from a long shift, you have somebody to cuddle next to on the couch and watch television.

But before I joined him, I changed out of my scrubs. I used to always spend the rest of the evening in my scrubs after a shift, but Adam can't stand it when I wear scrubs in the house, even fresh ones. His logic is the scrubs are covered in whatever germs or bodily fluids I was exposed to during my time in the hospital—which is a fair assessment. So I took a minute to sift through my drawers, trying to find something that struck that perfect balance between comfortable and something he would approve of. Because I was not changing again.

I finally selected a stringy tank top with a pair of sheer sweatpants. As a rule, Adam doesn't like me in sweatpants, but he makes an exception if they're "sexy" sweatpants.

When I got back into the living room, I immediately saw the approval on Adam's face and breathed a sigh of relief.

I had expected to plop down next to Adam on the couch to watch *This Is Us*, but instead, he reached for the remote and shut off the television. I immediately got a sick feeling in the pit of my stomach. I must have done something wrong.

I wracked my tired brain, trying to figure out what I did to upset him. Was I later than usual from work? Did he catch me flirting with another guy? I'm not sure if I'll ever figure it out without him telling me. Last week we fought for two hours because I borrowed some of the milk from his shelf in the fridge. I don't know how he figured it out. I wouldn't have ordinarily, but I was dying for some corn flakes and I was all out of milk. I was so careful—I put it back in exactly the same place he had it, even turned at the same angle.

But I hadn't done that again. I was sure of it. I only borrow his stuff if I'm desperate.

"So I've got some exciting news," he said.

He was smiling. I hadn't done anything wrong.

I allowed my shoulders to relax. "Oh…?"

I assumed he was going to tell me something about his book, so I was surprised when he said, "I bought us a house."

What?

That was the last thing I expected him to say. He'd been complaining recently about the construction work outside and how it made it hard to focus on the revisions he was doing on his novel. But I had expected him to say he wanted to start looking at houses maybe. Not that he'd already bought one. I mean… what the heck?

"You bought a house?" I managed.

He nodded. "And I sold this apartment."

What?

I felt like the wind had been knocked out of me. The apartment I was living in now belonged to another person? How was this possible? I looked around the room, a sense of growing panic squeezing my chest. How could he do this without telling me?

"Adam," I said as calmly as I could. "Why didn't you tell me you were selling the apartment?"

"I wanted it to be a surprise." His voice was a deadpan, as if selling your apartment right out from under your wife was a totally normal thing to do. "I thought you'd be pleased. Now we have a house and you didn't have to deal with the hassle of selling the old place and buying a new place. It was quite stressful."

"But don't I get a say in where we're going to live?"

He shrugged. "I bought it with *my* money. And I own this apartment. So really, it's my decision, isn't it?"

I took a deep breath, trying to calm myself down, but my head was buzzing. All I could think was that if he respected me at all, he would never have done something like this.

Then again, I could yell and scream all I wanted, but it wouldn't change anything. He's sold our home. He's bought a new one. What could I do at this point aside from starting a horrible fight?

"Where's the new house?" I finally asked.

"Montauk. In Long Island."

At the moment he told me, I didn't have a sense of where Montauk is. If I did, I would have been far more upset than I was. The second I looked it up on a map later, I almost fainted. Do you know where Montauk is? It's practically in the Atlantic Ocean. As far as I'm concerned, we may as well go live in Siberia.

"You'll love it, Vicky." Adam's voice softened and he put a hand on my knee. "It's a huge house with lots of bedrooms, a finished attic for me to work in, a giant garden… and a backyard where… you know, the children can play."

He knows my buttons—I have to give him that. He knows how excited I've been about the prospect of trying for a baby. And we have agreed that we don't want to raise a bunch of kids in a tiny Manhattan apartment. If we want to have three or maybe even four kids, it would cost a fortune to live in a place where we wouldn't all be living in bunk beds.

A yard. A garden. Lots of bedrooms.

When he put it that way, it didn't sound so bad.

Adam could tell he was swaying me. "Come see it with me," he said. "If you hate it, then… I'll back out of the sale. But please just look at the house."

So tomorrow we're driving out to see the new house. He has absolutely sworn that if I hate it, we don't have to live there. Of course, we can't stay put because he already sold our apartment.

I still can't believe he did that. But that's just the sort of man Adam is. He makes a decision and then… he just does it. I wish he didn't do that, but maybe after he gets used to being married, he'll get more used to consulting me on things.

In the meantime, I'm actually pretty excited about seeing the new house. I haven't lived in a house since I was a child. Adam keeps talking about how great it is and how I'm going to fall in love with it for sure. I can't wait!

September 2, 2017

It occurred to me today that I haven't made many huge decisions in my life.

Most things were obvious. Go to school. My nursing degree was a no-brainer because I've wanted to be a nurse ever since my mother's battle with cancer—she had the most fantastic nurse on the inpatient unit and I was inspired to be that kind of great nurse. Then when a friend suggested nurse practitioner school, I somehow just knew it was the right decision—I didn't even have to think about it. I had always wanted to live in Manhattan, so when I got the job in the ER, it wasn't a hard decision whether to take it. And even though I had a few moments of doubt before getting married, that decision too seemed obvious in the end.

And once again, it seems like another big decision is being made for me.

Adam rented a car and drove us out to the house in Montauk today. Did I mention how far away Montauk is from Manhattan? Like I said, Siberia. As we were making the drive, it occurred to me what this meant. If we decided to take this house, I couldn't continue working in the ER. The commute would be ridiculous. I'd have to look for another job closer to the house—and who knew what was available around there.

I pointed that out to Adam during the drive and he nodded. "Would that be the end of the world?"

He had a point. I took the job only a year out of NP school, and I never believed it would be my job for the rest of my life. But now that I've been there for over three years, I wouldn't mind if it were my job for the rest of my life. I like that ER. I like the patient population. I like the people I work with. I don't want to leave.

Then again, working at new places exposes you to new experiences. That's what people say anyway. Adam did, at least.

"I'd have to look and see what jobs are available around Montauk," I said.

"Or," he said, "you could just… stay home."

I sucked in a breath. "What?"

"Is that a bad thing?" He took his eyes off the road to glance at me. "The house is huge and just taking care of it will be a full-time job. And soon we're going to have a houseful of kids to take care of, right?"

Oh right, that's another thing—I've quit my birth control pills. My period came back right away. I have a clockwork twenty-five-day cycle, and we made love a lot this month. As crazy as it sounds, I could be pregnant right now. Every time I think about it, I get this excited feeling in my stomach. Deciding to get pregnant is yet another no brainer.

As much as I love my career, I always dreamed of staying at home with my children. Considering I lost my mother so young, I don't want to miss even a nanosecond of my children's lives, because really, you don't know how long you're going to have.

"I want to support you," he said. "I make more than enough money to support our family. Please... let me do this."

"I'll think about it," I promised.

After about a hundred hours of driving, we finally got to the house. I gasped when I saw that there was a gate surrounding the place—I've never lived in a gated home before. I never thought of myself as the sort of person who would live in a gated estate. The garden was enormous, although terribly overgrown, and there was a small shed at the edge of the property. (Could that become my she-shed? I've heard she-sheds are the new thing!)

We were definitely in the middle of nowhere. I've never lived in a place so far away from... well, everything. Our nearest neighbor had to be a mile away. When I took my phone out of my pocket, the screen announced that I had no service.

As I walked into the foyer of our new potential home, the first thought I had was that if I screamed, nobody would be able to hear me.

"What do you think?" Adam asked.

"It's..." I hesitated, looking around for the first time. "It's beautiful."

I meant it. The house was beautiful—and huge! The living area was bright and airy, and there was a white staircase spiraling up to the next level. When I looked up, I saw a chandelier dangling over my head—an actual *chandelier*! I had never imagined living in a place that had a chandelier. After years of tiny Manhattan apartments, I wanted to throw my arms out and spin around, reveling in the fact that I wouldn't knock into something. And then, before I could stop myself, I was doing it. I was spinning. Spinning!

I didn't want to love it as much as I did.

Adam grinned at me as I finally stopped spinning because it was making me ill. "You love it," he said.

"I do, but…" I wrung my hands together. "My job…"

His eyes darkened. "It's just a job, Victoria. Can't you find a new one?"

"But…"

"Or is there some other reason you want to stay that you're not telling me?" He raised an eyebrow. "Mack, for instance?"

Oh no. Adam has this irrational jealousy of Mack, which he manages to bring up at every opportunity. Well, I suppose it isn't *entirely* irrational since Mack *was* in love with me. But ever since I got back from Vegas, Mack and I have been pretending that conversation never happened. It's a bit awkward though—another point in favor of leaving.

"Is that it?" he asked. "You don't want to be away from your *boyfriend*?"

I could hear the bitter edge creeping into his voice, and I knew we were on the brink of a really big fight. I also realized Adam absolutely would storm off and leave me in this house. In the middle of nowhere with no phone service.

"It has nothing to do with Mack," I said quickly. "I just… I need to think about it. Can't I have a chance to think about it?"

He narrowed his eyes at me. "What's there to think about?"

And that was that.

So it looks like we're moving. I'm giving up my life in Manhattan for something entirely new and different out in Long Island. I'd like to say it's temporary, but once we pop out a few kids, there's no way we'll ever move back.

This will be forever.

September 10, 2017

Today was my last shift in the ER.

We're moving tomorrow. Adam hired another moving company, and they're coming tomorrow morning to haul all our stuff out to Montauk. We'll dart ahead in the new BMW Adam bought last week. It's the X35i, which supposedly handles very well in snow—we'll need it when the winter hits and we're trapped under two feet of white powder. It's still only early September so it feels like the winter is very far away, but I know it's right around the corner.

I'm trying not to feel sad about the fact that I'm

leaving forever and it's unlikely I'll take the time to drive three hours back to the city very often. Carol threw me a mini-party at the nurse's station, which we managed to enjoy for about five minutes before the ER started getting backed up again.

Today I'm savoring every single patient interaction. Even the ones with the drug-seeking patients who claim they dropped their Dilaudid in the toilet and why can't I give them a few pills to tide them over? (Why do people only seem to drop narcotics in the toilet? How come blood pressure pills never end up in there?) My last patient of the evening was a little old lady who tripped on an acorn and might have broken her wrist. It took all my self-restraint not to hug her.

"And as I was lying on the ground," the old woman said to me, "the squirrel ran by my head, and I swear to you, Miss Victoria, he was laughing at me!"

It turned out to be a distal radius fracture and I turned her over to orthopedic surgery, then got to work on the last of my charting. I took my time, interrupted every few minutes by someone who wanted to give me one last hug or tell me how much they enjoyed working with me. It's funny—you don't realize how much people like you until you're leaving.

Mack wasn't working today. I checked right when I came in to see if anyone knew if he was on duty and they said no. So I figured that was that—I would never see Mack again. And that was for the best. I was married after all, and he'd made it pretty clear how he felt about me. It was easier not to have some awkward goodbye.

"I'm going to come to visit you," Carol promised me when she hugged me one last time. We were both getting teary-eyed—I'm going to miss her so much! "And you're going to come out here with the baby, right?"

I laughed. "I'm not pregnant yet."

"Not this month. But I bet Adam will knock you up before winter."

I finally pulled my hoodie sweatshirt on over my scrub top and headed out of the ER for the very last time. I felt a jab of sadness when I passed the hot dog cart where I got food poisoning twice. (Shame on me—I thought the first time was a fluke.) It was the end of an era. The end of my life as a single girl in the city, and the start of my life as a suburban housewife. Well, for now, at least. I'm still planning to check out the job market out there.

"Vicky! Hey, Vicky, wait!"

I froze, a bubble of happiness in my chest. I turned around, but I already knew who was calling me. "Mack!"

He was jogging down the block, his black hair even more disheveled than usual. He was smiling, but there was something sad in his smile. The way his face looked was a reflection of the way I was feeling right now. Smiling, but about to burst into tears any second.

"I'm so glad I caught you." He took a second to catch his breath. "Carol only texted me an hour ago that it was your last shift and you're moving tomorrow."

"Yeah…"

We just stared at each other. It had been a little awkward between us since Mack admitted his feelings for me right before the wedding, but all that awkwardness suddenly melted away. He ran a hand through his hair. "I'm really going to miss you, Vicky."

"Me too," I said, and I meant it with every fiber of my being.

He looked like he wanted to say something more, but instead, he leaned forward and hugged me. It was a Mack Bear Hug—I'd had them before, but this was the best one I'd ever had, and probably also the last. He was so big and warm and he smelled like Dial soap and fresh air. I realized I was clinging to him and we just stayed in that hug for… well, a while.

There's nothing wrong with that. I mean, Carol and I hugged a lot too today.

When we finally separated, Mack's eyes were a little moist. "If you need anything out there, just call me. Okay?"

"Um, you know it's three hours away, right? And you don't even have a car."

"I don't care."

And I stared up into his brown eyes, I got this sick feeling in my chest. Like I'd made a terrible mistake.

That night in the bar, when Mack told me how he felt? I should have ended it with Adam. I should never have married him. I should be with Mack. I made the wrong decision.

But the feeling passed. Yes, I chose Adam over Mack. There's nothing I can do to change that now. I mean, I'm not going to leave my husband.

So I said goodbye to Mack, and that was that.

CHAPTER 34

I have been working here for nearly two months and in all that time, I haven't once seen Victoria smile.

I've made an effort. I crack jokes in her presence. I try to smile as much as I can to set a good example. But it doesn't seem like it's ever going to happen. Especially today. While I'm helping her eat lunch, she looks like she's closer to bursting into tears than smiling as she dutifully opened her mouth for a bite of puréed beef.

"This Thursday is Thanksgiving," I say brightly. "We'll dress you up real pretty and have dinner together. You, me, and Adam. It will be delicious."

I can't imagine puréed turkey is going to be that delicious, but I'm not going to say that.

Victoria lifts her one good eye to look at me. She looks so sad. I used to think she had a dream life before her accident, but I don't think so anymore. If the things she's writing in her diary are true, it doesn't seem like she was very happy with Adam at all.

It seems like he was horrible to her.

But he isn't like that at all around me. It's hard to imagine that these two men are even the same person. It's like the Adam she describes in her diary is an entirely different man who happens to have the same name as the man I've been sharing a bed with.

I don't know what to think.

"Listen," I say to Victoria. I put the spoon down on her plate. "I was thinking... Maybe I could find Mack for you."

Her eyes widen.

"Would you like that, Victoria?"

She doesn't answer me. I had hoped for something— maybe not an outright smile, but at least some of the sadness disappearing. Maybe she doesn't think I can find him. And the truth is, I'm not entirely confident.

"What's his last name?" I ask.

Her mouth opens like she's about to speak. I lean in, hoping to catch any piece of information that might help me find this guy. "Mmmmmmmm."

I realize now what she's trying to do. She's trying to say his name, but she can't. She has so much trouble with M words, so I guess I shouldn't be surprised. But if that's the case, I doubt I'll get his last name out of her. Oh well. It was worth a try.

"I'm going to find him," I promise her.

It's the least I can do.

CHAPTER 35

Google is not helpful. Of course, all I've got to go on is that he's a paramedic named Mack who worked in Manhattan. Google mostly turns up a lot of links for EMT schools, and a few links for Mack trucks. The Internet is not going to get me what I want to know.

So I decide to call Mercy Hospital, where Victoria used to work. They'll probably know who he is.

As I'm dialing the number, I wonder exactly what I'm hoping to accomplish here. If I do find Mack, then what? Obviously, he loved her very much… but it's been a long time since he confessed his feelings to her. He might have another girlfriend by now. He's probably not still thinking about Victoria. And even if he is, would he still love her the way she is now?

But I get this feeling the man Victoria described in her diary would still love her like this. That's what I believe anyway.

When I get through to the emergency room, an

impatient sounding woman answers the phone. I can already tell this isn't going to be easy. "Hello? Mercy Emergency Services."

"Hi." I squeeze the phone in my right hand. "I... I was wondering if you could help me...I'm trying to find an EMT..."

"From what company?"

"I... I'm not sure," I stammer. "But his name is Mack."

"Last name?"

"I... I'm not sure."

"Do you have a complaint about this EMT?"

"No, no," I say quickly. I don't want to get the poor guy in trouble. "But it's imperative that I find him. It's... well, it's an emergency. I know he brings patients to your emergency room a lot, so I thought maybe you could help me get in touch with him..."

I hold my breath, bracing myself for the woman to hang up on me. But instead, she says, "And what did you say his first name is again?"

Oh my God, she's going to help me. It's a Thanksgiving miracle. "Mack."

I have about two seconds to celebrate before the woman says, "There are no EMTs who come here by that name."

"Are... are you sure?"

"Very sure. I've worked here for a year and I sign off when the patients come in from the ambulance."

I want to ask her one more time if she's sure, but it's obvious she is. Nobody named Mack works there, at least for the last year. He may work somewhere else now. Maybe after Victoria left, he decided to leave too.

I'm not sure what else to do. I suppose I could start calling all the ambulance companies to try to track him down, but given I don't even know his last name it seems like it might be difficult. It doesn't look like I'm going to be able to find Mack for Victoria.

Chapter 36

Victoria's Diary

September 28, 2017

Today was an odd day.

We've been living in the new house for two weeks. It still doesn't feel like mine—it's like I'm a guest here. I haven't had a chance to look for work, because unpacking has been such an ordeal, and the house itself is a lot of maintenance. We had to get the cable and internet hooked up, and Adam got a Microcell so we have decent cell phone service, although I was insistent on a landline. Considering we're in the middle of nowhere, it just makes me feel more secure.

I do have a car now. Adam surprised me with a Honda Civic. It's a reliable car, but considering what a fuss he made about ensuring his own car functioned well in the snow, I'm not sure why he bought me a tiny vehicle that only has front-wheel drive. Once the snow starts to fall, I'm going to be trapped here. But he reasoned I shouldn't be driving in heavy snow anyway. *You haven't driven in years, Victoria. You're out of practice.*

Anyway, it was a moot point. You can't return a car.

Because I won't be working in the foreseeable future, Adam set up a joint bank account for the two of us. I canceled my credit cards and got a joint one with him. I've been so independent since I was in college, it feels weird to be relying on another person for financial support, but Adam was so insistent than he wanted to "take care" of me. And truth be told, I've been working since I was in high school—it'll be nice to take a break for a little while.

Adam also hired a gardener, because the front lawn is an embarrassing disaster and I don't exactly have a green thumb. At first, I was happy he took on the responsibility of hiring someone, but I wasn't so happy when I saw who he hired. Our new gardener is a breathtakingly gorgeous young woman named Irina who is from some eastern European country. She has long, white-blond hair, and legs like a giraffe. She barely speaks English, but she still manages to find all of Adam's jokes far more hilarious than they actually are.

I also had to buy some extra furniture, because the pieces we had from our old apartment looked ridiculously sparse in this vast space. Adam had to approve everything I bought, which of course was reasonable, but he's very picky. I wanted to buy a sofa, and I had to show him—no joke—over a hundred photos of couches online before he agreed to one. Then the sofa arrived a few days ago, and the second he sat on it, he hated it and accused me of having bought "the wrong one." I supposed it was possible since there were so many. Anyway, this morning I was waiting around for the company to take back this sofa and bring a different one. That's when Peter showed up.

Peter is Adam's agent. He's in his fifties and is a nice enough guy, meaning he doesn't try to hit on me. He showed up in a suit and tie, looking mildly annoyed at having to drive all the way out here from wherever he lives, and even more annoyed when I said Adam had stepped out.

"Do you want to wait here?" I asked him.

He snorted. "I guess so. Where else would I go?"

I went to the kitchen to throw together a plate of food for our guest. I had gone to the supermarket last week and found it bafflingly huge compared with the smaller shopping centers I used to go to in the city. Most of the time I'd just go to the convenience store down the block for ninety percent of my groceries. But there was nothing convenient about where we were living.

I made a plate of crackers with mascarpone cheese and raspberry jam, but when I set them down on the coffee table, Peter didn't even glance up from his phone.

"Hey," I said to him.

He still didn't look up. "Yes?"

"Can I ask you something about Adam's parents?"

Ever since we moved out here and started trying more aggressively for a baby (I've even bought an ovulation kit), I've been thinking more and more about my in-laws. I know Adam is mad at his parents, but it's time to bury the hatchet. Maybe if I could reach out to them, they would feel the same way. I mean, who isn't tempted by the idea of grandchildren?

Peter raised his eyes from his phone. "What about them?"

"Do you know where they live?"

His brows bunched together. "Do I... what?"

"Or a phone number," I said quickly. "Any information at all..."

"Victoria..."

"I know Adam is angry at them, but if I could just talk to them—"

"Victoria." Peter's voice was more firm this time. "Adam's parents are dead."

My next argument froze on the tip of my tongue. Adam's parents were... *what*? "Dead?"

He arched an eyebrow. "You don't know that?"

"No, I..." My head was spinning. "Are... are you sure?"

He laughed darkly. "I was at their funeral. So yes, I'm pretty sure."

Their funeral? It was a joint funeral? Did that mean they died together?

Against my will, my mind went to Adam's first novel,

All in the Family. The protagonist with the grudge against his horrible family. Plotting out their "accidental" deaths. Getting away with it scot-free.

"How did they die?" I murmured.

"Car accident. Just one of those things."

Well, at least they didn't die from carbon monoxide poisoning like the family in Adam's book. I chewed on my lip. "What about his brother?"

Peter leaned back against the couch and sighed heavily. "Adam really never told you any of this?"

"Peter, please…"

He sighed again. "He killed himself a few months after they died. Buried a gun in his throat."

All of a sudden, I felt like I was going to throw up. And then a second later, I was running to the kitchen sink and actually throwing up. Of course, Adam chose that exact moment to stroll into the house, whistling a tune to himself as he walked through the door.

From the kitchen, I could hear Adam and Peter talking softly. I couldn't even imagine what Peter was saying. I crouched down on the kitchen floor, clutching my temples. I felt dizzy and nauseated. I wanted to get out of the house, but I didn't feel like I could drive right now and there wasn't anywhere I could walk to. That's the problem with living in the middle of nowhere.

After about five minutes, Adam wandered into the kitchen to find me on the floor. His eyes widened. "What are you doing down there?"

"I… I don't feel great."

A smile touched his lips. "Are you pregnant?"

Right. Because I was randomly throwing up in the middle of the day. It hadn't even occurred to me, but now that it did, I was surprised by how much the idea filled me with panic. My first thought was: *Oh please God, don't let me be pregnant. Please…*

I wiped my lips with the back of my hand and struggled to my feet. "I don't think so."

"Hey, how come the couch is still out there? Weren't you responsible for getting rid of that goddamn thing?"

I could see the fight brewing in him and I cringed. But before he could start laying into me, I cut him off: "Adam, are your parents dead?"

He opened his mouth, probably deciding whether or not to lie. Something I'm starting to realize about my husband is that he's quite a good liar. I've caught him in lies here and there, and it bothers me that I can't tell when he's lying. The only way I ever know is when it's so blatant that it's obvious—and even then, he rarely 'fesses up.

"Yes," he finally said. "They are."

"Oh my God!" My voice was loud enough that Peter could probably hear, but I didn't care. "Why didn't you tell me?"

He at least had the good grace to look embarrassed. "I'm sorry, Vicky. I should have told you."

"Darn right, you should have."

He raked a hand through his hair and leaned against

the kitchen counter. "I just... I had that falling out with them like I told you. And before I had a chance to make things right, they got in that accident. It was devastating. I... I couldn't deal with it, so I pretended like they were still around." He lowered his eyes. "I was going to tell you the truth, but I was embarrassed about having lied. I didn't think you'd ever know the difference."

And that seems to be the essence of our marriage sometimes. He lies to me because he thinks I won't ever know the difference.

"Adam," I said quietly, "if this is going to work between the two of us, you have to be honest with me from now on. I mean it. We're *married.*"

He nodded slowly. "Right. Of course." He took a step towards me. "I'm so sorry, Vicky. I should never have lied to you. I won't do it again."

I let him put his arms around me and gradually relaxed into his embrace. I was still angry he lied to me, but I gave him a pass. After all, it must have been incredibly traumatic having his parents die on him before he could make things right. My parents are gone, but at least they knew how much I loved them.

When Adam pulled away, he brushed a strand of hair from my face. I've been wearing my hair down all the time now because that's how he likes it. If I ever put it up, he complains.

"Hey, Vicky," he said. "One other thing."

I nodded. "Yes?"

"Don't you dare ever talk about me to Peter behind my back again." His jaw twitched. "Okay?"

"Uh…" I searched his face, hoping for any trace of humor. "Okay. Sorry."

He mumbled something under his breath as he grabbed a bottle of wine from one of the shelves in the kitchen, then went back to the living room. I stayed in the kitchen, waiting for the deliverymen to arrive and pick up the sofa.

I took a pregnancy test later in the afternoon. It was negative.

I cried with relief.

November 18, 2017

This morning I got it into my head that I should join a gym.

When I was younger, I never had the money to join a gym—I could barely afford sneakers to run around the park by my house. And then when I was working and I had more money, I didn't have the time. Well, now all I've got is time and money. It's been two months and I still haven't been able to find work out here (although to be fair, I haven't been looking that hard). Adam also hired a maid who comes twice a week so I don't have to do much cleaning. And now that it's gotten cold, Irina has started doing cooking instead of gardening. Apparently, she's multitalented.

So this is my day:

I get up around nine or ten. I take a shower for at least forty minutes. I make myself an extravagant breakfast, then plop myself down in front of the television with a bag of chips or something equally nutritious. And… that's about it till lunch. I'm getting dangerously addicted to some of the game shows. Like *Family Feud*. (That is such a great show. I think I would do really well at fast money.)

Then when I've finished lunch, I go outside. Shop a little. Okay, shop *a lot*. I'm quickly filling our house with junk. My wardrobe is a little bit out of control. So many shoes…

I'm afraid to even get on a scale lately. But this morning I had trouble buttoning my jeans. And I'm not talking about my skinny jeans. I'm talking about my comfortable jeans that I wear on days that I'm not leaving the house and I don't care who sees me. I couldn't button *those* jeans.

So I had two choices. I could either go out and buy all new clothing in a size larger (or—let's face it—two sizes larger). Or I could join a gym and hopefully fit back into my clothing

I located a gym about five miles away from the house, so I took a trip there right after lunch. Okay, I stopped at McDonald's for lunch first. I figured I'd have one last Big Mac and fries for the road before I got back to being healthy again.

The gym looked perfect. It was small but seemed to have a good amount of workout equipment. It was bright and new looking, and the people working out didn't seem like they had perfect bodies—there's nothing worse than running next to somebody who looks like a fitness model. I felt like I fit in pretty well here. So I approached the cheery blonde named Taylor working at the front counter and told her I wanted a membership.

Over the next fifteen minutes, I allowed myself to not only agree to a one-year membership, but also signed up for weekly Zumba classes, swimming, and kickboxing. I also signed up for something called slow flow vinyasa, whatever that is. If they had asked for my firstborn, I probably would've handed that over as well.

"Now we'll just need a credit card to put on file for you," Taylor said cheerfully.

I reached into my purse to pull out my wallet. I looked in the slot where I usually keep my credit card, but it was gone. Panic squeezed my chest. "Oh my goodness," I said. "Where is my credit card?"

A tiny crease formed between Taylor's light brows. "It's been stolen?"

"I think so." I looked inside my wallet and saw the cash was all still there. "Shoot, I'll have to call the credit card company." I looked up at her. "Can I sign up without the credit card?"

She frowned. "I'm afraid not. We're required to have a card on file. But I can save your paperwork and you can come back when you get a new one."

I was annoyed about the hassle, but I was even more anxious about telling Adam about the missing card. And I had to tell him. This was our joint credit card, so if I needed to get a new one, he would have to get a new one also. He was going to be absolutely furious when I told him it was gone. I cringed in anticipation of that conversation.

Maybe I could find it. Then I'd never have to tell him it was missing.

I racked my brain trying to think of how it could have disappeared. It didn't seem likely somebody would have pickpocketed me, took out my credit card, but left the rest of my wallet with all my cash. The last time I used the card was two days ago, at the mall. Was it possible that I left it at a department store?

I spent the next two hours retracing my steps for the last several days, trying to think where I might've left it. Then I started desperately calling every store I've ever shopped at to see if I left my credit card there. No luck.

So I drove around for a while, not eager to get back home. I was going to have to cancel my credit card and find out if there were any unauthorized purchases on the card. I had no choice. Adam was going to be furious.

When I finally got back home, Adam was downstairs in the kitchen. He was with Irina, helping unpack some groceries she had bought. They must not have heard me come in, and I spent a second of watching my husband with our gorgeous east European cook/gardener. Adam was standing far too close to her, and when he said something, she grabbed his arm and laughed.

Then he leaned in and whispered something in her ear, and she laughed harder.

That was when I cleared my throat.

"Miss Victoria!" Irina exclaimed. The woman had the gall to look pleased to see me. "You are home! Please, do you want to see new groceries? I plan dinner for tonight."

I shook my head. "No, thank you." I took a deep breath. "Adam, could I talk to you for a minute?"

I was dreading telling him about the credit card, but I didn't have much of a choice. If somebody stole my card, I had to report it and cancel it ASAP. He would be angrier if I waited. So really, there was no way to win at this point.

We went upstairs to the bedroom, and I tearfully explained everything that happened. At first, I was trying to make myself cry because I thought he might be more sympathetic, but then I realized the tears were real. I told him the story of my desperate attempts to locate the card. I swore I would take care of calling the credit card company and getting a new card and doing whatever I had to do to fix this.

I watched his face, already bracing myself for a temper tantrum. But to my surprise, he didn't seem upset at all.

"Your credit card wasn't stolen," he said. "I took it from your wallet."

My mouth fell open. He took it? Why would he do

that? "You did?"

He nodded. "I don't think you realize how much money you've been spending the last couple of months, Victoria. I am now the sole breadwinner, and frankly, it's offensive that you take such liberty with my money. I discussed this with a few people, and I think the best thing would be to give you a cash allowance so you don't overspend."

I couldn't believe what I was hearing. A cash *allowance*? Did he think I was a child? "I can't function without a credit card, Adam. How am I supposed to buy things online?"

"You can buy things online," he said. "Just send me the link, and if I think the purchase is appropriate, I'll buy it for you. Maybe I could set up a way to approve your purchases."

I could almost feel my blood pressure going up. True, Adam had a lot more money than I did going into our marriage. But I had *some* money. I never had to ask permission before buying a stupid lamp. Now I regretted having put my money in a joint bank account. I had wanted to keep a separate account, but he insisted it wouldn't be fair otherwise. After all, why should I get access to his money if he couldn't have mine?

"It will be a very generous allowance," he said. "Two hundred dollars a week. And that's not including online purchases, of course."

"I can't live on two hundred dollars a week!"

He frowned. "Why not? Irina buys all the groceries. I pay the mortgage and the cleaning bills. What expenses do you have that will cost more than two hundred dollars a week? Gas? Clothes? *McDonald's*?"

My face burned. Cheap shot. "You pay Irina more than two hundred dollars a week."

He narrowed his eyes. "Right. But she's actually *working*. You just sit around on your ass and do nothing except spend my money."

My cheeks burned. It was his idea for me to stay home, and now he was throwing it back in my face. But if I pointed it out to him, he wouldn't get it.

"What if I have a larger expense one week?"

He shrugged. "Then you should save up your money. Or if you were irresponsible and haven't been saving, you can ask me for a loan. I think this will help you learn about money management."

I took a deep breath. I hated the situation, but on the other hand, maybe it wasn't entirely unreasonable. I *have* been buying a lot of things lately, partially out of boredom. "How about two-hundred-fifty dollars a week?"

He smiled tolerantly. "How about this? When you get pregnant, we'll go to two-hundred-fifty dollars a week."

Right. We're still trying to get pregnant. So far, no luck. I'm using the ovulation test every month, and we always have sex right when we're supposed to and I stay in bed for an hour after with my knees up. I'm taking prenatal vitamins and I've given up alcohol and caffeine.

Unfortunately, I got my period a few days ago, so my tight jeans are not from a baby bump—just fat.

I haven't admitted to Adam that every time the pregnancy test is negative, I feel that flash of relief. I don't entirely understand it, because I do want a baby. I really do.

"Fine," I said. I didn't want to argue. Arguments with Adam were never quick. If we started fighting, it would go on for days. "Anyway, I went to try to join a gym today. Can I use the credit card for that?"

"A gym?" His face darkened, and I got a sinking feeling that I wasn't going to avoid an argument after all. "What do you want to join a gym for?"

I couldn't for the life of me figure out what he was so angry over. What was wrong with joining a gym?

"I want to try to get back in shape," I said. "I've gained a little weight."

His eyes flicked down to my abdomen. "Yes, I've noticed."

Great. I couldn't help but visualize Irina's perfect, svelte figure.

"But why do you need to join a gym?" he said. "The only reason people join a gym is to flirt with other single people. Is that what you want? Are you joining a gym to meet men?"

"No!"

"Don't lie to me, Victoria," he spit. "Why do you think I had to hire all women to work here? You flirt with any man who comes within a mile radius of you."

"Gee, I thought you hired Irina so *you* could have somebody to flirt with?"

I shouldn't have said that. By now, I am very aware of what sets Adam off. And I knew that would be the beginning of a huge fight. But I couldn't help myself. I mean, how dare he hire such a beautiful woman to work in our home then accuse *me* of flirting?

"I'm not flirting with Irina," he said. "I don't know how you could think that. You're, like, insanely jealous of any woman who's prettier than you."

"I'm not…" I started to say I wasn't jealous of Irina, but that wouldn't be true. I *was* jealous of her. Of course I was. Who wouldn't be? "Listen, I just don't know why you had to hire somebody who looks like her."

"I don't even notice her appearance. You're the one who's obsessed with it."

"Obsessed?" I noticed the volume of my voice was getting very loud, and Irina could likely hear from downstairs. "I'm not obsessed! But I could see you whispering sweet nothings in her ear in the kitchen."

"Sweet nothings?" His eyebrows shot up. "We were just talking about dinner plans. Jesus, you're really out of your mind, you know that?" He shook his head. "This is why I can't trust you at the gym. I'm glad I took charge of the credit card. Go get some running shoes and go jogging."

His voice had adopted that cold tone that guaranteed

he wouldn't be speaking to me for the next few days. At this point, I wasn't even sure if I cared.

Okay, fine. I care. You don't know what it's like to share a house with somebody who is actively not speaking to you. He can be so hostile.

I bit my lip. "Can I have my two-hundred dollars for the week?"

"Yeah, right." He snorted. "I'll give it to you Sunday. Every Sunday, you'll get your money. So just be patient for once."

So right now, I've got fifty-three bucks in my wallet that I've got to make last until Sunday. (I'm not sure if he's going to give me the money on Sunday morning or Sunday evening.) I don't know what to do at this point. I'm not sure if I should try to look for a job, knowing by the time I get settled, I might get pregnant and need to leave soon. I'm going crazy with boredom, but once I have a baby, that will occupy a lot more of my time.

I guess I'll go get those running shoes. Well, I'll get them on Sunday when I've got some money.

December 2, 2017

I just had a huge fight with Adam.

He had some meeting with his publisher today, and our cleaning woman, Maggie, doesn't come on Tuesdays. So he asked me if I could iron one of his shirts.

It seemed like an easy enough thing to do. I took the iron from the closet with the ironing board and ironed his shirt as best as I could. I'm not exactly a professional at doing the laundry, but I thought I did an adequate job. But then when he came out of the shower and I showed him the freshly ironed shirt, he freaked out. Apparently, I ironed it wrong. He kept showing me something about the crease and how I had ruined the shirt forever. He ended up throwing the shirt in the trash, which didn't even make sense to me. Maggie could have ironed it later and fixed whatever I did wrong.

"Are you bad at everything?" he asked. "Because I really can't figure out what you're capable of doing correctly, aside from sitting on the couch, watching television, and eating. And spending my money, of course."

"Well, maybe I should go back to work then." I said it like a threat, as if I hadn't already sent out a bunch of copies of my resume everywhere within driving distance. I was beginning to think I was going to have to widen the radius of my search. I didn't want to have to drive an hour and a half to work, but maybe it would be worth it. It would be better than staying here. And I could have money again.

"You sucked at that too." He held up his left hand. "Look at the scar I've got on my hand because of you."

"You have a scar on your hand because you sliced yourself with a knife."

"They probably would have fired you if you hadn't quit," he went on like I hadn't said anything. "You're really lucky you have me to take care of you." He sneered at me. "That's all you were looking for, wasn't it? A man to take care of you so you'd never have to lift a finger again."

"That's not true."

"Of course it's true!" he snapped. "Our whole marriage is just a scam of yours."

And with those words, he picked up the photograph of us on our nightstand—the one taken just minutes after we got married. He hurled it to the floor and the glass inside the frame shattered into a million pieces. I backed away because I was in my socks and I didn't want to get glass in my feet.

"Clean that up." He gave me a dirty look. "I need to figure out what the fuck I'm going to wear."

I wanted to throw something at him. The iron was still on the ironing board, and even though I had turned it off, the metal was still very hot. For a moment, I was seized with the urge to pick up that iron and go right for his face. That would teach him a lesson.

But instead of attacking him with the iron, I went downstairs to get a broom and Dustbuster to clean up the broken glass.

Adam was gone by the time I got all the glass cleaned up. He didn't even say goodbye when he left—I only knew he was gone because the front door slammed behind him. As soon as I heard that sound, I collapsed onto our bed. I buried my face in my hands, and the tears started to come. I still love Adam, but sometimes I think I hate him. Sometimes I feel like I could murder him with my bare hands.

I had been sobbing for about five minutes when my phone buzzed in the pocket of my sweatpants. I took it out and saw a message from Mack.

How is it going?

It was such a simple, innocent message, but it only made me cry harder. Mack was thinking about me. He was worried about me.

I picked up the phone, unsure what to write back. I could tell him everything. But what good would that do? It wouldn't change anything. With my luck, Adam would probably find out about our whole conversation.

I'm OK, I finally wrote.

He wrote back almost immediately. *Just OK?*

I couldn't bear to say anymore, so I just wrote: *How are you doing?*

OK. Then: *I miss you.*

I sucked in a breath. *You know I'm married, right?*

I miss you platonically.

I smiled at the screen, despite everything. Mack and I texted back-and-forth for the next half an hour, and my tears eventually dried up. It was nice talking to a friend. I still haven't made any friends around here. Anytime I talk to Adam about joining something, he doesn't want me to do it. There was a book club at the library, and he was furious when I asked him about it. He wanted a list of everyone who would be attending. When I said I couldn't get him a list like that, he told me I couldn't go. He still brings up that book club as an example of my insane behavior, like I asked him to go to a sex party.

The book club is meeting this week and I've already read the book. Maybe I'll go. Adam is already furious with me, so it can't make things worse. I just feel so isolated out here.

No, I better not.

Chapter 37

I took Victoria's Honda Civic to the minimart a mile away because it's the only place that's open on Thanksgiving and Adam realized we didn't have enough butter. (That declaration scared me, considering I bought an entire four-pack of butter last week.) He picked up the turkey and other groceries yesterday, so our refrigerator is stocked. He got up early this morning and has been seasoning the turkey and hovering over it like it's a newborn baby

He looked so cute this morning while he was rubbing oil and butter and sage and rosemary all over the turkey while singing to himself. I watched him for a moment, feeling a rush of affection until I remembered what I had read in Victoria's diary. This is all an act—the real Adam is an angry, violent, and jealous man.

And then I ran out of the house without even saying goodbye.

When I return with the butter, he's just getting the turkey in the oven. He straightens up and gives me a hug and kiss, which I accept rather stiffly. But he's so excited about the turkey that he doesn't seem to even notice.

"Turkey is good to go," he says.

"Great." I look up at his smiling face. "Hey, it's… um, it's too bad your parents can't be here."

I watch his expression carefully. "Yeah, well," he says. "They like to go to my uncle's house. He's one of those outgoing people who loves to entertain and he makes this huge spread. That way my mom doesn't have to cook."

Is he lying? I want to shake him and ask if his parents are dead. But would he really make up a whole story about their Thanksgiving plans? Because if he did, he has serious problems.

And what about that phone call the night of the big storm? If he wasn't talking to his mother, who was he talking to?

I tried to find Adam's book, *All in the Family*. I'm curious if it's as bad as what Victoria described. But I couldn't find any copies in the house. I even looked at the supermarket but didn't find any there either. I thought about reading it on my phone but finally decided against it.

I have to end this relationship. Or whatever this thing between us is. I can't do this anymore to Victoria. And I can't do it to myself. I don't know who this man is. The only positive thing I can say is that it doesn't sound like he was physically abusive to Victoria.

But if I end it with him, will he fire me? I couldn't entirely blame him. And then what will Victoria do without me? I'm sure she would rather have me around than him taking care of her all the time.

Adam wraps his arms around me and pulls me close to him. He whispers into my hair, "You know what I'm thankful for this year?"

I shake my head.

"I'm thankful for you." He squeezes me tighter. "I don't know if I ever really told you how unhappy I was before you showed up here. My life was empty. I mean, I had my writing, but I couldn't even focus on that."

"You mean since Victoria's accident?"

He lets out a long sigh and pulls away from me. "There's something I should tell you."

If he tells me his parents are dead, I'm quitting.

"Victoria and I weren't happy together." He rubs his hands over his face. "I mean, we were at first. When we were first dating. But after we got engaged, she became a different person. And then after we got married, it got much worse. But... I didn't see a way out..."

He looks off into the distance. I don't know what he's talking about. Victoria described in detail how horrible he was to her. Was he not aware of that at all? Maybe that's why she seemed different to him.

"Well," I say, "given how difficult things were, it's good of you to take care of her like you are."

He lets out a breath. "Yeah, that's the thing..." He toys with the turkey baster on the counter. "I've been doing a lot of thinking. I wanted to be there for Victoria, but it's just too hard. I think… after the Christmas holidays, I'm going to start calling some nursing homes in the area. It's for the best."

He must see the ashen look on my face, because he quickly adds, "You can keep staying here, obviously. I'm not kicking you out. You can keep working here if you want or find another job. But your room is yours as long as you want it. Or… my room."

"I… I don't know," I murmur. I feel very ill, like I might throw up.

He reaches out to touch my arm, but I yank it away. I don't want to be near him right now. "I'm going to give Victoria her breakfast," I mumble.

His brow furrows. "Trust me, Sylvia. This will be for the best. For everyone concerned."

But I don't trust him. Not even a little bit.

CHAPTER 38

Victoria's Diary

December 12, 2017

I was almost jumping up and down with excitement all day today because Carol and her boyfriend Jeff were coming out to visit tonight. She said she wanted to come out before the holidays.

Getting people from the city to come here is no easy task, but Jeff drives for Uber anyway, so it's not that big a deal to him. I mean, it's definitely far, but he's used to spending long periods driving. Meanwhile, I haven't made it into the city once in the three months we've been living out here. I suggested it once to Adam, and he got so upset that I never mentioned it again.

I bought a new dress especially for tonight. Well, I bought it partially because most of my old dresses are too tight now. I finally got on the scale last week and discovered I had gained fifteen pounds since we moved out here. I wish I could join a gym, especially now that it's too cold to go out running. But since that's not a possibility, I'm planning to ask Adam for some sort of exercise machine. Maybe an elliptical. It's way too expensive to buy on my allowance.

Anyway, I saved up my money for the last two weeks so that I could buy this slinky black Michael Kors dress with a slit up the right thigh. When Adam saw me in it, his face lit up and I decided the money was worth it. It seems like it's impossible to make my husband happy these days, so if a dress is enough to do the trick, it's worth every penny. I also wore the snowflake necklace Adam bought me when we were first dating.

Except as I hung it around my neck, I got a sudden jab of sadness—my life had become so different since the night Adam gave me that necklace. Some of it is good, obviously. We're married now. Living together. We're trying for a baby. But somehow, when I look back on my life before I got that necklace, I want to burst into tears.

"You look amazing," he told me as he kissed my neck. "I'm so lucky."

Adam has been in a spectacular mood this week. Things are moving forward really well with his new book. The proofs will be out very soon and he can't wait for me to see. He's been really sweet and generous, and incredibly affectionate. And not only was he immediately agreeable to Carol coming over, but he even offered to cook an elaborate Italian dinner. In spite of the knife injury that brought him to the ER, he used to sometimes cook for me back when we lived in the city—he wasn't too bad at it. But the truth was, I was just happy to have Irina out of the house for the evening. I couldn't bear the thought of Adam flirting with Irina all night, in front of my friends.

Carol and Jeff arrived looking tired from the drive, with both their cheeks pink from the cold. Carol was hugging an apple streusel to her chest, which was from my favorite bakery in the city. The sight of her familiar face made me nearly burst into tears yet again. I threw my arms around Carol and hugged her for way too long.

"I miss you guys so much," I told her.

She pulled away from me and looked me over head to toe. Her face brightened. "So when are you due?"

My face felt like it was on fire. "I'm not pregnant."

Carol looked like she wanted to crawl under a piece of furniture. "Oh my God, I'm so sorry, Vicky! Please don't take it personally. You told me you were trying and I just assumed…"

"Nobody could blame you," Adam spoke up. "All she does is sit around and eat, so this is the result."

"You look great, Vicky," Carol said quickly. "I just… I thought you told me you were pregnant somehow. That's all."

Nice save. Except we all knew the truth. I don't look great. I look like a mess.

Adam and Jeff went to watch some game on television

while I gave Carol the grand tour. We started with the first floor and worked our way upstairs. She oohed and ahhed over the entire house—she must have told me a hundred times how jealous she was. Although I don't think she was *that* jealous. No Manhattanite wants to live at the very tip of Long Island.

The tour finally concluded in the master bedroom. Carol shook her head as she scanned the vast suite. "This is like a dream house," she said. "I can understand why you wanted to live here."

Of course, I didn't want to live here. Adam bought the place without telling me. And I had to give up my entire life in the city to be here. There hasn't been a day gone by when I didn't wish I had made another choice.

"You're so lucky," she sighed. "This incredible house. Married to Mr. Perfect. And I bet you really are pregnant! You just have that glow about you."

"Yeah. Um, so how is everyone back at the hospital?" I was sick of talking about myself and how great she thought my life was. "Any gossip?"

That got Carol going. She told me all about how one of the nurses got caught making out in the supply room with a married doctor. And one of the nurses is pregnant. She was going on and on, but as she was talking, I realized there was only one person I was really curious about. And I was getting frustrated that she never mentioned him.

"How is Mack doing?" I finally asked when there was a break in the conversation. I tried to sound like I couldn't care less.

She shrugged. "Fine. Same."

"Oh. That's good."

She paused thoughtfully. "He asks me about you."

My heart leaped in my chest. "He does?"

"Yeah. Like, once a week. He tries to be all casual about it." She narrowed her eyes at me. "Hey. Did anything ever happen between the two of you?"

"No!" I didn't want there to be any whiff of something going on between me and Mack. For all I knew, Adam was listening at the door. "We were just really good friends. That's it. I haven't heard from him in ages. I was just curious, that's all."

She grinned at me. "He's pretty cute though, right?"

"If you like that type…" I looked down at my watch. "Let's go check on the food."

Back down on the first floor, Adam and Jeff were having beers and completely immersed in a football game. They were joking around and Adam was being his usual charming self that made everyone love him and waitresses give him their phone number. Mr. Perfect—that's my husband.

Carol sat down on the couch while I went to check on the food in the kitchen. It looked like Adam had sort of forgotten about it when he got immersed in the game. The tomato sauce he had been cooking appeared over-reduced—nearly burned—and he hadn't even started on the pasta yet. I knew I should go out to the living room and tell him his sauce was about to be ruined, but I also knew if I said that, he'd get angry at me. I did *not* want to fight in front of Carol and Jeff.

Finally, I decided the best thing to do would be to at least get the pasta started. That way I would be helping— plus we didn't want to eat too late since Carol and Jeff had a long drive ahead of them back to the city. I got the water boiling and tossed in the spaghetti. Just as I had set the timer, Adam wandered into the kitchen.

"What are you doing?" he asked.

"I got your pasta going for you."

Any trace of a smile dropped off his face. "And who gave you permission to do that?"

"It's not a big deal. It's just pasta."

"Right. But *I'm* cooking the meal." He raised his eyebrows at me. "When we're at a restaurant, do you go into the kitchen and start messing with the stove?"

I wrung my hands together. It was clear that my attempts to avoid a fight had not been successful. "No…"

"First you make me entertain your annoying friends… then you embarrass me with your appearance…" He ticked off my offenses on his fingers. "Then you try to ruin the dinner I've spent all evening cooking…" He shook his head. "I don't even know why I put up with you. You're lucky I'm a nice guy."

"Look." I bit my lip. "All I did was boil some pasta. I thought it would help you."

"I see. So you didn't think I could handle the meal

without your help?" He snorted. "Well, if that's how you feel, how about this? Why don't you just finish cooking the entire meal all by your fucking self?"

And then he took one of the ceramic plates on the drying rack and hurled it at the wall, where it shattered into a million pieces.

He spun around and left the kitchen, knocking over the box of spaghetti in the process. The box was still half full, so spaghetti spilled all over the floor in a spectacular mess. Adam either didn't notice or didn't care. In any case, he didn't stop. I bent down to pick up the pasta, wincing when the house shook as the front door slammed.

Carol came running in, and I made up an excuse about how I had dropped a plate and broke it—clumsy me. I only hoped she didn't notice the dent in the plaster on the wall. As for Adam, I told her he had to run out to get some last-minute ingredients. She seemed like she bought it and helped me clean up the mess on the kitchen floor.

Of course, an hour later, Adam still hadn't returned. I pretended he called me and told me his car broke down. We managed to salvage some of the dinner, at least, and we had that apple streusel for dessert. I was so upset that I ended up eating like three pieces of it. Carol kept telling me it was no big deal, but I still feel humiliated over the whole thing. I can't believe he ran out on me for something so ridiculous and small. The worst part is that it doesn't even surprise me.

And now it's midnight. He's still not back.

My husband has a temper. I have to accept that. I knew that starting the spaghetti was going to upset him. I shouldn't have done it. I knew that! What is wrong with me??? By now, I have a good sense of what sets him off, so I just need to be very careful not to do those things.

Where *is* he? It's midnight, for goodness sake!

I'm going to go downstairs and have some more of that apple streusel.

CHAPTER 39

Victoria is dressed in a billowy flower-printed dress that I found in her closet. Something tight is out of the question because of her feeding tube and it would not have been flattering with the way she often slumps in the chair. I have a feeling the dress used to be more snug on her, but now it hangs loose on her bony frame.

I also spent some time on her hair. I combed it out and put in the oil treatment again, and it looks lush and shiny. I thought about trying to tie it back, but I think it's most flattering when it's loose.

Now I'm working on her makeup. I put a layer of pink lipstick on her crooked lips, and now I'm doing my best to cover the scar on her left cheek. I don't think there's anything I could do to conceal it entirely, but it looks a lot better than when I started.

Victoria is allowing me to put on the makeup, but she looks utterly unenthusiastic. I can't entirely blame her. As much as I chatter about how much fun this will be, I'm not looking forward to it either.

Part of me wants to duck out and leave Victoria and Adam to have Thanksgiving alone as a married couple. But the more I read of her diary, I feel like that is not what Victoria wants. She doesn't want to be alone with him. And I don't want her to be alone with him either.

"There." I dab on the last of the concealer—I've used half the container and the scar is still very visible. "All done."

Victoria just stares at me.

"You look beautiful." I grab the mirror I found in the bathroom and hold it up to her face. "Take a look."

Victoria glances briefly at the mirror, then turns away. She never seems very happy when I show her a mirror. She either looks away or frowns at herself. Sometimes she touches the scar. I wish Adam had shelled out for her to get plastic surgery. I know he thinks she doesn't notice, but he's wrong.

"I just…" I chew on my lip. "I want you to know that I'm not going to… I mean, Adam is your husband, not mine. I'm going to tell him tonight that I'm not going to…"

For the first time since I came in here, Victoria's eyes show a spark of interest.

"It's not right," I say. "It was a mistake and I'm sorry. I'll tell him tonight."

"Be…" She's focusing so hard on what she wants to say that some drool comes out of the right side of her mouth, smearing her lipstick. "Be... care..."

For once, I know exactly what she's trying to say. *Be careful.*

I leave Victoria to find some nail polish in the bathroom. That's the last thing I need to complete her look for the evening. I want Victoria to look really beautiful tonight. Like her old self, as much as possible. It's important to me.

Maggie must have moved the nail polish when she was cleaning. I look in the usual place in the closet within the bathroom, but it's not there anymore. I search through the other shelves, trying to find the bag of multicolor nail polish tubes. I find more makeup, but not polish. But one thing I do find surprises me.

It's a black bag of medications.

I never was sure where Adam kept Victoria's medications. He always just seems to have them ready to administer. I pick up a bottle from the black plastic bag and see the date of the most recent refill. It was less than a month ago. These aren't old medications. These are the ones he's giving her right now.

I read the name of the medication off the bottle: Quetiapine.

Adam said that Victoria was only on medications to keep her from having seizures. On a whim, I take out my phone from my jeans pocket and type the name of the medication into the search box. The Wikipedia page for "quetiapine" pops up and I click on it.

Quetiapine is not a medication to prevent seizures. According to the Wikipedia page, it's an antipsychotic used to treat schizophrenia and bipolar disorder. It's also used for sleep due to its highly sedating effect.

Well, that explains why Victoria is so tired after she gets her medications.

There are more bottles inside. I recognize the name of the medication on the next bottle. Valium. It's what my mother used to sometimes take when she was feeling anxious. After she took it, she would often be very groggy and go straight to bed.

Why is Adam giving Victoria a bunch of medications that knock her out?

I hear footsteps outside and quickly shove the black bag back into the bathroom closet. A second after I get them in there, Adam appears at the bathroom door. He's wearing a green button-down shirt that brings out the color of his eyes and makes him look achingly handsome. "Is Victoria almost ready? The turkey is just about to come out of the oven."

I straighten up and nod. "I was going to paint her nails, but maybe I'll hold off. I don't want her fingers to smell like nail polish during the meal."

"That's fine." He adjusts his shirt collar. "But don't forget to clip her nails. I don't want to get scratched when I'm doing her medications."

I pick up the nail clipper from the shelf near the sink and hold it up. "Yep. No problem."

"Amazing. You're the best, Sylvia."

As soon as he leaves the room, I slide the nail clipper back onto the shelf.

Chapter 40

Our Thanksgiving banquet is almost ready.

I've changed into something a little fancier than my jeans and sweatshirt, but not much—I didn't bring any fancy clothes with me and I'm not about to go foraging in Victoria's closet, even though Adam assured me it would be fine. Also, I don't want to show up Victoria. This is her home, and she deserves to be the best-dressed person here.

The only thing left to do is to bring Victoria downstairs for the feast. Except when I get upstairs, it seems like that part is not going to be so easy.

Adam is attempting to lift Victoria the way he does when he brings her downstairs for me to take her for a walk. But she is resisting him as violently as she can. She's shoving him away and yelling, "No! NO!"

I'm impressed by how effectively she is resisting him with only one working arm that doesn't even seem to work very well. She even gets her left leg into the mix. She finally lands one good kick at his shin, and he takes a step back, swearing under his breath. His face is bright pink.

"For Christ's sake, Vicky!" He rubs his shin. "We've got a whole meal downstairs. Don't you want to enjoy it with us?"

"No." She shoots me what seems like a meaningful look. "No. *No.*"

Adam glances over at me. "She really kicked me hard. I don't know what to do."

"No, " Victoria says again. "No. I... *No.*"

"I think it's pretty clear she doesn't want to come downstairs," I say.

He grits his teeth. "She doesn't know what she wants."

"I think she does."

He narrows his eyes at Victoria. "Fine. If you don't want to come, just stay up here. But we're not bringing you food. You're going straight to bed."

I hate the way he's talking to her like she's a child. I want to volunteer to bring Victoria some food later tonight and help her eat, but Adam seems determined to make his point. So he sends me downstairs while he gets Victoria into bed, gives her some tube feeds, and administers her medications. Usually, it takes him an hour to get through her bedtime routine, but he's downstairs in half an hour. It makes me wonder what he skipped out on.

In the meantime, I've brought all the food out to the dining table and set our places. As his eyes rake over the table, I feel a twinge of anxiety. I remember how he exploded when Victoria started the spaghetti that night.

Will he blow up at me for bringing the food out? He's already in a bad mood over Victoria refusing to come downstairs. So I brace myself.

"Hey," he says. "You brought all the food out."

I take a step back. "Yes…"

A smile touches his lips. "That's great. Now we can eat right away."

I let out of breath—there was no explosion. Of course, Adam has never yelled at me for anything. If I didn't read Victoria's diary, I would think he's the most mild-mannered guy I've ever met. You never know what's lurking under the surface, I guess. And I'm scared about what he's going to say when I tell him that he and I can't be together anymore.

But I must tell him. It can't go on like this any longer.

I wait until we're both stuffed with turkey, stuffing, mashed potatoes, and green beans. And wine. Lots of wine. The dinner was nice. Adam seemed a little bit miffed about the Victoria situation in the beginning, but then he settled down and we had a nice conversation. It was a lovely night. But I couldn't stop thinking of Victoria upstairs in her bed.

"This was really fun," Adam says to me as he leans back in his chair, full and contented. He casually rests his hand on top of mine.

"Yeah." I ease my hand away from his as subtly as I can. "It was… nice."

"All I want to do is go straight to bed…."

Okay, this can't wait another minute. I have to tell

him. It's wrong not to.

"Listen, Adam," I say. "There's something I need to tell you."

He's quiet for a moment, studying my face. "I know."

"You know?"

"I'm crazy about you, Sylvia." He rubs at the stubble on his chin. "But I'm not completely oblivious. I know you don't feel the same way."

"It's not that I don't feel the same way exactly, but…"

"It's Victoria," he says without my having to say it. "I know. It's a weird situation. I shouldn't have put you in that position." He shakes his head. "In my defense, I wouldn't have done it if I wasn't so goddamn lonely."

He's not angry. He's not yelling at me or exploding. He's making me feel sorry to be ending things. I know he's been very lonely. And I know that our brief relationship made him happy.

"No hard feelings." He sticks out his hand so I can shake it. "Friends?"

I reach out to grasp his hand. His feels warm and firm in mine. Am I making a mistake? Maybe Adam has changed from the guy who blew up at Victoria over nothing. He doesn't seem that way at all right now.

But either way, this is the right thing to do. I can't stay with him. He's *married* to Victoria.

Adam and I work together in silence to clear the dishes away from the table. I stash the leftovers in the fridge, then I go back out to get the glasses we used. On the way out of the kitchen, my eyes are drawn to that dent on the wall. The one Adam claimed was caused by moving the refrigerator.

Victoria said in her diary that he threw a plate and it smashed into the wall, creating a dent.

I stare at the imperfection in the plaster. Was it caused by a refrigerator or a plate? I can't tell.

I'm not sure if I'll ever know for sure what happened in this house.

CHAPTER 41

After Adam goes off to bed, I sneak down to the kitchen. I peek inside the refrigerator and find all our leftovers still stuffed inside. I scan the contents for a moment and pull out the apple pie.

The apple pie is one of the only things that isn't homemade. Adam picked it up yesterday from the supermarket. I grab a knife and cut a small slice. Then I dump it into the food processor and hit purée.

When the pie reaches the right consistency, I pour it out into a small bowl. Then I quietly sneak up the stairs to Victoria's room.

Just because she refused to come to our awkward little Thanksgiving dinner, that doesn't mean she shouldn't get to eat tonight. I'm sure Adam gave her some tube feeds, but she should at least get to try some of our gigantic feast. That is, if she's awake.

I open the door to Victoria's room without knocking. In the dim moonlight, I can see her lying in bed, her eyes shut. She's asleep. I tiptoe over to the lamp by her bed and turn it on. Her eyelids flutter open.

"It's Sylvie," I say. "I brought you some pie."

I look down at the bowl in my hand. The pie looked so much more appetizing before it was ground up into one big mush. I wish she could try it whole, but Adam said she would choke.

"Would you like to eat some pie?" I ask.

Victoria looks down at the bowl in my hand. She's quiet for so long, I'm almost worried that she's falling asleep again with her eyes open. But then she speaks: "Did you…?"

"I spoke with him," I say quickly. "It was fine. He was… nice. He's been really nice to me."

Victoria makes a noise I've never heard before, something between a laugh and a snort, but she's not smiling. She never, ever smiles.

"Anyway." I force a smile of my own. "Do you want pie?"

"Sylvie," she says.

I scoop up a little bit of pie with the spoon. "Yes…?"

"Get the…" She pauses to swallow her saliva. "His gun. Get it."

What? "Victoria," I say quietly, "I can't…"

"Get it." She stares straight at me. I've never seen a woman less interested in having a bite of pie. "Or… Or else…"

I lower the spoon. "I'm sorry…. I can't…"

Before she can say anything else, I take the bowl of puréed pie and go back to my bedroom. I curl up under the covers and eat the pie myself. Actually, it isn't half bad.

CHAPTER 42

Victoria's Diary

December 20, 2017

I don't even know what to make of what happened today.

I was sitting on the couch, watching television, when Adam came home. He gave me a look when he saw me sitting around, but what else am I supposed to do? Irina does all the cooking and Maggie does all the cleaning, so where does that leave me? I had one job interview a few weeks ago that was over an hour's drive away with traffic, and then they never called me back. I tried going running a few days ago and nearly slipped on a patch of ice. It's been a particularly snowy and cold January, and it's just too slippery to run anywhere.

I suggested to Adam that I might take a class. There are some night classes at the local high school. But he kept insisting that I only wanted to take the class to meet men, so he wouldn't let me use the credit card.

So my days are filled with game shows in the morning and binge-watching television series on Netflix in the afternoon. And a lot of snacking, which I try my best to conceal from Adam. Unfortunately, I had three sour cream and onion potato chips in my mouth at once when he walked in, and he gave me a really dirty look. He doesn't like it when I snack between meals. I also knew he didn't approve of what I was wearing, which was my comfy sweats. I thought he was going to be out all day or else I would have dressed differently. I always make sure to have a nice outfit on when he gets home.

"So you've just given up on yourself," he said. "Is that it?"

I brushed potato chip crumbs off my sweatshirt and sat up straight. "No…"

He shook his head in disgust. "Go get changed."

I knew this was a discussion that had the potential to escalate quickly, so I went upstairs to our bedroom without argument. He was right, anyway. I looked like a mess. My sweatpants and sweatshirt weren't even clean—there was a big stain on the shirt. Embarrassing. But I hadn't thought it mattered since I was just hanging around the house.

I sifted through my clothing, trying to find something he would deem acceptable. I pulled out a pair of designer jeans I purchased a couple of months ago, when my old jeans became too snug to fit me, even with the top button left open. I bought a couple of new pairs two sizes larger than my old pairs.

Except when I put these new jeans on, they were too tight to button. The only pants I have that fit me anymore are my sweatpants.

I was screwed. If I came back downstairs in sweatpants, it would be a massive argument. I had to problem-solve—fast.

So I kept the jeans on and wore one of my longer shirts to hide the fact that the button was open. I didn't know how I was even going to sit down with those tight jeans on.

That reminds me—I'm going to have to save up my money to buy some new clothes yet again. There's no way I can ask him for money to buy new pants because I can't squeeze into my old ones anymore. That's an argument I don't want to have.

Anyway, when I came back downstairs, Adam was fiddling with a small black briefcase he had been carrying when he came into the house. He had placed it on the kitchen table and was now peering inside.

"Is that the proof of your book?" I asked. I still haven't even caught a glimpse of the new book yet—I don't even know the title.

He shook his head. "Nope. It's a gun."

"A... *what?*"

There are two kinds of people in the world. People who are comfortable with firearms. And people who look at a gun and are filled with absolute, crippling fear. Guess which one I am.

He opened up the case entirely so that I could see a pistol embedded in the foam. I instinctively took a step back. I had never been this close to a gun before. And honestly, I never had any interest in being this close to a gun. I would have been perfectly happy to go my whole life without ever being in the same room as a gun.

"Why did you buy a *gun*?" I nearly screamed at him.

"Vicky." He lifted his green eyes to meet mine. "We are in the middle of nowhere. Completely isolated. If somebody breaks in here, we'll be sitting ducks. We need this for protection."

I hugged my arms to my chest. "Do you even know how to use it?"

He laughed and removed the gun from the case. I took a step back. "Of course I do. My father took me to a gun range when I was a teenager for firing practice. Everybody should know how to shoot a gun. It's in the second amendment."

"I don't want to even touch that thing."

He rolled his eyes. "You know, I'm not here all the time. You should know how to use this."

"I'd rather not."

He held the gun in his right hand and pointed it in the direction of the wall. "Well, what if some strange man comes into the house while I'm gone?"

I just shook my head.

"You'd probably like it." He swiveled the gun toward

me. I stared into the barrel and my stomach dropped. "You'd probably think he was attractive and fuck him."

My mouth was almost too dry to get out any words. "Please don't point that thing at me."

"It's not loaded." But he put it down. Thank goodness. "Come on. At least let me show you how to use it. We don't have to go to a firing range or anything."

I hated the idea of having a gun in the house. But at the same time, he did have a point. We were in the middle of nowhere. If somebody broke in, they could do whatever they wanted to us and we'd be defenseless. A gun might level the playing field.

"Fine," I said. "One lesson."

So Adam showed me how to load the cartridge of the gun with bullets. The gun was heavier than I thought it would be when I held it in my hand. The whole thing felt very surreal. He turned the safety on, then he nodded at the front door. "Get your coat. I'll show you how to shoot."

"We're going to fire the gun?"

He rolled his eyes. "What good is a gun if you can't fire it?

I have no intention of ever firing that gun. Not ever. Maybe I could threaten somebody with it. I could shake it in a threatening way. But when push comes to shove, I don't think I could ever pull the trigger. But of course, when Adam gets it in his head he wants to do something, it's very hard to dissuade him. So I got my coat and followed him outside.

It snowed yesterday and most of the snow still hadn't been cleared away. Our entire gigantic front yard was a bed of white powder. I was wearing my boots, but they sunk so deeply into the snow, my feet got drenched instantly. I desperately needed a new pair of boots but I hadn't saved up enough money to get decent ones. Also, I stupidly left my gloves in the house.

Adam pointed to a tree in our massive lawn right next to the shed where we kept the gardening supplies. (My she-shed dreams have never come to fruition.) It was about twenty feet away. "I'm going to have you aim for that tree."

He explained to me what I had to do. Hold the gun with my right hand and my index finger resting on the side of the cylinder. Then wrap my other fingers around the front of the grip. Tuck my thumb in like I'm making a fist. Then take my left hand and wrap it around the front of the right hand. By the end of the lesson, my fingers were bright red from the cold.

Adam demonstrated the grip himself, so I could observe somebody who knew what they were doing. Of course, he had on his nice warm leather gloves. He pointed the gun in the direction of the tree. "You need to squeeze the gun as hard as you can without making the barrel shake," he explained. "Then you want to bring it to eye-level when you point at the target."

Without any warning, he squeezed the trigger.

I always knew guns were noisy. But I wasn't prepared for how terrifyingly loud the sound was when that stupid gun went off. I let out a yelp and jumped back about two feet, which Adam found hilarious. My ears were ringing. I could see the splintering in the tree and realized he had hit his target.

"Now it's your turn," he said.

He handed the gun to me. I tried my best to grip it the way he had just shown me, but my hands were shaking too badly. My fingers were now completely numb. He laughed at the way I was shaking, and he put his arms around me to help steady my grip. It didn't help.

"Pull the trigger," he told me. "Remember—steady, even pressure."

I knew he wasn't going to let up until I fired the stupid gun. So I pointed at the tree with my shaking hands and squeezed the trigger.

It was even louder when I was the one firing. I felt the recoil in my right shoulder and then a jab of pain.

"You missed the tree," Adam said with a smirk. "I think the bullet hit the shed."

"What a shock," I muttered. My ears were still ringing.

We went back into the house, and Adam showed me where he was keeping the gun: right on top of our bedroom closet. So in summary, I will now be sleeping with a gun six feet from my head. I made him absolutely promise we are going to keep it unloaded and not touch it unless we are certain there's an intruder in the house.

As much as I hate having a gun in the house, I

suppose he does make a good point. We are in the middle of nowhere. If I call the police, how quickly could they possibly arrive? Maybe it isn't a terrible idea to have a gun for protection.

Anyway, it's not like I have a say in the matter.

CHAPTER 43

If there ever was a time to get the gun out of Adam's closet, it would've been back when we were sleeping together. Now that we're not, I have no excuse to be in his room, digging around. The opportunity has passed.

Not that I have any intention of digging around in his room for that gun. No matter how many times Victoria tells me I should.

I have trouble sleeping after reading Victoria's diary entry. It's so hard to read about what happened to her. Before I started reading, I believed she was happy until the moment she fell down the stairs. Now I know she wasn't. And with every entry, it just seems to get worse.

I'm scared to see what else he did to her.

Maybe she didn't really fall down the stairs. Maybe he pushed her.

I get out of bed early. It's too early for Victoria to be awake, so instead, I head downstairs and put on my coat. It's so early that I run into Eva on her way inside. She gives me a look like she thinks I'm scum. And maybe I am.

"Where you go?" Eva narrows her eyes at me. "Are you leaving?"

"No, I…" I just have to get out of here for a few minutes. "I'll be back."

When I get outside of the house, the cold air hits me like a slap in the face. If it were to rain, the rain would come down as snow. Maggie has warned me that we're due for our first blizzard soon. I'm dreading it.

I bury my hands deeper into my coat pockets and start walking all around the path that circles the house. All the leaves have been cleared away, at least. Adam never hired a gardener and instead did the work himself. I saw him going out with a rake not that long ago. There are still branches threatening to trip me, but it's not as bad as it was. I pause when I get to the tree Victoria showed me the other day. I walk closer to it, staring at the splintering of the wood where the bullet pierced.

This is what Victoria described in her diary. Adam shot the tree.

Then I look at the shed next to the tree. I step closer, but before I get within a couple of feet of it, I see that familiar pattern of splintered wood on the shed as well. A bullet went into the shed too. That's the bullet Victoria fired when she was trying to hit the tree and missed.

It happened. Just like she described.

Just like I found that dent in the wall of the kitchen.

I'm scared of what else I'm going to read in her diary.

I don't want to read anymore.

But I must.

CHAPTER 44

Victoria's Diary

December 28, 2017

Today while Adam was upstairs working, Peter showed up with the proof copies of the new book.

I was so excited about it. I loved Adam's other two books, both of which have gone to the top of the *New York Times* bestseller list. According to Peter, this book is even better than the other two. He keeps saying it's going to be the biggest book of the year. I have been dying to read it.

"Do you have the book?" was the first thing I asked Peter when I opened the door for him.

He laughed. "Eager, are you?"

I laughed too, but it was true. When Adam told me the proof copy would be ready this week, I became obsessed with it. I wasn't even irritated by the fact that Irina was prancing around our kitchen in a skimpy tank top and shorts, humming to herself. Tell me—who dresses like that in the middle of winter?

I called upstairs for Adam to come down. He had given me a heads up Peter was coming today and hinted very strongly that I better be dressed nicely. He even gave me an advance on my weekly allowance. So yesterday, I bought some new clothing. I bought everything a size larger than what I needed. Optimistically, I was hoping to lose some weight, but realistically, I didn't see how it was going to happen until the spring.

I could practically hear the drum roll playing as Peter pulled the thick hardcover novel out of his suitcase. The white capital letters on the cover immediately jumped out at me:

THE VIXEN

The Vixen? What was that about?

Even though I knew Adam was going to be angry that I looked at the book before he came down, I grabbed it out of Peter's hands. Below the big block letters, there was a photograph of a woman on the cover. A woman with blond hair. The same exact shade and style as mine. The resemblance was unmistakable. And then the tag line:

She betrayed his trust. Now she'll pay.

My hands were shaking. I nearly ripped open the cover to read the inside flap with the book description. *The Vixen*. A wife who betrays her husband repeatedly. And now? Now he gets *revenge*.

What. The. Heck.

Adam came down the stairs, also dressed up in a nice pair of tan slacks and a button-down shirt. He looked devastatingly handsome when he was dressed up. He's every bit as attractive as he was that first day I met him. Whereas I look like an entirely different person. I'm afraid to even look in the mirror lately because I barely recognize myself.

"The book!" He cocked his head to the side as he saw me holding it. "Vicky. I thought you promised you were going to wait for me."

I was too shaken to even get defensive. I was still trying to wrap my head around the whole thing. My husband has written a book about a man who is betrayed by his wife. And then he seeks revenge on her.

This doesn't make me feel good.

"You wrote about me," I said in a shaky voice. "This book is about *me*, isn't it?"

He looked down at the cover of the book. He snatched it out of my hands. "What are you talking about?"

"This book is clearly about me!" I nearly screamed the words. "Just look at the cover! It's me!"

"Adam didn't design the cover," Peter said. Of course, he would defend Adam.

"That's right," Adam said. "I'm just seeing it for the first time now."

"Oh… fiddlesticks!" Not for the first time, I regretted the fact that my parents had instilled in me such a deep distaste for swearing. Because I really wanted to swear at him right now.

Adam's lips settled into a straight line. "Victoria, let's not have this discussion right now."

Peter flashed an uncomfortable smile. "Actually, I think I might head out now. Adam, give me a call when you've had a chance to go through it."

As much as I didn't want to fight in front of Peter, I got an uneasy feeling after he left. Adam wrote a book about me. About how I was a cheating wife who had betrayed him repeatedly. That's how he sees me.

He wrote that book about his family. Now they're dead.

Does that mean he's going to kill me?

With Peter gone, Adam locked the door behind him. He turned to face me. "Victoria, you need to calm down."

I pointed to the book. "Is this really what you think of me?"

"No, of course not!" He shook his head. "It's fiction. My imagination. If you read it, you would see it's not about you at all."

"Well, let me read it then."

He hesitated a moment, then nodded. "Fine. You can read it." I started to reach for the book, but then he held it away from me. "But first let me show Irina. She'll be really excited."

I sucked in a breath. "Seriously? You need to show our *cook* before you let your wife have a look?"

His eyes darkened. "What is it about you and Irina? You have to stop being so jealous. It's insane. She's a nice girl."

I wanted to scream at him again, but there was no point. Adam wasn't going to stop flirting with Irina. So I let him go into the kitchen to show her the book. I watched her throw her arms around him excitedly. *You are so magnificent, Adam!*

That's what Adam loves. He wants everyone to tell him how great he is. He doesn't get enough of that from me so he has to go to Irina.

I did finally get my hands on a copy of the book. And since I didn't have anything better to do today, I've been reading it nonstop in the bedroom. I finished it five minutes ago.

It is the most horrifying thing I have ever read.

That is to say, it's brilliant. The characters are so vivid, they just leap right off the page. The plot is so twisted and clever, every time I think I figured it out, there's another twist. And the character of the wife—Nicki—well, she is the epitome of a gold-digging, cold-blooded bitch who gets exactly what is coming to her in the end. She suffers a horrible, agonizing death.

I don't know what it means that Adam wrote this book. I have never been unfaithful to him, but Nicki is unfaithful to her husband repeatedly, especially with a man named *Jack*. As soon as they get married, Nicki quits her job and stays home to spend all of the protagonist's money.

Nicki has committed every single offense that Adam has accused me of.

He's written this book to send me a message:

Be careful. Or else you will end up like Nicki.

And believe me, I don't want to end up like Nicki.

January 9, 2018

On nights when the snow is very bad, and even sometimes when it isn't, Adam has allowed Irina to spend the night in our guest bedroom. His logic is that she has a long drive home and he doesn't want her to get into an accident. And it's not like we need the extra room. (Especially since I am failing spectacularly at getting pregnant.)

I want to be a generous employer who is fine with an employee spending the night for the sake of her safety. Except last night at three in the morning, when I woke up to use the bathroom, Adam wasn't in our bed.

I pulled on my pink terrycloth robe and crept out into the hallway. I walked slowly to keep the floorboards from making noises, which they tend to do. I was hoping I'd look downstairs and find Adam making himself a late-night snack in the kitchen. But unfortunately, when I got to the guest bedroom, it was obvious the occupants inside were very much awake.

In fact, I could hear giggling.

I froze, not sure what to do. I wanted to bust in and

catch him in the act. But then what? It was three in the morning and my car was buried under a foot of snow. I couldn't just leave. And if I asked Adam to leave, he'd surely refuse. After all, he owns this house—I don't.

On top of that, I couldn't bear the sight of my husband with another woman. Even thinking about it made my entire body burn with humiliation. If I walked in on that, it would destroy me.

So I decided to confront him in the morning.

I don't know how, but I eventually managed to drift off again. And when I woke up again, Adam was beside me in bed. It was like he'd never left. If I hadn't had so much water to drink before bed, I would have been none the wiser.

"Hey, Vicky." Adam kissed my neck and then let out a loud yawn as he cuddled closer to me. "You're nice and warm."

Before I knew it, he was kissing me more aggressively, tugging at my oversized nightshirt. I recoiled at his touch. "Please, Adam... not now."

"You're not interested." He yawned again and pulled away. "What a shocker."

"Why don't you pay Irina another visit then?"

He rubbed his eyes. "What are you talking about?"

I sat up straight in bed, clutching the blankets to my chest. "You were in her room last night."

"No, I wasn't." He sat up too, looking at me with his sincere green eyes. "I don't know what you're talking about."

"I heard you."

He shook his head. "Maybe you dreamed it? Come on, Vicky. You know I would never do that."

One minute ago, I had been a-hundred-percent certain about what I heard. But now I was doubting myself. He looked so earnest. Maybe I really did dream it all. It's certainly possible. Because nobody is that good a liar, are they?

"Of course," he added, "if I did do it, nobody would blame me. I mean, look at you. You're like a house. It's not exactly a turn on."

I felt the heat rush into my face. "Well, sorry."

He snorted. "I know most women let themselves go when they get married, but you took it to another level. Honestly, you're really lucky I *don't* cheat."

With those words, he got out of bed and went to the shower before I could muster a response.

Did I imagine it all? I closed my eyes. I could visualize myself outside of the guest room. I could hear laughter. Whispers. It wasn't just Irina in there. She had a guest—a male guest. But it didn't necessarily have to be my husband. Maybe she had a boyfriend over, and Adam had been upstairs working in the attic the whole time. Or maybe I dreamed it, like he said.

I shrugged my housecoat back on and left the bedroom to go make breakfast. Maybe I'd make pancakes with cut up slices of banana, like I used to sometimes when

Adam and I were first dating. It was true he wasn't being a great husband lately, but I haven't been a great wife either. We haven't even been married a year yet, and it feels like all the romance has been sucked out of our marriage.

I wondered if maybe we needed to rekindle what we used to have. Starting with a candlelit... breakfast. Well, breakfast, anyway.

Except before I even got to the stairs, I ran smack into Irina.

She was wearing a robe too, except hers was red and sheer and barely grazed the top of her thighs. The skin of her long legs was flawless. If I had to guess her age, I would have said twenty-two or thereabouts. She had high cheekbones and clear blue eyes. From any distance, she was one of the most beautiful women I'd ever seen.

"Miss Victoria," she said. "Hello."

"Hello, Irina," I muttered.

She hesitated, her light brown eyebrows scrunched together. "I heard your conversation with Adam. About how you heard him in my room."

"Oh..." I averted my eyes. "Well, I didn't mean to assume..."

"You heard correctly," she said in her thick East European accent. "Your husband was in my room last night. For many hours." And just so there's absolutely no confusion, she added, "We made the love."

"Oh." I blinked at her. "I... I see."

"You do not deserve him." Her glassy blue eyes stared

right at me. "He is wonderful, brilliant man. And you... I see what you do. You lie around house like the slug. You do not lift one finger. You just watch the television and get fat."

My mouth fell open. When I imagined confronting Irina, this was not how it went in my head. "I..."

"He says you are disgusting," she continued, even as I wanted to stick my fingers in my ears. "He says he feels nothing for you anymore. He is sorry he married you and he feels trapped." Her eyes narrowed. "Soon he will leave you. And you will be kicked out on the street with nothing."

My mouth was still hanging open. It took a few tries for me to kickstart my lips back into action. "You're fired, Irina."

Her eyes widened and two circles appeared on either cheek. "You cannot fire me! I will tell Adam."

She pushed past me, jostling my shoulder roughly in the process. She marched right to the bathroom and opened the door without knocking. I heard her high-pitched accented voice yelling at Adam. A moment later, he emerged from the bathroom, his hair damp, a towel wrapped around his waist.

"Vicky," he said. "What happened? Why would you fire Irina?"

I was speechless. I couldn't believe what was happening right in front of me. What had my life become? "I fired her because you're sleeping together."

Adam grunted. "And I told you, we're *not*." He frowned at me. "You have to get this jealousy under control, Victoria. You're sick. You need to see a therapist. Get on medication."

For a moment, I thought of that gun up in our closet. I imagined grabbing it out of the closet, pointing it at Irina's pretty face and pulling the trigger. I might have missed the tree, but I wouldn't miss at such close range. I imagined her beautiful, smug face exploding in a spray of blood.

Of course, I wouldn't really do that.

Adam spent the next hour calming Irina down, then he returned to the bedroom to scream at me for my jealousy being so out of control. He also informed me that I didn't have the right to fire anyone without his permission. Then he stormed out, slamming the door behind him.

I don't know what to do anymore. I should leave Adam. I'm sure I should. But it's not that easy. I don't have anywhere to go. I don't have any money aside from about forty dollars left of my allowance this week. My car won't even make it out of the gates with this snow.

I'm trapped.

CHAPTER 45

I have so many questions I wish I could ask Victoria, but I know she won't be able to answer any of them.

After reading about Adam's latest book, *The Vixen*, I put down Victoria's diary and started reading that instead. I've been reading a little bit of it every day for the last week when I can steal an hour or two. There were no copies in the house, so I've been reading it on my phone, which makes my temples ache from eye strain.

In spite of that, I've been devouring this book. Adam said that he thought he was "lucky" to have become a best-selling author, but he wasn't lucky. He's talented. He's really freaking talented. I haven't ever read anything like this book.

I can see why Victoria was worried the book was based on her. The villain, Nicole, is the wife of the protagonist, and she's an absolute psychopath. She tortures the protagonist by spending all his money and flirting shamelessly with other men while at the same time growing insanely jealous of anyone he even glances at. When she starts outright cheating on him, that's when he's had enough. He plots his revenge.

I don't know if Victoria's personality in any way resembled Nicole before her injury, but it seems like in Adam's head, there were certain similarities. At the very least, he believed she was cheating on him. Physically, there's no doubt they are similar.

Their nicknames are even similar. Vicky. Nicki.

And the names of the other man. Mack. Jack.

What happens to Nicole in the book is nothing short of horrific. Even though I'm reading it on my tiny little phone, my eyes are pinned to the screen. In any case, the protagonist definitely gets his revenge. By the end of the book, Nicole is in two pieces. Literally.

As I scoop mashed potatoes into Victoria's mouth, I try to imagine how she must have felt while reading that book. I also wonder if there was any truth in it. I mean, Victoria did have a terrible accident, but it was nothing like what happened to Nicole.

A dollop of mashed potatoes slides out of the right side of her lips. I reach out with a napkin to wipe it away. I look down at the plate, which still has about a quarter of the food left. "Are you getting full?" I ask.

Victoria nods.

"One more bite and we don't have to do tube feeds," I tell her. That's a big motivating factor for her. She hates those tube feeds.

Victoria looks down at the food, then back up at me. "Sylvie," she says.

I smile at her. "Just one more bite."

"Irina," she says.

My hand freezes in mid-air. That's the first time she has said the name Irina, even though she wrote about her extensively in that diary. And Maggie told me Victoria was jealous of Adam's relationship with Irina. I remember how when I tried to ask Maggie where Irina had gone, she was so evasive.

"Irina," she says again. "Irina... Glen Head."

I don't know what Victoria is trying to tell me. You really appreciate the English language when you're trying to have a conversation with somebody who can only speak in one or two-word phrases. Maggie had told me Irina was from Glen Head. Does Victoria want me to find her?

"Do you want me to look for Irina?" I ask. "Is she in Glen Head now?"

"Yes." She nods but looks hesitant. She's never going to eat any more of the potatoes, but that's okay. She had most of them. "But... no. She..."

I lean forward, waiting eagerly for her to spit out the rest of the sentence. But before she can say another word, there's a rap at the door. I lift my head and see Adam standing there. He's got the dreaded syringe in his right hand.

"Is this a good time to do the medications?" he asks.

Victoria shoots me a pained look. She hates getting

those medications more than anything. I thought at first it was because it hurt her going in, but now I suspect it's because of how they make her feel after. Those medications knock her out. I'm not sure whether or not that's the purpose of them, but that's what they do. She spends half her day asleep because of those medications.

"I… I guess so." I stand up to let Adam have room to get to her. "We're done eating."

"Great." He winks at me as he approaches Victoria. "All right, Vicky. We'll make this quick."

I should probably mention the fact that I haven't clipped Victoria's nails in over a week. I could warn him.

But I don't.

He reaches down to pull her shirt up and get to her feeding tube. I see the strange look in Victoria's good eye, and I instinctively take a step back. Adam is too focused on the feeding tube, so he doesn't notice.

And then she lunges at him.

CHAPTER 46

Adam screams.

There's blood. There's actual blood where Victoria's fingernails break through the skin of his face. He swears at her, tosses the syringe on the bed, and runs out of the room, clutching the side of his face. Victoria watches him, a satisfied look on her face.

"I better go check on him," I mumble.

It turns out she didn't get his eye, so he should count himself lucky. When I get to the bathroom, he's got a wet cloth on the right side of his face. There's blood soaking through it.

"What the hell was that?" Adam barks at me. "I thought you were clipping her nails."

"I did," I lie.

"Not enough." He pulls the wet cloth off the side of his face and I see three bright red scratch marks across his cheek, oozing blood. "Jesus Christ. I look like I got mauled by a tiger."

"Listen," I say, "why don't you let me give her the medications from now on? She won't fight me like she does you."

Even though those scratches on his face look very painful, he hesitates.

"You can crush the medications and put them in the syringe," I say. "I'll just inject it. I think she would prefer that."

He puts a fresh piece of toilet paper on his wounds and winces. "All right. Fine. But just... be careful. I don't want this to happen to you."

It won't. That's one thing I'm sure of.

I go back to Victoria's bedroom. She's sitting calmly in her wheelchair, watching me. I go over and pick up the syringe from the bed. I shake it, and I can see white particles running around the fluid. Her medications, ground up.

"You don't want to take this, do you?" I say.

Victoria shakes her head, her eyes never leaving my face.

I open up the window next to her chair. An ice-cold breeze shoots into the room. I hold the syringe out the window and press the plunger until the contents are dispensed to the ground below. Then I close the window again.

"Okay?" I say.

For the first time since I started working here, she smiles.

CHAPTER 47

Victoria's Diary

January 13, 2018

This morning while Adam was upstairs working, I got a text on my phone from Mack:

Hey, I'm going to visit some friends on the island. Are you up for a visit?

It took all my self-restraint not to scream out: *Yes! I miss you so much! Come now! Save me!*

Of course, I haven't seen Mack in almost six months. I'm amazed he's thinking about me at all, much less willing to be my savior. He's not even really coming to see me—he's just passing by on the way to see some friends.

That would be nice, I finally wrote. *What day?*

He wrote back instantly: *I'm flexible. What day works for you?*

Adam has a meeting out in the city on Thursday. He'll

be gone all day. And Irina isn't around on Thursdays. Not that anything suspicious would happen, but Adam surely wouldn't see it that way.

Thursday afternoon?

Thursday works. Text me your address and I'll be there around three.

I texted him the address. And right after, I deleted all the texts from my phone. I don't even have Mack's number saved in my phone anymore. Adam wouldn't keep paying for my phone unless he had my password, and he checks my phone periodically. I can't take a risk.

My only fear is that he might find this diary. If he did... well, I don't even want to think about it. I hide it very well. He won't find it.

For the first time in what feels like months, I have a little bubble of happiness in my chest. I'm going to see Mack! I can't wait!

January 17, 2018

I breathed a sigh of relief this morning when Adam left to go to his meeting in the city. I had been convinced something would come up at the last second and he would cancel, and then I would have to figure out what to do when Mack arrived. If he showed up while Adam was here, Adam would go nuts. I'd have to cancel.

But fortunately, everything went according to plan.

As soon as Adam left, I hurried upstairs to change. I had a few new outfits I bought that fit well enough, but when I looked at myself in the full-length mirror in the bedroom, I felt ill. I looked *terrible*. I was bloated, my blond hair was limp and dull, I had purple circles under my eyes, and my skin was blotchy. There wasn't much I could do about my hair, so I just twisted it back behind my head like I used to wear it in the ER. I spent half an hour applying makeup to conceal the circles and the blotchiness. I had variable success.

It would have to do.

At a few minutes after three, the doorbell rang. I ran over and flung the door open, and there he was. Mack. Looking the same as he did when I last saw him—his black hair still messy, his smile slightly crooked. At the sight of him, I forgot about worrying how I looked and just threw my arms around him.

He laughed and steadied himself, as if I had any chance of knocking a big guy like Mack off his feet. He hugged me back. His arms felt so good and warm and safe. I wanted him to carry me away from this place. A hard lump formed in my throat.

"It's so good to see you," I managed. I pulled away from the hug, even though I didn't want to because I couldn't let him get the wrong idea. Surely, he had a girlfriend by now. And he was just popping in on his way to visit a friend, after all.

"Same here." He grinned at me and his eyes crinkled.

"It's not the same without you in the ER. Everyone misses you."

I nodded, not trusting myself to speak.

"You look great," he said. Clearly a lie.

"Thanks," I mumbled. I cleared my throat. "Well, come in. I'll give you the grand tour."

I showed Mack around our giant house. He was politely enthusiastic, but I could tell he didn't care that much. He kept trying to ask me questions about how I was doing, but I did my best to deflect. What was I supposed to tell him? I spend my days watching television? My husband is cheating on me with the cook?

"What's new with you?" I asked as we concluded the tour in the living room. I sat down on the couch and he settled down next to me.

"Well…" He got this grin on his face and I knew exactly what he was going to say. He met some wonderful girl and he was going to marry her. The thought of it made me want to throw up, even though I'd of course be happy for him. "I got into medical school! I'm going in the fall."

"Mack!" He had talked a lot about going to medical school, but he had worried about being too old. I could tell he really wanted to go though. It was his dream. I was so thrilled he went for it. "That's amazing!"

"It *is* amazing." His grin widened. "Of course, I don't know how I'm gonna pay for it. I'm going to have to keep working ambulance shifts while I'm in school. And I'll be almost thirty-five when I graduate. But…"

For the second time since he arrived, I threw my arms around him. He hugged me back, but this time when I pulled away, I realized our faces were only a few inches apart. And before I could stop myself, I had leaned in to kiss him.

There was a momentary flash of surprise on Mack's face, but he didn't push me away. Just the opposite. He kissed me back. And kissing Mack was... well, amazing. He was eager but gentle. It made me realize how much I had grown to dislike kissing my husband. There was a part of me that still loved Adam, but a larger part of me despised him.

It was Mack who pulled away first. He was blinking his brown eyes and looking at me with his brow furrowed. "Vicky," he said softly. "I didn't expect..."

My face burned. What was I thinking? Why did I kiss him that way? If he had ever really had feelings for me, they were surely long gone. And my current appearance wasn't going to rekindle them. "I'm sorry," I mumbled. "I know I look disgusting."

His eyes widened. "What are you talking about? Vicky, you're gorgeous. How could you say..." He shook his head. "But you're *married*. And I..."

And that's when I burst into tears.

I told him everything. Everything. He put his arm around me and listened with a crease between his brows the entire time. I told him how much I hated being stranded out here in the middle of freaking nowhere. How

I couldn't find a job. How Adam wouldn't even let me have a credit card. How he was almost certainly cheating on me with Irina. How I didn't think I could take even one more minute sometimes. I talked and talked until my voice was hoarse and the tears finally dried up.

"Jesus Christ." Mack ran a hand through his hair. "Vicky, I can't believe what you're telling me. You've got to leave. Now."

I buried my face in my hands. "I have nowhere to go."

"Bullshit." Mack squeezed my shoulders. "Carol will let you stay with her. And... well, if you want, you can stay with me. But my point is, you've got a place to go."

"I have no money."

"So what? Vicky, we're going to help you. *I'm* going to help you."

He wanted to help me. Even though he didn't have enough money to pay for school, he was still willing to share what little he had.

I wiped my eyes with the back of my hand. I couldn't even imagine how awful my face looked right now. All the makeup had surely wiped off. "I didn't mean to dump all this on you. You're probably late for meeting your friend."

Mack was quiet for a few moments. He picked at a frayed thread on his jeans. "There's no friend. I came out here to see *you*. Carol told me what happened at that dinner and I was worried about you."

Of course, that made me cry all over again.

"Look." He squeezed my shoulders again. "Go pack a

bag. We'll go right now."

"Did you drive out here?"

He shook his head. "I took the Long Island Railroad and got an Uber from there."

I glanced out the window. The sun had dropped in the sky and it had started to snow. Adam would be home before long. I imagined him coming home to find me gone. Or worse, coming home to find that I was in the middle of packing, with another man in our living room. He'd be beyond hurt.

"I can't go now." I lowered my eyes. "Once I leave here, I can't come back. I've got to have some time to pack and to tell Adam I'm going."

He frowned. "So tell him when he gets home. I'll wait."

"I can't." I was having trouble articulating this, but I had to make him understand. "Mack, he's my husband. I owe him at least an explanation."

He chewed on his lower lip. "What if he hurts you?"

"He's never laid a finger on me. He wouldn't do that."

"I don't trust him, Vicky."

"Please." I put my hand on his. "I have to do it my way. Trust me on this."

He looked at me for a long time. I could tell he didn't think any of this was a good idea, but he doesn't know Adam the way I do. Even at his worst, Adam has never threatened to hurt me. He'll yell and scream, and that will be it. "You tell me when you're going to have this conversation with him. I'll rent a car and I'll wait outside for you. Okay?"

Before I could answer, I heard the lock turning in the front door. I yanked my hand away from Mack. Damn, Adam was home early. He wasn't supposed to be home for at least another hour or two, but sometimes I think he gives me misinformation to keep me on my toes. And this time, he managed to catch me.

I stood up quickly, brushing off invisible dust from my skirt. Mack didn't budge from the couch. He had a dark expression on his face, and I was a little worried that the second Adam walked in the door, Mack was going to punch him square in the nose. And I have to admit there was a small part of me that would've really liked to see that.

Adam's eyes widened when he saw Mack sitting in our living room. His right hand clenched into a fist, and a muscle twitched in his jaw. "Victoria," he said. "You didn't mention we were having visitors."

Mack finally got to his feet. He turned to face my husband. "It wasn't planned. I just happened to be passing by."

"You just happened to be passing by Montauk. Interesting…"

Mack shrugged. I wished he would play along, just to make things easier for me when he left.

"Well, have you had the grand tour then?" Adam asked. His right fist had loosened and he was undoing the knot on his tie.

"Yes. Vicky showed me around."

"Wonderful." Adam smiled. I don't know how he was able to be so charming when he was undoubtedly seething under the surface. "Can I offer you a drink then?"

"No." Mack cast a glance in my direction. "I should probably... I guess I'll head out now."

Please take me with you. I got this horrible sick feeling in my stomach that I had made the wrong decision. Maybe it wasn't too late to go with Mack. But if I went now, I would have to leave everything behind. And I couldn't have a conversation with Adam with another man in the room.

"I hope you've got four-wheel drive on your car," Adam commented. "The snow is getting pretty heavy out there."

I glanced out the window again. He was right—the snow was really starting to come down. Big white flakes were falling quickly outside the window. Our lawn was already covered in a layer of white powder. By tomorrow, I'd be trapped here. Again.

"I'm going to call for an Uber," Mack said. "I'll just have them take me to the railroad station."

"Out here? In this weather? Forget it." He strolled to the kitchen and poured himself a glass of wine. "You'll be waiting an hour—if you're lucky. And it will be a blizzard by then."

Mack scratched at the back of his neck. "Well, I don't have much of a choice, do I?"

Adam took a long sip of the red wine. He swirled it around in the glass. "Just let me finish this and I'll give you a ride to the train station."

"You don't have to do that."

"It's no problem. My car handles really well in snow."

Mack's eyes were wary, but Adam had a good point. The snow was getting bad and if he had any chance of making it back to the city tonight, he had to leave right now. Otherwise, he could be stuck out here for days.

"Fine." Mack nodded. "Let's go."

I had a terrible feeling about this. I didn't like the idea of Mack and Adam being alone in Adam's car. Of course, I wasn't sure who I was worried about exactly. Mack had at least three or four inches on Adam and a good fifty pounds. I knew how strong he was, and I had no doubt he was easily capable of defending himself against my husband's temper.

So maybe it was Adam I should be worried about. If the subject of my welfare came up, I was worried Mack might give Adam a black eye. Would he still be able to go to medical school if he had an assault charge against him? That could wreck his entire life. I never thought of Mack as being particularly hotheaded, but I could see how furious he was when I told him how Adam had been treating me. I could see the way he was looking at my husband.

Adam went upstairs to use the bathroom while Mack pulled on his heavy coat. He kept casting nervous looks in my direction.

"I'll stay if you want," he said in a low voice.

"Here?"

"I don't know." His eyes went back to the window, where the snow was falling heavily. "Maybe we could find a hotel or something. Or I can spend the night here. I just... I don't think I should leave, Vicky. I'm really worried about you."

"I'll be fine." I reached out to take his hand for a split second before Adam came back down. "I promise. Don't do anything stupid."

He opened his mouth to say something else, but it was too late. Adam was already coming down the steps. And before I knew it, the two of them were going out the door.

January 18, 2018

It's weird... I was expecting a big blowout fight with Adam when he got back from dropping off Mack, but instead it was just the opposite. He didn't even mention the fact that he discovered another man sitting on our sofa when he got home. And he was nice. He told me he was going to cook me dinner, since Irina wasn't around. And then he served it to me over candlelight.

The whole evening made me wonder if leaving him would be a mistake.

I want to talk it out with Mack. Unfortunately, we've been having trouble connecting. He sent me a text to let me know he was on the train back to the city, but nothing else since. I keep looking at my phone anxiously, waiting to hear from him. Of course, the second I get a text from him, I'll have to delete it immediately. I can't risk Adam seeing it.

But as nice as Adam is being lately, it doesn't change anything. I know who he is. His nice guy act is all temporary. Maybe he was worried I would cheat and now he feels like he has to win me over. But once he feels secure again, he'll go back to being who he was before. A cheating bastard with a horrible temper.

So this morning I sent Mack a text message: *Rent a car for next Friday.*

I've got less than a week to tell Adam I'm leaving him.

Chapter 48

There's a big storm coming. The first of the year.

I went to the grocery store this morning, and you would think the apocalypse is coming. When I tried to reach for the last loaf of bread, a woman almost elbowed me in the face. I let her have it. It's not worth having an elbow in the face over a loaf of bread.

Maggie is cleaning the kitchen when I get back to the house, working at twice her usual leisurely pace. "I want to get out of here before the snow starts," she says.

"Is it really going to be that bad?"

"Well, the forecast is calling for two feet of snow." She wipes down the counter. "So yes, it sounds like it's going to be bad. You guys are definitely going to lose power again."

And this time, I'm *definitely* not cuddling up with Adam. No chance of that.

"When is it going to start?" I ask.

Maggie glances down at her watch. "The forecast said by noon, the snow will start. By three or four, you'll probably be trapped here. At least, with your little car. Adam's BMW might do a little better, but by tonight, the roads will be a disaster."

I get an uneasy feeling. At least with the last storm, I knew that as soon as the rain stopped, the roads would be accessible again. The thought of being trapped in this house for days is unsettling to me. Especially after all the things I now know about Adam.

As if reading my mind, Maggie says, "You should come stay with me and Steve."

"What?"

She nudges me with her arm. "Come on. Our place gets plowed pretty quickly and doesn't lose power as easily. Our sofa is really comfortable. We can have a Netflix marathon. Do you like *BoJack Horseman*? We're addicted."

"I don't want to impose…"

"You won't be! Really, it will be fun."

I'd be lying if I said I wasn't tempted. Maggie's warm little apartment seems so inviting compared with this giant estate. I feel so isolated out here.

But I can't leave. Because if I do, Victoria will be all alone here with Adam. I can't do that to her.

"I'm sorry," I say. "I appreciate the offer, but I think I should stay here and help with Victoria."

She shrugs. "Okay, but I'll be here another couple of hours in case you change your mind."

As I put away the groceries, I look out the window at the lawn surrounding the house—soon it will be coated in a thick blanket of snow. I think of that night Mack came out to see Victoria here. It was snowing that night too. He told her he was going to come back for her, but he obviously never did.

Why didn't he come back for her? Or did he come back and she had changed her mind about leaving?

Or maybe something else happened before she could go.

I look out the window and see a single snowflake fall from the sky. It's begun.

CHAPTER 49

The snow is coming down hard by dinner time. When I look out the window, all I see is endless white. It's scary. Maggie is long gone. If I wanted to leave here, I wouldn't be able to. We're trapped.

Adam comes down to the kitchen while I'm preparing Victoria's dinner. He's got an arm full of blankets, which he deposits on the kitchen counter. "I brought these for you," he says. "You know, in case the heat goes out."

Who is he kidding? The heat is definitely going out.

"Thanks," I say.

Adam gingerly touches his right cheek. The scratches Victoria made with her fingernails have scabbed over. "Let me know when Victoria is ready for bed. I put the syringe with her medications on her dresser."

"Okay, no problem."

He taps his fingers against the counter. "Thanks for taking care of the medications. It's really important she gets them."

"Yes. I know."

"If she doesn't, she could have a seizure."

"Don't worry. I'll take care of it."

I shut down the food processor and scoop out the contents onto the plate. Adam watches me for a moment, then he walks away. He seems to trust me at least.

Even though I haven't given Victoria her medications in a week.

I climb the stairs with the plate of food. When I get there, Victoria is watching television, her right eye intently glued on the screen, even though her left is looking in a different direction. Even so, she seems much more alert than she did a week ago. She doesn't sleep all morning anymore. She's eaten her entire breakfast three days in a row. Long enough that I'm starting to feel guilty about the oatmeal.

"Good evening," I say as I step into the room.

Victoria's eyes instantly go to me. That's another change I've noticed. Before, when I spoke to her, she would take her sweet time looking in my direction. Now she seems hyper-aware of everything around her.

"Sylvie," she says.

That's another thing. She talks a lot more now. I wouldn't say she talks a *lot*. She still says one word or maybe two-word sentences, each of which is a struggle for her. But before, there would be entire days when she wouldn't say even one word, and half the time that word didn't make sense. Now she always has something to say.

It's very hard not to come to the conclusion that Adam has been drugging her. The only question is why.

"It's dinnertime!" I announce brightly.

Victoria looks at the plate of food and crinkles her nose. I can't entirely blame her. I put too many peas into this purée and it looks sort of like vomit. But it doesn't taste bad. I sampled it.

"It tastes better than it looks," I tell her.

She turns away from me, out the window. "Sun," she says.

"You see the sun?" I smile at her. "Because I sure don't."

She winces. "No. It's…"

"Snow."

She nods, relieved. "Yes. Snow."

I look out the window, watching the giant flakes fall. It's beautiful, but also frightening. "There's sure a lot of it."

She nods again. "Can't… stuck."

I laugh. "Yeah, I think we're stuck here together."

Her brows knit together. She looks up at my face and blurts out, "You have to get the gun, Sylvie."

I stare at her. It's the longest sentence I've ever heard her say. "Victoria…"

"Closet," she says. "Get it. Bring it… here."

"Victoria, I can't…"

Her blue eyes fill with tears. "Get it. Or he'll…"

I don't know what she's talking about. Even within the pages of her diary, she never described Adam being violent towards her. He never threatened her with a gun. That was what she said to Mack, anyway. There's no reason to think we are in any danger. Not unless Adam catches me poking around his bedroom.

"Let's just have some dinner, okay?" I say.

I see the frustration in Victoria's face. If she could, she would go get that gun herself. That much is obvious. But I'm not going to let anything happen to her.

And in a few days, the storm will be over.

CHAPTER 50

Victoria's Diary

January 22, 2018

I can't stop shaking.

At about ten in the morning, I was sitting on the sofa, watching television, when there was a knock at the door. It was a loud rap that made me jump in my seat. I didn't feel any better when I got to the door and saw a police officer standing there.

"Is this the Barnett residence?" the officer asked. He was in his forties with a craggy appearance. His hairline was receding, but it suited him.

My mouth was so dry that when I opened it, no sound came out. I cleared my throat. "Yes…"

"My name is Detective Patterson," the officer said. He didn't offer me his hand. "I'd like to ask you a couple of questions if you have a moment."

"Uh…" My heart was pounding so hard, I felt dizzy. Why was there a policeman at my door? It had to be some sort of mistake. I haven't committed any crimes. Have I? "Of course. Please come in."

Detective Patterson followed me into the apartment just as Adam was coming down the stairs. Even though I was about to have a heart attack, he seemed completely unperturbed by the fact that there was a policeman in our house. He flashed one of the smiles he uses when he's trying to charm someone. I know it so well by now.

"Officer!" he exclaimed. "Is there anything we can do to help you?"

Detective Patterson nodded. "We're trying to track down the whereabouts of a friend of yours, Mrs. Barnett."

I got this buzzing in the back of my head while the detective explained the details. It was about Mack. He didn't show up for work when he was supposed to for two days in a row. Mack a reliable guy and this was very unusual behavior for him. So one of his coworkers went to his apartment to check on him, but he wasn't home. Nobody has heard from him in five days.

Not since the night he came out to Long Island.

"A Carol Webber said that he came here to visit you, Mrs. Barnett," the detective said. "Did you see him that night?"

I glanced over at Adam. He still had that bland smile on his face. I couldn't read his expression at all. But there's nothing unusual about that.

"Yes," I said. "He was here."

Detective Patterson nodded. "What was the purpose of his visit?"

"Mack and my wife were coworkers and friends," Adam answered for me. "It was just a social visit."

"And when did he leave the house?"

"It was getting close to six," I said numbly. "Adam gave him a ride to the train station. Because of the snow."

The detective turned to Adam. "Did you see him get on the train?"

Adam shook his head. "He went to buy a ticket, but the train wasn't coming for a little while. He told me not to wait, so I drove home. The snow was getting pretty bad by then so I didn't want to risk getting stuck."

I hazarded a glance up at the detective. He didn't look the slightest bit suspicious. "It does look like Mack bought a train ticket with his credit card," he said. "But I'm not certain if he got on the train. I'm trying to get in contact with the ticket-taker from that night."

A thought occurred to me. "He sent me a text from the train. So he must've gotten on the train."

"Do you have the text on your phone?" the detective asked.

"I…" I bit my lip and glanced at Adam. "I deleted it."

I wasn't about to tell the detective that I deleted all my text messages from Mack as soon as I got them. For the first time, I saw a flicker of interest on the detective's face.

I wrung my hands together. "Do you think he's

okay?"

Detective Patterson hesitated. "I hope so. Hopefully, he just decided to take a trip and didn't tell anyone. It happens. But I'm concerned that he might've gotten attacked on the train or maybe even at the train station."

"You think so?" Adam raised his eyebrows. "Mack is a pretty big guy."

"He's big, but he's not bulletproof."

Bulletproof. At the detective's words, I thought back to the revolver hidden away in the top shelf of the closet. Before Adam gave Mack a ride to the train station, he disappeared for a short time. Was it possible that he...?

"Well." The detective heaved a sigh. "If you do hear anything from Mack, please let us know right away. His family is very worried."

I watched the detective walk out the front door. I felt like I was going to throw up. Adam drove Mack to the train station and nobody ever heard from him again. Yes, I got that text from him on the train. But how could I be sure he's the one who sent it?

Adam closed the door behind the detective. My stomach clenched as he locked it and threw the deadbolt. "Well," he said. "Looks like your buddy went missing."

"What did you do?" I croaked.

"Mack and I had a really interesting conversation in the car," Adam went on as if I hadn't spoken. "Seems he felt I wasn't treating you properly. I don't know where he got that idea. I tried to correct him, but he didn't seem that interested in listening. Not until the very end. But then, of course, it was too late."

I closed my eyes. *No. Please, no. Not Mack...*

"That police officer was right," Adam said. "He wasn't bulletproof."

I clasped my hand over my mouth. "You didn't..."

Adam smiled at me. It was the most horrible thing I had ever seen. I can't believe there was ever a time when I had found this man attractive.

"You monster!" I hissed. "How could you..."

"Oh, it was easy." He took a step towards me. "And you know what the best part is? Your fingerprints are all over the gun. *Your* gun, actually. It's registered in your name."

I remembered that day he took me out for target practice. He had been wearing leather gloves, while my hands were bare. He was right—my fingerprints are all over that gun.

"Don't worry," Adam said. "They won't find him so fast. Not unless you misbehave again."

Adam still had that smile on his lips. I wanted to scratch his eyes out. But as I stared at him, I realized I was totally and utterly trapped. I can't ever leave him. If I ever try, he's going to tell the police I'm a murderer.

I sunk onto the sofa, my hands trembling. I didn't dare look up at him.

"Do you understand me, Victoria?" he said.

I didn't say a word.

"Do. You. Understand. Me." There was a menacing edge to his voice. "Answer me, Victoria."

"Fuck you," I whispered.

It felt so good to finally say those words to him.

Quick as lightning, Adam reached out and seized my wrist. I had told Mack before that Adam had never laid a finger on me, but today that changed. I could feel the bruises blossoming on my forearm.

"Don't you *ever* make a fool of me like that again, Victoria," he hissed. "Or I promise you, you will live to regret it."

When he let me go, there were angry red marks on my wrist where his fingers had been. He stormed off and I heard a door slam behind him. I buried my face in my hands and sobbed like the world was ending.

Adam killed Mack. He murdered the only man who ever truly loved me, just because he tried to help me. And if I don't do exactly what he says, I will be next.

And the worst part is, I'm not even sure if I care anymore.

February 15, 2018

In the last few weeks, I've been in a trance. I haven't left the house in all that time, but to be fair, the snow is so bad that I don't think I could even if I wanted to. My Honda Civic isn't going anywhere in the snow.

My life is on autopilot. I lie in bed till nearly noon. When I finally drag myself out from between the sheets, I go straight to the couch and turn on the TV. I don't even know what I watch. It doesn't matter. I grab a bag of chips or cookies or whatever from the kitchen and shove them into my mouth one by one. I don't even taste it.

Nothing matters anymore. I'm just going to let myself rot on the sofa. Maybe if I make myself disgusting enough, Adam will leave me alone.

This morning, he came out to the living room to yell at me. He stood over me, his fists on his hips. "Look at what you're doing to yourself," he said. "Get off the couch. Take a shower, for God's sake."

I didn't budge.

"Victoria." I wouldn't even look up as he spoke to me. "Get up off the goddamn couch this minute. Do you hear me? Quit watching television. I want you to get cleaned up and put on some respectable clothing. You're an embarrassment."

I didn't say a word.

"Victoria!" He was shouting now. "Fucking answer me!"

When I didn't answer yet again, he reached for the heavy metal ashtray on the coffee table. For a moment, I was certain he was going to throw it at my head. I imagined the dent it would make in my skull. I imagined everything going black.

I welcomed it.

But instead, he hurled the ashtray at the television set. The screen smashed and the picture went black. He probably expected a reaction to that, but if he did, he was disappointed. I just kept on staring at the black screen. Adam watched me for a minute, then he gave up and stormed out of the room.

February 22, 2018

I spent the last two hours packing my bags.

After what Adam did to Mack, my entire life felt pointless. I couldn't think straight anymore. But in the last few hours, that fog has finally lifted. I've never been thinking more clearly than I am at this moment.

This morning, I took a pregnancy test. It was positive.

I don't know how long I've been pregnant. With everything else going on, I had stopped checking. I can't even remember the last time Adam and I have had sex. If I had to guess, I would say I'm three months along. In six months, I will have a baby.

I don't care what happens to me. But I can't let that monster get his hands on my baby. I can't let him destroy my child's life the way he's destroyed mine. If I'm going to be a mother, I have to protect this baby. And that means getting away from Adam Barnett. Forever.

I don't know where I'm going to go. I have no money. I had stashed my engagement ring in my jewelry box, hoping I could hock it, but it's gone. Adam probably took it. If he finds out I'm pregnant, I'm not sure he'll let me leave. So it has to be now, before I'm showing.

Maybe Carol will take me in. Maybe I could find some sort of shelter for victims of domestic abuse. My boss at the hospital said I could come back anytime, so once I get my job back, I'll at least have some cash coming in. I'll be able to afford a place to live. And hopefully afford some childcare when the baby comes.

It's ironic. I started this diary to tell the story to my future children of how I met their father. And now I'm telling the story of how I left him, for the sake of my future child.

I don't care what I have to do. I'm going to protect this baby. That's why no matter what, I need to get out of this house. I need to get away from Adam. The snow has finally cleared away enough that I could get out of here in my little Civic.

To my future child: if you are reading this, I did it all for you.

I'm leaving your father. Tonight.

CHAPTER 51

I can't stop shaking.

The power went off an hour ago and I've been using a flashlight to read the end of Victoria's diary. Because it is now over. Her last entry was about how she was going to tell Adam she was leaving him. At some point between writing that entry and now, she fell down the stairs and nearly died.

The heat is off too. I'm buried under three blankets, but I still shiver. It's cold in here. When I look out the window, all I can see is white.

We'll be stuck here for days.

I'm trapped in this house. Trapped with Adam, who is a psychopath with a gun. I should have listened to Victoria. I should have taken it while I had the chance.

No wonder that woman at Mercy Hospital never heard of Mack. He went missing nearly a year ago.

What if Adam finds out I haven't been giving Victoria her medications? What will he do to me? Especially now that we're all alone here, with no witnesses.

Suddenly, I feel stifled by the blankets on my bed. And I have to pee badly. After a moment of contemplation, I push the covers away and slip out of the bedroom, still holding my flashlight

The hallway looks endless by the light of the flashlight. The floorboards creak beneath my feet with each step. I hug my body for warmth as I walk down the hallway. God, it's cold. It's like the wind goes right through this house. I hold my breath as I pass Adam's room and…

The door is open. And the room is completely black.

I shine the flashlight inside the room. The bed is empty. I hear a creak above me and realize he must be up in the attic. He must still be working in his office up there.

That means I could search his closet.

I shouldn't though. Adam has been nothing but kind to me during the time I've worked here. If he finds me rifling around his things, God knows what he'll do. It's better to just cross my fingers and hope the storm passes without incident.

You have to get the gun, Sylvie.

I could hear the urgency in Victoria's voice. Does she know something that I don't? Maybe the storm is an opportunity for him. Maybe he's been waiting to be alone with her. Of course, he's not entirely alone with her. I'm here too.

I have no idea what he plans to do. I only know he's killed someone once before.

I take a deep breath and enter Adam's bedroom. His closet is the one on the left-hand side—it's much smaller than Victoria's closet. I should have a much easier time finding things in here. I take one last look out the door to make sure the coast is clear and turn the doorknob to the closet.

It's a completely normal closet, but any closet looks ominous by flashlight. He's got a row of suits hung up and some dress shirts. He has a row of shoes neatly lined up at the bottom of the closet. I don't see anything down there that looks remotely like a gun. I shined my flashlight all over the bottom of the closet, searching.

But he wouldn't put it at the bottom of the closet. He'd put it at the top, wouldn't he? So there would be no chance somebody in a wheelchair could get to it.

I aim the flashlight at the top of the closet. I see a shoebox up there.

I grab the shoebox. I shove the flashlight under my armpit and rip it open. And there it is, lying nestled in the white paper. A revolver.

There's a loud creak from above, and I almost drop the shoebox. A second later, I hear footsteps. And the footsteps are getting louder.

Oh my God. He's on the stairs.

If he sees me with this shoebox, I don't know what he'll do. Yes, I'm the one with the gun, but I don't know how to fire it. Much like Victoria, I've never held a gun in my hand. He could pluck it right out of my hand and kill me with it before I could say boo.

The footsteps stop for a moment. He's at the bottom of the stairs. He's on this floor.

I rip the gun out of the box and stick it into my waistband. By some miracle, it doesn't go off and blow a hole in my foot. My hands are shaking like crazy as I close the cover of the box and shove it back into the closet. I pull my shirt down over the gun just as the door to the bedroom swings open.

Adam has a flashlight of his own and I shield my eyes from the glare of it as he enters his room. When my eyes have a second to adjust, I realize he's doing the same thing.

"Sylvia?" He sounds baffled. "What are you doing here?"

"I…" I'm stealing your gun. "I was looking for another blanket. It's freezing in my room."

Wow. Good job thinking on the fly.

"Yeah, it's really cold." He shivers. "Sorry about that. I'll go get you another blanket. They're actually in the hall closet."

No kidding.

Adam retrieves another blanket for me and sends me on my way. I return to my bedroom, but I can't sleep. First of all, I've got a gun stuck in my waistband and no idea where I should put it. The door to my room doesn't even lock. If Adam notices the gun is missing and finds it in my room, I'm scared of what will happen.

I need to ask Victoria what to do.

I wait long enough that I assume Adam must be in bed. Then I tiptoe out of my room and into hers next-door. A few weeks ago, Victoria would have been dead to the world at this hour. But since I stopped giving her those medications, she's much more awake at night. When I come into her bedroom, she's in bed but her eyes are wide open. I shut the door behind me so that nobody can hear us.

"I got it," I tell her. I only realize now that my voice is shaking. "I got the gun from his closet."

I raise the waistband of my pants and shine a light on it so she can see. Once again, I catch that glimmer of a smile on her lips.

"I don't know what to do with it now though," I say.

"My…" I follow the direction that Victoria is pointing with her shaky left hand. She's pointing at her closet. "T… tunk."

I shine my light into Victoria's closet. Sure enough, there's a trunk on the ground. It has a combination lock on it, but it's unlocked.

I open up the trunk and find some clothing inside. I stuff the gun inside a shirt and push the shirt back into the trunk. I close it but hesitate before snapping the combination lock into place. "Do you know the combination?"

"Nine… Five… six."

I look back at her face. This is a woman who had a severe head injury. Am I really trusting her to remember a three-digit lock combination? "Are you sure?"

"Yes."

Well, what's the worst that could happen? If she remembered the combination incorrectly, then at least nobody will be able to get the gun. Unless…

"Does Adam know the combination?"

Victoria snorts. "No."

I straighten up, taking one last look at the trunk on the ground. I hope I did the right thing. I hope Adam doesn't discover the missing gun and go completely crazy.

I look back up at Victoria, who still has that smile on her face. I guess she's relieved. I don't blame her, after what she's been through.

"Good night, Victoria," I say.

"Good night, Sylvie."

CHAPTER 52

After leaving Victoria's room, I go straight to the bathroom and open up the closet. I find that black plastic bag of medications and search through it until I find the Valium. I wrench open the bottle and swallow two of them dry. I've never had that medication before, so I'm guessing two will be enough to knock me out.

That's when I notice my phone is ringing within my pocket. My service has been down for hours, but now it's back, at least for the moment. I pull my phone out of my pocket and look at the number. I don't recognize it.

It must be Freddy.

Ordinarily, I would let any calls from Freddy go to voicemail. But something makes me put pick it up.

"Sylvie!" He sounds thrilled and shocked that I picked up. "Are you okay? How are you holding up in the storm?"

I can't even begin to describe what's been going on here. I'm not even going to try. "It's fine."

"You sound funny."

I walk down the hall to my bedroom and close the door behind me. "I don't sound funny."

"You do. Are you sure you're okay? Do you need me to come out there?"

Yes! I realize at this moment that I desperately want him here. The only person I've ever been close to in the last seven years is this man. Why did I send him away? Why have I been so angry at him when he didn't even do anything wrong aside from doing what I told him to do? Everything has been my fault, not his. I *need* Freddy.

But I can't say all that to him now. And I certainly don't want to make him drive out here in the middle of a blizzard. "That's okay."

"Are you sure? I think I should come."

I lie down on my bed and shut my eyes, waiting for the Valium to take effect. "I'm fine. I don't need you here."

"That's what you said last time."

 He'll never forgive himself for that. I told him I could face my father alone and he let me do it. And because of that, our lives were changed forever. "This time I mean it though."

He's quiet for a long time on the other line. I remember how in high school he used to call me before bed and sometimes we would just stay on the phone together until we both fell asleep.

"If you need me there," he says. "Just call me. I'll be there in an hour."

"That's not physically possible."

"I'll find a way."

I'm starting to feel drowsy. It's a nice sensation. Sort of like floating. "Freddy?"

"Yes?" His voice sounds far away.

"If we had a child now, what do you think it would be like?"

Anyone else would think I was out of my mind, but Freddy doesn't. I bet he wondered the same thing. "Well," he says thoughtfully. "It would be a girl, like you. And she would have blue eyes like you, but dark hair like me." I pull the covers over me as I shiver. "Her favorite food would be pizza and her favorite animal would be unicorns."

"Unicorns aren't a real animal."

"Sure they are. That's what she would say, anyway."

Freddy keeps talking. Telling me all about the child we would've had if I had let him stay with me that night. Eventually, my eyes drift shut and I doze off while listening to his voice.

CHAPTER 53

It's still snowing in the morning. I don't know how that's possible. How is there still snow in the sky? It seems like all precipitation in the universe is sitting right in our yard. There's so much snow, I don't even think we could open the front door.

Our power is still out, and so is the heat. I've been walking around the house, trying to get a signal on my phone again. So far, no luck.

When I come down to the kitchen to make some breakfast for Victoria, I'm bundled up in my warmest clothes and a pair of boots for good measure. I'm still freezing. When Adam comes down to the kitchen wearing equally warm clothing, a chill goes through me. But it's not from the cold.

"Victoria is out of bed," he tells me. "I bundled her up as much as I could and put some blankets on her lap." He rubs his arms. "I'm sorry it's so damn cold in here."

"It's okay. Not your fault." I empty a container of

baby food onto a plate because I can't heat the oatmeal. I wonder if now that Victoria is more alert, maybe she could handle something more solid. Of course, I can't ask him that. "I've almost got her breakfast ready."

"Thanks, Sylvie." He smiles at me. "I'm grateful for your help. I don't know what we would do without you."

But there's something a little off about his smile. Is there a chance he knows I took the gun from his room? He couldn't possibly. Well anyway, he can't get it back.

Not unless he knows the combination to that trunk.

I swallow. "That's what I'm here for." I glance out the window. "Do you have any idea when the snow will stop?"

He shrugs. "It's supposed to keep going all day today. We're probably stuck here at least another two days. Why? You got somewhere to go?"

There's a teasing tone in his voice, but again, I feel uneasy. I don't like the idea of being trapped here with him for two days. And if I need the police, there's nothing I could do. We have no phone service.

Without answering his question, I push past him and head up the stairs to Victoria's bedroom. The door is open and I see her sitting in her wheelchair, bundled up in a heavy sweater and three blankets over her body.

"Cold, huh?" I comment.

She immediately looks up at me. "Heat... out?"

I nod. "Yes. But don't worry, we'll keep you bundled up."

My eyes fall on the closet, where I stashed away the

gun last night. Did I really steal a gun from Adam's closet last night? It doesn't sound like something I would do.

"Do you think he knows we took it?" I blurt out.

Victoria raises an eyebrow at me. "*You* took it."

"Right, but…" I look down at the trunk in the closet again. Maybe I shouldn't have put it in there. Maybe I should have kept it in my room. "Anyway, do you want breakfast?"

She regards the plate of food I'm holding. "What?"

"Apple purée. And peach cobbler."

Victoria makes a face, and I can't say I blame her. The apple purée doesn't look particularly appetizing, and the only thing about the peach cobbler that resembles an actual peach cobbler is that it is roughly peach colored. I tried it once and it was pretty disgusting.

"I'm sorry," I feel compelled to say.

"Not… your…" Victoria frowns, searching for the word.

"Fault?"

She nods quickly. "Yes. Fault."

Despite how gross the meal is, she agrees to eat it. For the first time though, she's able to feed almost the entire meal to herself. Usually her left hand is very shaky and she loses interest quickly in the food, but this time she scoops puréed apple quickly into her mouth and is done within five minutes.

She seems better. I should be happy. But everything in this house is giving me a horrible feeling, like I should run away and never come back.

Unfortunately, that's not possible. I'm trapped here. At least until all this damn snow is gone.

CHAPTER 54

There isn't much to do in this house.

There's no Internet and no television. So I find a book downstairs in one of the many bookcases and read to Victoria most of the morning. Then after lunch, we do the same thing, but by around mid-afternoon, her head is sagging to the side and she seems to be falling asleep. I feel like doing the same. Between the cold and the lack of stimulation, I'm exhausted.

I leave Victoria in her chair and head back to my bedroom. Just as I get there, my phone starts ringing in my pocket, and I almost yelp in surprise. I've had no phone service all day. I'm excited to finally get it back. I pull out the phone and see Maggie's name on the screen. She must be checking up on me.

"Sylvie!" she cries. "You guys got phone service back!"

"Only just now. And it probably won't last."

"I just wanted to see how you were doing. Is everything okay over there?"

I can't even begin to describe to her how terrified I've been. "Yeah. Fine."

"I have to confess, Sylvie." Maggie lowers her voice a notch. "I spent the night there once during a storm a long time ago, and it was… I mean, by the time I was able to leave, I was ready to run screaming. The fights the two of them had… It was intense. Obviously they don't fight anymore, but it's hard to forget what it used to be like."

I look up to make sure the door to my room is closed. "I heard Adam would throw things."

"Adam?" She laughs. "No—you got it wrong. Adam would *dodge* things. Victoria was the one who would throw things. It was like she was *possessed*."

I frown. "What are you talking about?"

"Sylvia," Maggie says quietly. "You know Victoria was…"

I squeeze the phone in my fist. "Was *what*?"

She hesitates. "She's crazy."

What?

"Not just crazy." Maggie takes a breath. "She's dangerous."

CHAPTER 55

What? What is Maggie talking about? Victoria isn't crazy. *Adam* is crazy. Victoria was the victim in all this. Maggie is the one who's got it all wrong.

"What do you mean?" I ask carefully.

"Oh God," Maggie moans. "I shouldn't tell you this, but… well, where do I begin? She was always starting these horrible fights with him. She would scream at him at the top of her lungs. I saw her throw a freaking toaster in his head and it made a dent in the kitchen wall. Can you believe that?"

I picture the dent in the wall of the kitchen downstairs. But no. *Adam* did that. When he threw a plate at the wall.

"She… she did?"

"Yes!" I can picture Maggie's wide eyes. "She was intensely jealous of the cook, Irina Brunner. Half the fights they had were over her. She would call Irina a whore and accuse him of sleeping with her. I don't know if they were sleeping together or not—I don't think so—but she would be jealous of any woman he spoke to. I tried to dress as dowdy as possible and just stay out of her way, because I didn't want to arouse any jealousy on her part."

"But…" I think back to more details from the diary. "She couldn't have been that crazy. I mean, she worked as a nurse practitioner in a busy emergency room."

"Yeah. Until they fired her."

"They… fired her?"

"It's something I used to hear the two of them fighting about. She blamed him for losing her job, but it's pretty clear they let her go because she was so nuts. And she couldn't get anyone else to hire her because of what happened there. Apparently, she was really unprofessional and used to have temper tantrums where she would throw things."

Oh my God, could that be true? No. Maggie has to be mistaken…

"And the worst part…" I hear Maggie's voice waver. "One day, she brought home a gun. Like, an actual *gun*. With bullets and everything. Adam was so freaked out. He was begging her to get rid of it, but she kept saying they needed it for protection." She pauses. "I'm hoping after her accident, he got that gun away from her."

He did. And I just gave it back.

"And then there was this one night when they were having a particularly brutal fight," she says, "and Irina didn't come in the next day to work even though she was supposed to. A few days later, the police showed up asking about her. It was so scary."

"What…" My voice can't seem to get out the next words. I have to swallow before I can speak again. "What are you saying?"

Maggie's voice is hushed. "I swear to God, Sylvia, I think Victoria might have killed Irina."

No. No no no…

"I was going to go to the police myself and tell them what I knew," she says softly. "But then Victoria was in that accident and… well, there was no point after that. I figured we'd probably never find out what really happened to Irina."

My head is buzzing. My breaths are coming quickly, and I hug my knees to my chest. "Maggie, I gotta go."

"Are you okay, Sylvia? You sound funny."

"I gotta go. Now."

Without waiting for a response, I hang up the phone. My fingers are tingling and I feel like I'm about to have a panic attack. With shaking hands, I type into the search engine of my phone:

Irina Brunner. Long Island. Disappearance.

Immediately, a bunch of hits come up. It's true. It's all true. Back in February, twenty-two-year-old Irina Brunner disappeared without a trace.

Mack wasn't the one who disappeared. It was Irina. Who knows if Mack even existed. Probably not. He was probably all a figment of her wild imagination.

And I just gave Victoria back the gun that killed Irina. And stopped giving her the antipsychotics that had been part of her daily medication regimen.

I've got to get that gun back. Before something terrible happens.

CHAPTER 56

Victoria is asleep. I saw her nod off myself. All I need to do is slip into her room, open up the trunk, and take back the gun. Very easy.

I take off my boots and creep over to Victoria's bedroom in my stockinged feet. I had left the door open, and she's still dozing when I peek inside the room. The trunk is about two feet away from her. Is it possible to get over there, open it up, and take out the gun without her knowing it?

And even if I do wake her up, does it matter? Half her body is paralyzed. She won't be able to stop me.

I tiptoe over to the trunk and kneel beside it. I turn the numbers to the combination Victoria said. Nine. Five. Six.

The lock doesn't open.

"Sylvie?"

I jerked my head up at the sound of Victoria's voice. She's staring down at me while I fumble with the lock. I straighten up and plaster a smile on my face. "I just wanted to…" I clear my throat. "I thought maybe my room would be a safer hiding place for the gun."

She shakes her head. "Safe. There safe."

"Right." I scratch at my head. "Also, did you say the combination was nine, five, six? Because that doesn't seem to work."

She narrows her good eye at me. I'm not fooling her. Even with a brain injury, Victoria is not a stupid woman. She knows exactly what I'm trying to do.

"Sorry," is all she says.

"Do you think the trunk might be safer in my room?"

Her eyes are stony. "No."

I realize now who I'm looking at. I'm looking at a murderess. I'm looking at a woman who killed another woman because she believed that woman was having an affair with her husband. I'm looking at a woman who wrote down the world as she believed it to be in her diary, but it was all lies—and she got me to believe those lies to get what she wanted. I'm looking at a woman with a history of crazy paranoid behavior, who has not been getting her medications thanks to me.

And also, she knows I slept with her husband.

I look out the window. The sun has already fallen in the sky, but the snow is still coming down. I'm never getting out of here.

Victoria isn't dangerous anymore though. Not like this. The gun gives her a little bit more power, but I don't see how she could even get it out of that trunk with her shaky left hand. Although she did so much better with breakfast this morning…

"Anyway," I say brightly. "I'm going to start on your dinner."

She looks at me for a moment. "No baby food."

I don't know what I could feed her besides baby food since we have no power. But it doesn't matter. Because I'm not going to start on her dinner.

I'm going to find Adam. I've got to tell him what I've done.

Chapter 57

It's easier to find Adam than I thought. He's in his bedroom. He's got his flashlight on and he seems to be ripping apart his room. When he sees me at the door, he looks like he's about to jump out of his skin.

"Sylvia!" he cries. "Come in here a minute."

I step into the room, and before I can say anything, he shuts the door behind me. Even with the dim light of the flashlight, I can see how freaked out he looks. I can take a guess at why.

"Sylvia," he says in a low voice. "Do you... do you have any idea..." He rakes a hand through his hair. "Look, I've got to tell you something."

I can't stand another revelation right now. "Okay..."

"The thing is..." His eyes dart around the room. "There was a gun in my closet. I'm sorry I didn't tell you before. It was Victoria's and I never used it. Well, once I did—she made us go out and practice firing it. But it was hers. And after her accident, I just put it up in the closet."

He takes a shaky breath. "And now it's gone."

This is my cue to tell him everything. But the words are stuck in my throat. "Oh…"

"This probably sounds nuts to you," he mumbles. "I know. Half of what happened when I was married to Victoria seemed nuts to me. I thought she'd be better out here on the island, but it just got worse…"

"What got worse?"

"The paranoia." He sinks against the bed. "She was so insanely jealous. When I told the doctor about it in rehabilitation after her accident, he thought she might've been an undiagnosed paranoid schizophrenic."

Oh my God. "He did?"

"Well, in retrospect, it fit." He sighs. "He gave me this antipsychotic medication to try on her. So she's been getting that since the hospital, but it's hard to know if it works considering… well, how she is now. And it's kind of too late anyway."

And also, she's not getting it anymore. But we don't need to mention that part.

"The night of her accident…" He shakes his head. "I thought after she got pregnant, things might change. Maybe she'd trust me more. But nothing changed. Just the opposite—she was more paranoid than ever."

I don't know if I want to hear the rest of this.

Adam squeezes his fists together. "Then one night, when she was at the end of her first trimester, she just *lost* it. She started threatening me with her gun. Telling me she was going to kill me for cheating on her. I thought for sure she was going to pull the trigger, so when I saw a chance..." He lifts his green eyes, which look black in the dim light of the room. "We were at the top of the stairs. So... I pushed her."

He buries his face in his hands. I can't even imagine how horrible he must feel about the whole thing. He killed his unborn child. He nearly killed his wife.

"Please believe me," he says. "I wouldn't have done it if there were any other way. I thought about just letting her kill me. After everything I've been through with her, it almost didn't seem so bad..."

I sit beside him on the bed. "It wasn't your fault."

"Of course it was my fault," he insists. "I should've tried harder to get her help after she got fired from the hospital. I should have insisted. I could have..."

My heart is pounding in my chest. "Adam, I'm the one who took the gun."

Instead of looking angry, he just looks relieved. "You did? Why?"

"It's a long story, but... You can have it back. I think it's safer with you."

There are a hundred questions in his eyes, but he just nods. "Okay. Where is it?"

"It's in a trunk in Victoria's room."

"*What*?" He stands up abruptly. "It's in *Victoria's* room? What the hell is it doing in there?"

"Relax." I stand up and try to reach for his arm but he

shrugs me off. "It's safe there. Victoria is not going to get at it. She's paralyzed in half her body."

He turns to stare at me. "You don't know Victoria the way I do. You have no idea what she's capable of."

He crosses the room and yanks open the door to his bedroom. I expect him to dart down the hall, but instead, he freezes. I start to ask what's wrong, but then I see for myself.

Victoria is sitting in her wheelchair, right in front of his door.

And she's holding the gun.

Chapter 58

I don't know how she did it. A couple of weeks ago, she could barely keep her eyes open for more than twenty minutes. But after I left Victoria's room she got the gun from that trunk and wheeled herself down the hallway. She can't move her right hand, which is still motionless in the armrest, so it looks like she moved her chair using her left hand and her left foot to push herself down the hall.

She has a flashlight balanced in her lap, which makes the shadows on her face look almost ghoulish. Her right eye is pinned on Adam. The left one is gazing off somewhere else, but the right is like ice. I never want anyone to look at me the way she's looking at him.

Adam takes a step back and raises his hands in the air. "Victoria…"

"Don't." She shakes the gun with her left hand. It's surprisingly steady, considering her left hand is often shaky. I remember how steady she was when she fed herself breakfast this morning. Being off those medications really made a difference. "You… you…" She struggles to find the right words. But then she does: "I'm going to kill you."

Adam's eyes widen. "Please, Victoria." He sounds like he's choking. "Don't do this."

She snorts.

"I love you." He lowers his hands and puts them together, pleading. "Victoria, sweetheart. You know how I feel about you. Please don't do this…"

The gun doesn't budge from her hand. "Irina…"

"Nothing happened between me and Irina." His voice is slow and careful. "I swear to you, Vicky. Nothing happened."

"Bullshit!" Some drool leaks out of the right side of her mouth. "That's… bullshit. You and her…"

"No…"

"And… *her*!" Now suddenly, the gun is pointed at me. I had been trying to be inconspicuous. So much for that. "I know."

Oh God, Victoria is going to kill me. After she kills Adam, I'm next. Or maybe I'll be first. I don't know about the order, but it doesn't matter. Either way, I'm toast.

This is how it's going to end. I'm going to be murdered by a crazy woman in her own home.

Adam glances back at me. He hangs his head. "Victoria, I'm so sorry. I swear, I'll make it up to you— anything you want. Tell me what you want."

Thankfully, she pointed the gun away from me—for

now. She stares straight at him. "I want... you." His face brightens only momentarily and then she adds: "Dead."

She's going to kill him. She's really going to kill him.

He knows it. All the color drains out of his face. He looks like he's about to start crying. "Victoria, please... don't do this."

But she's not going to change her mind. I can see it in her eyes.

And then she pulls the trigger.

The gunshot is surprisingly loud. So loud that I am momentarily disoriented. But not as much as Victoria, whose entire wheelchair jerks back. I look over at Adam, who is still on his feet. He's not dead. I'm not even sure she hit him with the bullet. He looks behind him and we both see the defect in the wallpaper of the hallway.

The flashlight rolled out of Victoria's lap when she shot the gun. She's struggling to right herself. This is my only shot. If I don't do something now, she's going to kill Adam with the next bullet. And then me next.

So I lunge at her.

It was too dark to realize this, but she was only about a foot away from the staircase. So when I jump at her, her chair wheels backward and the back wheels slip on the steps. She realizes it's happening a second before I do and lets out an anguished scream.

And together, we go down.

Chapter 59

I'm at the bottom of the steps.

My head hurts. I think I bumped it on something way down. Maybe a step or two. My shoulder aches also. I haven't even tried to move from the ground and two things already hurt me. I'm scared to see what else will hurt when I try to get up. *If* I get up. Victoria fell down these same steps a year ago and never got up.

"Sylvia!" It's Adam's voice. "Sylvia, are you all right?"

He's asking me, not Victoria, even though she took the same spill I did down the steps. I muster up all my strength and sit up. The world spins around me for a moment, but then it goes still again. My head throbs.

"Sylvia." Adam is kneeling beside me, his green eyes wide. "Are you okay? Say something."

"Something," I say.

Adam tilts his head to look at something behind me. He clasps his hand over his mouth. His complexion turns green. "Jesus Christ."

I follow his gaze to where Victoria is lying on the ground, a few feet away from her wheelchair. Nobody's neck should be bent at that angle. Her eyes are slightly open, staring at nothing.

"I... I think she's dead," I say.

That's an understatement. She's obviously dead. She's the most dead person I've ever seen in my entire life.

"Oh, Jesus." Adam buries his face in his hands. "Victoria..."

"Adam." I wince at a sharp jab of pain at the back of my neck. It occurs to me that after a bad accident, you're not supposed to move because of a possible neck injury. Oh well, too late for that. "She was going to kill you."

He crawls on the floor until he's next to her. He leans over her body, and his eyes fill with tears. "I'm so sorry, Victoria," he whispers.

He wraps his arms around her limp body and my own eyes fill with tears. Yes, Victoria was not a good person. She was insanely jealous. She was violent. She was probably a murderess. But he loved her anyway.

"We've got to call the police," I say gently.

Adam sits up slowly, although he still has Victoria's limp hand clasped in his. "You can't tell them what she tried to do."

"Adam..."

"No, Sylvia. I don't want her to be remembered that way."

I glance over at the gun, which came out of Victoria's

hand during the fall and is lying on the floor a few feet away from us. That gun came so close to ending both our lives. "How are we going to explain *that*?"

"I'll hide it away somewhere. Nobody needs to know." He cups his hand over Victoria's white cheek. "*Please, Sylvia.*"

As much as I hate the idea of lying to the police, I see his point. It won't help anyone to know that Victoria threatened us both at gunpoint. And this is very important to him.

"Okay," I say. "I won't tell anyone."

CHAPTER 60

Because of the snow, it takes hours for the police to get to us. Thankfully, the snow does eventually stop falling and a plow is able to make a path to the house for the police and an ambulance to come. It's way too late for Victoria though. An ambulance isn't going to be able to help her.

I gave the police a statement. The power was out because of the storm and we couldn't see anything, so Victoria and I accidentally stumbled down the stairs when I was taking her to the bathroom. I survived the fall—she didn't. Adam and I agreed it was best to keep the story simple.

The police believed our story. I had been terrified they would be skeptical and ask a lot of questions and maybe ask me to come down to the station for further questioning, but they didn't do that. Maybe part of it was because Victoria was so ill beforehand. Maybe they thought her life wasn't worth much. But I disagree with that.

After the police were done with me, a paramedic named Drew examined me on the sofa. He acted like I was badly hurt, which I wasn't really, given I fell down the whole flight of stairs, and he's being very annoying about insisting I come with him to the hospital.

"You have a concussion, at the least," he says.

"No, I don't."

He gives me a look. "You fell down a flight of stairs. You need to get a CAT scan of your head."

My head is still aching. There's a huge lump developing on my forehead, but I don't want to go to the hospital. "I'm okay."

"Come on," Drew says. "It's hard enough to see what happened to Vicky. I don't want to leave here without having you fully evaluated."

I look up at him, surprised at how casually he used her nickname. Then I look over at Adam, who is still talking to the police. They look like they're wrapping things up and he walks them over to the open front door.

"Did you know Victoria before?" I ask him.

"Sure." He shakes his head sadly. "I used to see her all the time when I worked back in the city. I used to sometimes do shifts with this guy named Mack and he would always bring patients to Mercy Hospital—that's where she worked. I would tease Mack that it was because he had a crush on her and wanted an excuse to see her."

What?

"Mack?" My tongue feels numb. "You worked with

another paramedic named Mack?"

"Well, sort of." Drew toys with the stethoscope around his neck. "His name was actually Glen MacNeil, but everybody called him Mack. Why? Did you know him?"

I feel dizzy. I don't know if it's from what he's telling me or from the concussion. Maybe I really should go to the hospital. "This guy, MacNeil... Do you still keep in touch with him?"

Drew frowns. "That's the thing. Not that long after Vicky left, Mack just kind of... disappeared. Nobody knew what happened to him. And then right after, Vicky had the accident. A lot of bad luck right at once." He pauses. "Hey, are you okay, Miss Robinson? You look like you're going to be sick."

"Yes," I gasp. "I'm okay. I'm fine."

He squints at me. "I really think I should take you to the hospital."

"No. Please." The last thing I want right now is to be in the hospital. I don't want to think about anything that just happened. I don't want a bunch of doctors and nurses asking me questions. I can't take that right now.

Drew argues with me for a few more minutes, but then Adam comes back into the house. He looks as tired as I feel. He furrows his brow when he sees us together. "What's going on?"

"She had a bad bump on the head." Drew is appealing to Adam now. "She needs to go to the hospital, but she's refusing to go."

Adam frowns. "Are you feeling okay?"

"I'm fine," I insist. I look him in the eyes. "I swear. I don't want to go to the hospital."

Adam looks at me thoughtfully. "I think she's okay. I'll keep an eye on her tonight."

I wonder if I'm making a mistake. I wonder if this is my only chance to escape this place, and I'm giving it up. The truth is, I'm not sure what to believe anymore.

Drew looks between the two of us then lets out a sigh. "Fine. But if she starts getting lethargic or anything else worrisome, call 911."

I walk Drew to the door, just to make sure he leaves. The snow has nearly stopped, but the visibility is horrible outside. I'm probably safer here than driving around, even in an ambulance. It's not like an ambulance is immune to accidents.

"God, there's a lot of snow out here," he says.

He's right. As far as I can see, there's nothing but snow, aside from the lone path that's been plowed for the ambulance and the police car to get to us. There's a path to get out now, but not for me—the Honda I've been using is completely buried.

"Even your shed is buried," he comments.

"Yeah," I say, noticing the white mound that used to be the shed where we keep the gardening supplies. I can still see the door, but not much else.

Drew gives me one last long look. "You swear you're

going to be okay?"

"I swear," I lie.

And then he leaves. He gets in the ambulance and I watch him drive off.

I should go back inside the house now. It's absolutely freezing outside and I don't want to get frostbite, although the house isn't much better. All I want to do is lie down and sleep for the next twenty-four hours. My bed is calling to me.

But I can't seem to move. Something is tugging at my memory. Something Drew said to me.

The shed.

My heart is suddenly pounding in my chest. I can hear Victoria's voice in my ear:

Glen Head.

She kept saying it over and over. Except her voice was so slurred. I assumed that she was talking about the village in Oyster Bay, because I had recently seen it on a map. But now I realize what she was actually saying.

Glen shed.

Mack's real name wasn't Mack. It was Glen MacNeil. He disappeared almost a year ago and nobody was able to find him. And repeatedly, Victoria kept saying Glen shed.

I've got to get out to that shed. I need to know if I'm going crazy or if everything Victoria said was true.

I go back into the house. I don't see Adam—he must have gone upstairs. Thank God, because I don't know how I'm going to explain to him that I'm going outside in this mess of a storm. I put on my boots, a hat, and my coat, but I don't think it's going to be enough. But what else can I do?

It's got to be twenty degrees out. The wind slaps me in the face. It's only about thirty feet to the shed, but it feels like thirty miles. With each step, my legs sink deeper into the white powder. The snow comes up to the top of my thigh. It feels like it will take me an hour to walk these thirty feet, but I push myself to keep going.

Come on, Sylvia. You can do this. Just a little further.

By the time I reach the door of the shed, I am badly out of breath. The wood is coated in snow, but I can still see the splintered area where the bullet pierced the wall. Thank God it looks like the door opens into the house rather than out. I reach for the handle on the door, but it won't budge. It must be frozen.

I put both hands on the handle and push down with all my strength. Finally, it gives and I'm able to push the door open. I practically fall into the shed and a couple of gallons of snow come in after me. There's no chance of closing the door again. I'm not even going to try.

I've never bothered to go in here before. Adam told me the shed was used to store gardening supplies and hinted that it might not be safe. Maybe something will fall on me. I had no desire to see a couple of hoes or rakes, so I left the shed alone.

For the most part, he described the shed accurately. It looks like it's entirely gardening supplies. Rakes, a weedwhacker, something that looks like a lawnmower. It's a pretty innocent shed. Nothing remarkable. Certainly no dead bodies in here.

Maybe Victoria wasn't talking about the shed after all. Or if she was, maybe she was crazy and not making any sense. That's what I'd like to believe at this point. Considering she's dead and all. Because if everything in the diary was true after all, I should have let her kill Adam.

And then I see the trap door on the ground. Why would a shed have a trap door?

There's a padlock on it. I kick at it with my foot and it makes a loud clang. I bend down to get a closer look at the lock to figure out if there's a way to open it and...

Oh my God.

The smell coming from beneath the trap door is unbelievable. I couldn't detect it when I was standing, but with my nose close to the ground, it's unmistakable. It's the smell of decay. And Adam must know about it because he has been in the shed. He raked all the leaves, after all.

It's true. It's all true. Somebody's body is in this shed and it's rotting as we speak.

"What do you think you're doing?"

I straighten up, twisting my head around, which sets off a jab of pain in my temple. God, my head hurts—I should have gone to the hospital. But instead, I stayed here, like a fool. Because I wanted to know the truth.

Anyway, I don't need to look to see who's standing behind me. Only one other human being is out here tonight.

It's Adam.

CHAPTER 61

He followed me out here. He must have seen me leave the house and then came after me. And because of the wind and the darkness, I didn't even know he was behind me. Why didn't I look behind me?

I take a step back. He doesn't know how much I know. He thinks I'm still on his side. Maybe I could fake my way out of this

But then, by the dim light from the lone window in the shed, I see the look in his eyes.

"You lied to me," I blurt out. "You killed Mack. You said you didn't even know who he was."

"Yeah, well." Adam's eyes never leave my face. "MacNeil deserved to die. He was fucking my wife."

"You don't know that."

"Don't tell me what I know." Something glints in his right hand. Oh my God, it's the gun. I thought he got rid of it—yet another thing he lied about. "Victoria was a slut. She fucked everyone. You don't know what it was like to have a wife like that."

I just shake my head.

"And then I found out she was pregnant." He shakes his head. "I found the test stuffed in the bottom of the wastebasket in the bathroom. She didn't tell me, and there's only one reason why. Because it wasn't mine."

"That's not true—"

"Don't tell me what's true!" Adam is shouting now, but the sound is swallowed by the wind. "She was going to leave me, to go raise that bastard child of hers. Do you know how people would've laughed at me if I let that happen? I had to get rid of her. Just like I got rid of my asshole parents."

I just stand there, afraid to say anything else.

"Victoria got what she deserved." A smile touches his lips. "And I have to thank you for helping me finish the job. I had wanted to do that since she came home, but it would've been suspicious. Thank you for taking the blame. Great performance, by the way."

Another thought occurs to me. "What about Irina? Is she..."

I point down at the trap door.

"Oh, that was a whole different mess." He lets out a sigh. "Irina discovered what I did to Victoria. She was *blackmailing* me. At first, she just wanted to live in that house and for me to buy her a bunch of expensive clothes and shoes. But then she wanted more. A lot more."

That huge walk-in closet of Victoria's... I wonder

how much of that clothing belonged to Irina. "So you killed her?"

"I didn't have a choice, Sylvia."

I stand there, my fingers growing numb from the cold. I'm trying to figure out how this is all going to end, and I don't see any way that works out well for me. Adam has a gun. There's no way I could make a run for it with all the snow. I'm trapped here.

Oh God, he's going to kill me and put me in the room below the shed. And nobody will ever know.

I raise my hands in the air. "I won't tell anyone. I swear to you."

He snorts. "You don't think I'm dumb enough to believe that, do you?"

Worth a try.

"I *saved* you," I point out to him. "Victoria was going to kill you."

"Right. And now I'm going to save myself."

He lifts the gun and points it straight at my face. I cover my face with my hands, as if my fingers would be any protection from a bullet. When Victoria aimed the very same gun, she missed. But she had shaky hands. Adam's hands are completely steady and he's had practice shooting. He won't miss.

I remember how loud the gunshot was when Victoria shot the gun. I brace myself for the sound. It will be the last thing I ever hear.

Bang!

I jump at the loud noise. But it doesn't sound like it did last time. It's not as loud. And it was more like a clang than a bang.

I pull my fingers away from my face. Adam isn't standing in front of me anymore. He's on the floor, unconscious.

And Freddy is standing in the doorway, his dark hair plastered to his skull from the snow. And he's holding a large shovel in his hand. I look up at his familiar face and almost burst into tears.

"Looks like you needed me after all," he says. "And this time, I was here."

EPILOGUE

6 months later

I'm starting to get used to waking up next to Freddy
Ruggiero again.

He always sleeps with one arm over his head, like he's
raising his hand with an answer he knows in class (a rare
occurrence back when we were in school). He always keeps
the other hand on me. At the beginning of the night, he's
got me pulled close to him, usually with some sort of
spooning action going on. But even if we separate during
the night, he always manages to keep one hand on me. Like
he's afraid I'm going to drift away.

I watch him sleep for a little while. His black eyelashes
are like soot and unfairly long for a man. It's the only
pretty thing about Freddy.

I never thought we'd get back to this point. With all
the fighting and debt and the guilt over losing the baby, I
thought we would never get back to the point where we

loved each other again. Where we dared to talk about a future that didn't involve working our butts off for a minimum wage.

My alarm clock goes off and Freddy's pretty eyelashes flutter. He rubs his eyes with the hand that was flung over his head while keeping his other hand squarely on my thigh. I shut off the alarm.

"Sorry about that," I say.

He groans and rubs his eyes again. "It's so early…"

Freddy is not a morning person. "It's eight o'clock."

"But it's *Saturday!*" His dark brown eyes blink open. "And I was in class till ten o'clock last night!"

You could have knocked me over with a feather when the guy who graduated high school by the skin of his teeth and vowed he was done with school forever admitted that he was taking night classes to get a degree in computer engineering. Freddy has always been decent at computer stuff—he always knew what to do when mine broke down. So the field fits him. And it pays way better than the blue-collar jobs he's had since high school.

The amazing thing is that he's talked me into going back to school too. I'm going to start taking classes in the fall. Believe it or not, I'm really excited. I still don't know what I want to be when I grow up, but it will be nice to have options.

I lean forward and kiss him on the nose. "I have to go somewhere. But you can stay in bed."

He pulls me close for a deeper kiss. I swear, Freddy is

the only guy in the world who doesn't have morning breath. "Be home before dinner?"

"You bet."

An hour later, I'm taking the D train into Manhattan. While I sit on the subway, I browse the Internet on my phone to pass the time. As has become my habit, the first thing I do is check on the news sites for mentions of Adam Barnett.

After Freddy found Adam pointing the gun at me in the shed, he called the police. At first, Adam tried to lie his way out of the whole thing, like he always did. But the evidence was overwhelming. Ultimately, Adam pled guilty to the murders of Glen MacNeil and Irina Brunner. It was the smart thing for him to do. In exchange for his confession, they didn't pursue him for the attempted murder of Victoria... and avoided an extended media circus that was sure to result when a bestselling author murders two people. There was also an agreement that there wouldn't be any further investigation into the deaths of his parents and brother.

Adam is currently serving two consecutive sentences of twenty-five years to life in a New York state prison. So there is a tiny chance of him getting out of jail eventually. When he's eighty-five.

I find one news item about Adam, but it's a small one. All the proceeds for *The Vixen* are going to be donated to a charity to benefit battered women. I suppose it's a start.

My destination when I get off the subway is a little

brunch place out in Manhattan. I've been working so hard lately and spending most of my free time with Freddy, so when Maggie texted to invite me out for brunch, I jumped at the chance. I haven't seen her since Victoria's funeral. Last I heard, her boyfriend got a job closer to the city and they moved.

I make it to the crowded diner by a quarter to ten, just barely beating out the brunch rush. Maggie told me this place has the best French toast, although I'm partial to an omelet. Anything but oatmeal. I don't think I'll ever be able to eat oatmeal again.

Maggie has already gotten us a table. She's squeezed into a corner, somewhat isolated so that we can have a quiet conversation. Her red hair is loose around her face, and she looks prettier than she used to when she was cleaning that big house. Her green top is very flattering and she's got a beautiful sparkly necklace that I've never seen her wear before. She waves excitedly when she catches sight of me.

"Sylvia!" she cries. "Over here."

I squeeze past a family with their four young children and about two waiters carrying full trays of food to get to the table. I start to slide into the seat across from her, but before I can, she jumps up and hugs me. Typical Maggie.

"It's so great to see you!" she says excitedly.

We both settle down into our seats, and I peek at Maggie over the brim of the menu. She looks incredible. I can't get over it. Whatever she's doing right now agrees with her. I think something in that house in Montauk must've been sucking the life out of her.

"How is the new job?" I ask her.

Maggie told me in our last phone conversation that she has a new cleaning job out in Queens. She seemed happy enough about it. "Oh, you know. The usual. Nothing too creepy. How about you?"

"Just waitressing," I say. I don't mention the fact that I'm going back to school. I don't want Maggie to feel guilty she isn't doing the same.

Our waitress comes by and takes our orders. French toast with a side of sausages for Maggie and a western omelet for me. After the waitress is gone, she leans in and lowers her voice.

"Have you been to see him?" she asks.

"Who?"

She gives me a funny look. "Who do you think? Adam."

I shake my head. "No. Of course not."

I saw the news stories in which they showed Adam receiving his sentence, and he looked like death. A man like Adam won't do well in prison. He looked like he wished he were dead. If New York had a death penalty, he might have found a lethal injection preferable to spending the rest of his life behind bars.

"Have you?" I ask.

She toys with the diamond charm hanging off her necklace. There's something about that necklace that looks so familiar—it's bugging me. "Once," she admits.

"Really?" I look at her in surprise. "Why?"

She shrugs. "I'm surprised you haven't."

"Why? What do you mean?"

She snorts. "Come on, Sylvia. It's *me*. You don't have to pretend."

"Pretend what?"

My eyes go back to the necklace around Maggie's neck. And then it hits me all of a sudden why the necklace looks so familiar.

It's the snowflake. The same one Victoria was wearing on the day I first met her. The one Adam got her as a present.

How did Maggie get that necklace? Did she take it from the house? Of course, is that such a big deal? It was Victoria's necklace and she's gone now.

But something about Maggie wearing that necklace makes me feel very uneasy. I remember the word Victoria said to me that night during the first storm:

Mine.

It seems like Adam was very generous with his wife's possessions. Especially for certain women.

"Hey," I say. "Can I... ask you something, Maggie?"

She nods. "Of course."

I study Maggie's freckled face. There's been a question swirling around my head since that big storm and I haven't had the nerve to ask. Until today. "So you told me you saw Victoria throw a toaster at the wall, and that's what made the dent in their kitchen wall."

She laughs. "That's not a question."

I frown. "I guess my question is, did you really?"

All traces of humor disappear from Maggie's face. "Did I really what?"

"Did you really see it? Or did you make that up?"

She stirs her water glass with her straw. "I don't understand you, Sylvia. I thought we were on the same page."

"Same page about what?"

"You know what I mean." She shakes her head. "Everyone made like Adam was the villain in all this. But you and I know the truth. Look at Victoria. All she did was lie around and eat junk food. I saw it with my own eyes. And you... you saw the way he took care of her after she got hurt. Was she grateful? Of course not."

"So... she didn't throw the toaster?"

"No." Maggie folds her arms across her chest. "She didn't."

I feel dizzy all of a sudden, like I'm going to throw up.

"What did you do?" I whisper.

"MacNeil was a big guy. It was too hard for Adam to get him into the shed on his own." She sniffs. "Anyway, my job was to clean up for him. So when he asked my help cleaning up, I helped him." She pauses. "Just like you helped him get rid of Victoria."

For a moment, I can't find my voice. "That was an *accident.*"

"Yeah, sure. Whatever you say."

"It was!"

"Was it an accident when you slept with him?"

I don't even know what to say to that. "No… but…"

"Hey, I can't throw stones." She shrugs again. "I had the same relationship with him that you did. Why do you think Eva hated us both so much?" She runs a finger along the rim of her water glass. "He's incredible in bed, isn't he? And so considerate. Every time there was a storm, he'd call me to make sure I was okay."

My stomach drops. I remember when Adam was talking to his "mother" prior to the first big storm. But he couldn't have been—his mother was dead.

He was talking to Maggie.

"Steve is a nice guy and all," she goes on, "but there's no comparison. I would have dropped him for Adam in a heartbeat if Adam asked me to." She sighs. "Such a shame he got locked up. A crime, really."

The waitress comes by with our food. She drops the western omelet down in front of me and I stare down at the yellow lump of food. Maggie digs into her French toast with gusto, but my appetite is gone.

"I… I have to go…" I manage.

Maggie looks up sharply. "Sylvia, you're not considering… We have an understanding, don't we?"

I reach for my purse slung on the back of my chair. "I have to go."

But before I can stand up, I feel something close

around my wrist like a vise.

Maggie's skinny white hand is gripping my wrist to keep me from getting away. Her grip tightens as she leans in close to me. "Where do you think you're going?"

I glance at the other tables, to see if anyone is paying attention. Of course, this is New York. Everyone is minding their own business. Nobody is going to intercept, just like when that old lady started choking and I had to perform the Heimlich—that seems like ages ago now. "I just... need some air."

Maggie leans in closer so that I can smell cinnamon French toast on her breath. "You're the one who killed Victoria. If you say a word about me, you're going down too."

Her brown eyes are like ice. Her fingers are biting into my skin hard enough to leave bruises. She must be very strong if she was able to help lift a guy like Mack.

"Understand?" she says.

I nod. "Yes."

"Say it. Say you understand."

"I understand."

Her eyes study my face for a moment, then she lets me go. My heart is pounding in my chest so hard that I feel like I might drop dead of a heart attack. And the worst part is, there's nothing I can do.

There's no evidence whatsoever that Maggie did anything wrong. Like she said, Adam never breathed a word. I'm the one who pushed Victoria down the stairs. If anybody could potentially go to jail, it would be me.

It's her word against mine.

Maggie gives me one last look and digs back into her breakfast. How does she have any appetite right now? She pops a large chunk of sausage into her mouth and the fork comes away clean. She chews and swallows.

I watch as her eyes widen and her mouth opens. She looks like she wants to speak, but no sounds come out. The panic mounts on her face. I get a sense of déjà vu, again remembering that fall day when I saved that woman from choking.

Maggie is choking.

In the split second that follows, I imagine her face slowly turning blue. I imagine her collapsing to the ground as her lungs scream for oxygen. Then there would be an ambulance—too late. A trip to the hospital. Or maybe straight to the morgue. I see it all unfolding in front of me.

I was a hero once and look where it got me.

So this time I do nothing.

THE END

ACKNOWLEDGMENTS

When I finish the first draft of a book, the first thing I always say is, "I finished it, but it sucks." So thank you to all the people who helped me make this book not suck. Thank you to my mother, for your boundless and unbridled enthusiasm. Thank you to Kate, for the positive supportive as well as the awesome and thorough editing job. Thank you to Jen for your always insightful critiques. Thanks to Rebecca, for your great advice. Thanks to Rhona, for always being ready to look at another cover. Thanks to my amazing writing group. It's incredible to have that support in my life.

Thank you to the rest of my family. Without your encouragement, none of this would be possible.

And thank you to all my brain injured patients. I have been working in this field for over ten years, and I am only starting to appreciate how complicated the brain is. Thank you for allowing me to be part of your recovery.

Made in United States
North Haven, CT
02 April 2022

17804407R00250